BRAXTON'S CENTURY
VOLUME 2

JR STRAYVE JR

No part of this book may be reproduced in any form or by any electronic or mechanical means including information storage and retrieval systems, without permission in writing from the author. The only exception is by a reviewer, who may quote short excerpts in a review.

This book is a work of fiction. names, characters, places, and incidents either are products of the author's imagination or are used fictitiously. Any resemblance to actual persons, living or dead, events, or locales is entirely coincidental.

JR STRAYVE JR

Visit my website at: www.jrstrayvejr.com Printed in the United States of America First Printing July 2021

2021 JR STRAYVE JR

ISBN: 978-1-7371243-0-6

AUTHOR'S NOTE

IF YOU HAVE NOT HAD AN OPPORTUNITY TO READ VOLUME 1, YOU MAY WANT TO TAKE A MOMENT TO READ THIS:

Braxton, Prince of Wales, was born in England in 1860. The third son of Prince Richard and Princess Mercedes, he is happily the fourth in line to the throne. Braxton has his own plans for his future, and they do not involve being king of England. Their family – including the Princes Dominic and John and Princesses Dierdre and Carmen - reside at Aurelio Palace, a bucolic estate in the country, a day's carriage ride from London.

Braxton's Century Volume I begins in the young prince's 10th year, when his quest for excitement leads him to inadvertently set fire to the family castle's towering rotunda.

Princess Mercedes realizes Braxton's active imagination, constant thirst for new adventures and innate intelligence will lead him to places she will not be able to follow.

She worries for his safety, but also revels in his precocious mind, courage and inventiveness.

To escape the confines of his royal responsibilities, Braxton sets out on a course to win his own fortune and as a result, his freedom. Ambitious and with a head teaming with dreams, he decides to create his own empire, a commercial empire.

This burgeoning tycoon begins his career when still a young man, training a team of hand-picked thoroughbreds and winning the Queen Anne Stakes horse race. His next adventure, the purchase of interest in a railroad, was financed by the proceeds from the Queen Anne Stakes. He then proceeds with gusto to create a new life full of adventure, intrigue and romance. Over the ensuing 16 years he establishes a school for the working class, grows railroad systems, European trading companies, and international mining. Braxton is not averse to bringing down the rich and powerful. Also establishing a secret intelligence force, he identifies and targets anyone who might stand in his way.

These perceived "hindrances" to his successes receive a Machiavellian surprise at Carnivale in Venice. The "Mars" project. The reader will learn more about this as it is revisited in England at some future point.

The young man is viscerally charming to women and men alike. He spends an idyllic month on the island of Capri with his longtime friend and distant cousin, Aramis. We also learn of his adventures in Paris, Madrid, Lisbon, Vienna, Venice, Rome, St. Petersburg, and Moscow. But it is the Grand Duchess Valentina, the aging Russian czar's daughter, who haunts his dreams. As she and her cousin, Grand Duke Maxim, rule Russia as co-regents, will Braxton and Valentina ever have the time and opportunity to create their own life together? Which of his many "mistresses" – human and financial– will ultimately rule Braxton?

Braxton's Century Volume II will intoxicate the reader with more romance, intrigue and adventure. Come with Braxton as he lays claim to Japan, China, and Singapore, and perhaps, meets his match in India.

Will Valentina tame this powerful charismatic persona? Will Braxton continue to conquer the world of the 19th Century? Welcome to the sprawling saga of Braxton's Century, Volume 2!

CHARACTER LIST

List of Characters Integral to the Novel

Prince Braxton: 3rd son of the Prince and Princess of Wales

Prince Dominic: 1st son of the Prince and Princess of Wales

Prince John: 2nd son of the Prince and Princess of Wales

Prince Richard: Prince of Wales and Braxton's father

Princess Carmen: 1st Daughter of the Prince and Princess of Wales

Princess Diedre: 2nd Daughter of the Prince and Princess of Wales

Princess Mercedes: Princess of Wales and Braxton's mother

Grand Duchess Valentina: 2nd daughter of the czar

Grand Duke Prince Maxim: Nephew to the czar

Grand Duchess Mathilde: Daughter of the Austrian emperor

Viscount Lord Ramsey: Prince John's former lover & aide to Braxton

Prime Minister Hirobumi: Prime Minister of Japan

Master Seiko Higoshino: Braxton's teacher, aide and confidante

Joe Richards: American entrepreneur

Cosimo, Duke de Chiacontella: Braxton's Uncle and Mercedes's brother

Count Aramis de Chiacontella: Braxton's Cousin

1
———

MOSCOW & BEYOND

In the summer of 1886, the imperial co-regents, Grand Duke Prince Maxim and Grand Duchess Valentina, hosted a banquet for three hundred nobles in the Kremlin Palace's Hall of the Order of St. Alexander Nevsky. The snare had been laid.

A table covered in gold-flecked cloth ran the length of the white and gold gilded two-story hall. Gold plates, goldware, and shimmering crystal Baccarat glasses lay before bejeweled women and men, overdecorated in ribbons, medals, and corded aiguilettes. The orchestra played.

Well into the evening, many toasted and heralded Maxim and his co-regent, Valentina. The imperial cousins graciously accepted the praise, returning their compliments, not betraying what lay in wait.

The most vociferous of the fawning nobles were soon to feel less than welcome at this imperial fête.

Maxim smiled down the length of the table adorned with golden candelabras. From high above, massive, gilded chandeliers held hundreds of flickering candles alongside thousands of dangling pendulous faceted crystals.

Grand Duchess Valentina, seated at the table's far end, caught Grand Duke Maxim's eye. Valentina's jet-black hair was adorned with a shimmering tiara; her aquamarine eyes flashing as her facial muscles tightened, her countenance turned to ice. She nodded.

The time had come to extract revenge and rid the crown of a festering cancer.

Although 10 years older than his cousin, Maxim's physique was soldierly and fit. Signaling the Imperial Guard by rubbing his shoulder, the shoulder once injured by an assassin's bullet, the assassin present and known to many assembled at the table.

Several nobles taking note of his action tugged at their collars and swallowed hard. Some nervously chattered; some in a higher pitch. Several exhibited lines of sweat running over their foreheads and dancing across their cheeks. The fervid, hushed tones emanating from the damned began to permeate the room.

Maxim raised his glass, staring down the table toward the Grand Duchess Valentina. She acknowledged his lead and also raised her glass. Simultaneously, they sipped from their flutes, returning them to the table and continuing the conversation with their respective dinner partners. The orchestra played on.

Twenty-eight of the sixty Imperial Guards flanking the hall marched up behind fourteen noblemen and their wives.

The orchestra played on.

Conversations halted, except for those Maxim and Valentina were having with the loyal nobles seated nearby.

Maxim, taking note of the pause in conversation among the other nobles said loudly, "Please, continue!"

The fourteen nobles and their wives rose as the guards drew back their chairs. There was no fuss, no screaming, no pleading, fainting or theatrics. They knew their fate.

The orchestra played on.

The guards escorted their prisoners from the hall.

The remaining guests, unable to speak, sat silently.

Servants appeared and removed the now vacant place settings and chairs. Footmen and guests then moved together to re-arrange the chairs, causing it to appear as if the departed nobles had never existed.

Once again, banter and laughter slowly began to fill the room.

Food courses were presented, and wine was consumed.

The orchestra played on, filling the air with an elegant waltz.

That fateful night, having occurred months earlier, served to cement Maxim's and Valentina's autocratic powers over the Russian Empire.

———

Grand Duchess Valentina and the Imperial Court remained in Moscow for a few months following that fateful night. Her cousin Grand Duke Prince Maxim and Prince Braxton had departed Moscow continued their quest in search of income-producing natural resources for Mother Russia.

Valentina soon wrote to Braxton.

Dearest Braxton,

I so miss your arms around me. Every night when I go to bed, I think of your strong body against mine. I savor the memory of your warm breath against my face and neck. I yearn for your loving touch. It is only these recollections that relieve my angst, allowing me to fall asleep and dream of you.

It would be so nice for you to be here to help me with the decisions

I face alone every day. Both your and Maxim's absence sheds a brilliant light on the precarious situation in which the empire finds itself. Knowing you and my cousin have placed your confidences in me sustains me through each day. My father's counsel is slowly evaporating as he declines in health. I am alone.

I have never shared with Maxim my fears and doubts, so, please keep my confidences. I do not want to distract him from his mission and must remain strong and capable in his eyes.

I have made great progress in consolidating our position in the government. The rumors of what happened in Moscow appear to have discouraged malcontents and usurpers from challenging my authority. On more than one occasion I have replaced ministers I felt have agendas of their own that conflict with mine. One of my ladies in waiting has heard there are simple songs, ditties, going about comparing me to my predecessors, Catherine and Elizabeth. They were strong and decisive rulers. I trust this will work to my advantage.

Valentina went on in great detail to describe what was transpiring in St. Petersburg, closing with:

I pray soon that I soon will be rid of my role in the regency. Only then can we look to our future together.

With all the love I can give,
Yours, Valentina

———

Braxton wrote a letter to his brother, Crown Prince Dominic, to make excuses for not being able to attend his marriage to the Austrian Grand Duchess, Mathilde:

My Dear Brother,

I understand you are to be made Duke of Cambridge Congratulations! Another title and another honor. Thank God you have the broad shoulders to carry them all. Yes, you may hear a bit of sarcasm in my tone, but I am a trifle teasing. I understand an income comes with it. That is good! Marriage is expensive, or so I hear.

It pains me I will not be able to return to England for your marriage to Mathilde. As your devoted brother, there is nowhere else I would rather be on that glorious day when you are wed. Our bucolic days at the Aurelio Palace are a thing of the past and that saddens me. I have a tinge of guilt in taking solace that I will not have to bear the burden of kingship. I would not wish the burden of wearing a crown on anyone. But there is no doubt you will be a perfect husband and father and, subsequently, one day a great king. You remain in my prayers.

As to my goings-on, Maxim and I left Moscow weeks ago and are traveling through the Russian hinterland. It is a beautiful country.

The rolling fields, towering mountains and untamed rivers abound. The people are kind and very generous. They love what they perceive to be Russia. Albeit, they have no concept of the reality of Western Russia, its industrialization, westernization, economic and political chaos.

The peasant's lack of knowledge of such things brings to mind Thomas Gray's poem, "Ode on a Distant Prospect of Eton College," where he opines:

Since sorrow never comes too late, And happiness too swiftly flies.

Thought would destroy their paradise. No more; where ignorance is bliss,

'Tis folly to be wise.

Russia is locked in ages long past, as in medieval times.

Maxim and I have been overwhelmed with strategizing the implementation of efficient mining and lumbering. The harvesting of trees and preparing them for transport is a herculean effort. Rail is not available in most locales. Wagons pulled by teams of six horses are our only recourse. This arcane conveyance over primitive roads will eat into our profits.

We are making do and transporting the loads to the Black Sea where they are loaded on ships bound for Europe and the Mediterranean. It escapes me as to how we will ship wood to the Far East without rail service. The market there for building lumber is insa-

tiable. I am beside myself in my attempts to solve the dilemma of meeting the demand when plagued with fourteenth century transportation!

The good news is the consortium is beginning to see money trickle in. All funds are, of course, reinvested. I am using my own capital to finance the laying of track so we may be able to move some of our cargo via train in four to six months. There exists ample cheap labor. We pay them well and find them quite industrious, laying several miles of track each day.

Planning ahead, I have ordered freight cars specifically designed to carry timber. The cars will be converted to carry freight from Europe on their return trip after delivering the lumber. This will help defray some of the carrying costs. Our efforts require an incredible amount of machinery and supplies which we have purchased in England, Germany, France, and Belgium. Eventually, the two-way traffic will prove to be profitable for me. I think I neglected to mention the consortium is contracting with my company to carry all exports and imports associated with our endeavors.

The engineers are beginning to understand the situation and are becoming much more efficient. The German, Swiss and English engineers are working wonders. Profits will follow soon, I hope. And there is oil. I will tell you more about this as things move along.

In the meantime, Maxim is returning to St. Petersburg; affairs of state and such. I am not confident he will be rejoining me in the near future. Rumors of his uncle's rapidly declining health are rampant. I would imagine you have gotten wind of such rumblings.

Now, I must go. It is time for Maxim and I to trudge down into the mines. Frankly, I enjoy it. It is a bit intimidating heading below ground into the claustrophobic, dank and dirty underworld. But at the same time, I am living a life that affords me constant exhilaration and a sense of purpose. I have learned so much about myself as a man. I am blessed.

Know that I love you and cherish you as brother and friend. My regards to your special Mathilde.

Anxious to see you soon, Brax

The Duke of Cambridge answered Braxton immediately, advising he wished him to see their grandfather, the king, before he passed. It was time for him to return home. Unfortunately, the king passed away before Braxton received his brother's admonition.

Receiving the news of his grandfather's quick demise greatly saddened Braxton as he looked back on the many wonderful times he had spent with the old king. His most cherished memories were of days at the races and intimate afternoons with his grandparents at Buckingham Palace. Braxton knew he would be unable to return in time to partake in the funeral and other events surrounding the king's death.

I have spent so much time abroad chasing my ambitions, I have missed my brother's wedding and Grandpappa's last days.

I am needed here. Dominic is married and Grandfather buried. There is nothing I can do. But I will be there for Pappa's coronation next year.

———

Braxton's Japanese mentor, Seiko Higoshino, arrived at one of the eastern Russian mining camps following his auditing the Russians' art collections. These art works and artifacts had been confiscated subsequent to the attempted assassination of Grand Duke Maxim and the arrest of the government ministers.

Seiko sat opposite Braxton on the train at a utilitarian wooden work table in the administrative staff's cars. "Master Seiko, I trust you have rested from your long journey."

"Yes, my Lord. I am grateful for the days you allowed

me to recuperate after my trip. I must admit, I had not foreseen how vast this land is."

Braxton said, "I too, Master, am repeatedly amazed at what I learn and discover here. During your respite, I have had an opportunity to review the reports you sent ahead and those which you delivered on your arrival. The wonder contained within rivals anything I have seen here in Russia."

Seiko nodded his head in appreciation. "Thank you, my Prince.

By the way, I so appreciate your providing me with the Japanese tea. What they refer to as tea out here is somewhat lacking. I savor every sip."

"You are very welcome."

"The information on the marketability of exporting raw materials appears complete and the prospects encouraging. Iron ore is a priority. Germany, England, and France show promise in your analysis. Lead and copper rank second. Tin is certainly a growing market. Coal will have a market in the Balkans and central Europe. This will necessitate keeping our prices low so that we remain competitive."

Braxton handed Seiko a thick folder and said, "Please examine these numbers and return to me with your thoughts. Double check my numbers. If they look accurate, we can discuss setting our plans in motion. It is time we get our ore out of the ground and into market."

"Yes, I will do that. At the same time, may I suggest we notify wholesalers of the impending availability, my lord?"

"Yes, we should be able to come up with anticipated dates the prospective buyers can expect to take delivery."

"My Prince, the lumber wholesalers are asking for more lumber. Is it possible to increase volume?"

Braxton drummed his fingers on the table and said in a

frustrated tone, "The wood is cut and ready for shipment. We have millions of board feet sitting on the ground rotting, waiting for transport. We must increase transportation capacity." He paused and said, "That may take a while. We have over a hundred miles of track to lay first. Perhaps in forty-to-sixty days we can commence shipping via rail.

Please continue to take the orders. We will fill them eventually," Braxton sighed and looked out the train window.

"Yes, Highness."

Master Seiko then placed a medium-size, leather-bound box on the center of the worktable. Braxton lifted his brows, looking from the window toward the elegant box.

Seiko grinned a bemused smile and said, "Good news, Sir."

"It looks like good news, but I have no idea what is in it."

"Pictures! Many pictures!" Seiko laughed, grinning broadly. "And of course, catalogs. Twelve such volumes from the deceased nobles and eight from the less than honorable ministers having met the same fate as that of the nobles."

Braxton wrapped his arms around himself and said, beaming, "Well done, Master Seiko! Show me. Tell me more. You have been busy!"

Seiko opened the portfolio and placed the nobles' catalogs in one stack and the ministers' in another pile alongside it. One stood fifteen inches high compared to the smaller one standing eleven inches tall. He then handed the prince an inch-thick pile of lose papers.

"These papers are divided by families and contain an itemized list of all artifacts, paintings, statues, prints, religious icons, and many unique pieces, some dating back hundreds, perhaps a thousand years." Braxton looked down at the papers, then to Seiko, the box, and back at Seiko. "Truly?"

"Yes, my prince. I have noted the value alongside most items.

Some of them I could not value. For that, please forgive me. Many are, without a doubt, priceless."

"Did you have each item photographed?"

"Yes, Highness, but the quantity was so great I brought only the most important or unique items that have been photographed."

"Yes, that makes sense. Where are they now, the other photographs?"

"In the Paris house, with copies of the catalogs you have before you. For safekeeping."

"Excellent. Did you place them in the vaults we had built in the basement?"

"Yes, Highness."

"Hmm," the prince said, rubbing his chin. "With the slow economy and weak market, these items cannot go for the most favorable prices now. I hesitate to speculate what they are truly worth."

"That is correct, my lord."

"Too many treasures and not enough buyers." "Yes."

"Please let me have time to peruse what you have presented. I will take these items to my private car. Let us speak again tomorrow."

"Thank you, Master. You have once again exceeded my expectations."

"You honor me, my prince." Both men rose and bowed.

Braxton and Seiko met the following day and agreed the next course of action was to send a letter to Maxim and Valentina in St. Petersburg, informing them of their findings. Valentina's response arrived weeks later.

Dearest Braxton,

I truly hope this letter finds you well. Maxim sends his best, as does my father. As you can imagine, we were all stunned at the work your curator has accomplished in his audit of the confiscated property. The czar was impressed and grateful.

That is the good news. My father is in somewhat of a panic over our financial state and insists everything be sold at whatever price you can get for it. Maxim and I tried to persuade him otherwise.

Father is considering tossing his own vast collections on the market to raise cash. Per your thoughts, I have convinced him to reconsider. When I told him he ought to hold them in reserve, keeping them for a rainy day, the czar remarked, "The heavens are pouring rain now, what are you waiting for? Should we build an ark?"

Maxim and I finally convinced him to rethink his position. For the most part, he still has his wits. Fortunately, he has subsequently asked that I continue to handle the liquidation of the art for the crown.

I would suggest we take a middle road. Your Master Seiko has, as I said, done a remarkable job of cataloging and analyzing the inventory.

Perhaps you and he could serve as our agents?

Ascertain what items are most sought after by collectors at this time. Put them on the market. Some items should bring a good price regardless the economy. If we can show some money flowing in to the royal coffers, perhaps father will move on to other things.

Valentina closed her letter with more words of love and hope for their reunion soon.

Prince Braxton and Master Seiko met to discuss Valentina's letter. Seiko finished reading the part of the correspondence pertaining to the art and artifacts and placed it on the worktable between them.

"Masker Seiko, what are your thoughts?"

"It concerns me the czar and the co-regents are of different minds. If we should act as agents, that could place us dangerously in the middle."

"Your point is well taken, "Braxton said, staring down at his lap.

With a pained expression on his face, he looked up and said quietly, "We will have to be very careful to protect Russia's interests and seemingly appear to follow his imperial majesty's instructions."

Seiko, wide-eyed, his voice trembling, said, "Highness I beg your pardon, but what you said might be perceived as duplicity by some. I know that is not your intent."

The prince folded his arms and sat back in his chair. "Yes, that is a risk. One that we shall have to take. I believe Maxim and Valentina have instructed us to use our judgment. The czar wants to see cash coming into the treasury. I believe we can meet those expectations."

Braxton pushed several sheets of paper toward Seiko. "In these notes you will see that I have outlined a plan. Should the proposal be feasible and have the potential to put large sums of money in the czar's till, would you consider conveying our thoughts to the czar? You would have complete discretion and operational control."

"Humbly, my lord, I thank you for your confidence in me. I request that you let me study what you have given me."

"Excellent!" Braxton said grinning. "Let me provide you with a brief overview. We will transfer all the items to the Paris house. The vaults are large enough to hold a great number of them. Would you agree?" Seiko nodded.

"You will convert the first and second floors of the

manse into an art gallery. There is sufficient light, that infamous Parisienne light.

The pieces should show well there. We shall call it the 'Imperial Gallery.'"

Seiko's jaw dropped. "That is quite a task, but an excellent idea. All the best art is sold in Paris."

Braxton chuckled, "Thank you." He picked up one of the pages from his notes and took a moment to review it. "Here is where it could get dodgy. As we must raise some capital for the czar, I will provide you with sufficient funds to inflate prices during the auction. You will, of course, not purchase anything on my behalf that cannot be sold for a greater price in the near future. Remember, Master, while I appreciate art, art is not my business. Railroads, mining, and trade are. To me, art is to be appreciated for its beauty. It should, however, never tie up valuable capital that can be used to great advantage elsewhere."

Seiko rubbed the palms of his hands together thoughfully. "Perhaps we might resell the art in New York or San Francisco."

"Precisely! That is exactly what we shall do, which brings me to another idea. We ought to consider establishing galleries in New York, Chicago, San Francisco, Rome, Berlin, London, and maybe Sydney, Australia. God knows there is enough artwork to fill these new galleries twice over.

"As you know, the rich want to feel rich, particularly the newly rich, of which there are many in America. They naively rationalize their extravagant purchases, believing if it costs a fortune, it engenders status. You must know your buyers. I have resources available to provide information on many aristocrats and the wealthier nouveau riche."

Master Seiko sat transfixed as he listened to the prince.

"I will write a letter to the Aurelio Palace Academy to

provide you with graduating students who can assist you in your efforts. You will have students once again, teacher!"

Braxton and Seiko continued their discussion, digging further and further into the details. Two hours later, Seiko accepted the position as curator of the "Imperial Gallery."

———

Six weeks following the opening of the gallery in Paris, the pressure on the Russian Imperial Treasury began to ease. Income also began to flow in from raw materials and Russian lumber sales. Within a year, the Russian government was once again paying its bills on time. Within three years the treasury was restored to a manageable level that allowed the government to run its affairs efficiently and begin to make infrastructure improvements. Most importantly, the foundations of the military had been bolstered and modernized, assuring the security of the czar's throne.

Meanwhile, Braxton was becoming keenly aware foreign engineers and mining teams were, by necessity, running the operations themselves. Foreigners dominated and controlled the Russian labor. Braxton was concerned the overwhelming foreign presence would agitate the populace. Not so long ago, a significant German presence had created considerable animosity. Braxton also felt his own persona, while now not perceived as a threat, could be a catalyst for dissent. He subtly removed himself visibly from daily operational activities and remained out of sight whenever possible.

He worked closely with the most talented Russian engineers, giving them more and more authority in day-to-day operations. Within three months, Braxton had all but disappeared from the sight of Russian labor. When he needed to inspect mines and facilities it was done discreetly and without fanfare.

In efforts to "Russianize" the mines, Braxton had begun reaching out to engineering and mining professionals in France, Belgium, and America to staff training and education programs for the local populace and laborers. He solicited upper- and middle- class students in Moscow, Kiev, St. Petersburg, and Novosibirsk. He promised these young men a stipend and an education leading to well-paid employment. Commandeering the homes and facilities that had been confiscated from the treasonous Russian noblemen, Braxton founded training centers and provided housing for this new army of aspiring engineers and managers. These intelligent, eager, and ambitious students assimilated into the professional class overseeing the mining and logging.

Once the managerial and professional levels had begun to be staffed by Russians, Braxton decreased participation of foreign experts. Russia would never entirely be free from external professionals, but it would eventually provide native-born technocrats and supervisors for most of its mining, logging, and soon to be booming oil exploration and drilling.

With these systems in place, Braxton turned his attention further east to the promising oil fields. As Braxton was preparing to explore these potential fields, he was commanded by the government to return to England on the occasion of his father's coronation. During the train ride through Russia and into Europe he wrote to the woman who stirred his heart.

My Dearest Valentina,

I find myself racing across two continents, having delayed my departure by three weeks due to a sad and costly cave-in at the Rivkosky mine. Unfortunately, thirty souls perished. The experience has proven to be the most dreadful one I have ever experienced. The poor families have had their lives ruined. I hope you and Maxim do not mind, but I have committed funds from the treasury to help support the wives and children. It seems the right thing to do. At the same time, I am personally underwriting the construction of a school house to be built in the village. I simply could not leave any sooner than I did. Hopefully, my family will understand my arriving at the 11th hour.

I plan on being in England for a month or two and then returning to Russia. There is so much to do. I have brought a small staff with me to assist in my affairs.

The timing for my departure is a great inconvenience. We are at the beginning of verifying potential sites for oil, but my duties at home demand I leave. You cannot imagine my frustration.

At the same time, I am so looking forward to seeing my family. It has been almost two years. Of course, I want to be there to see my father and mother crowned.

Pondering the purpose of my trip and contemplating what might lay ahead has caused this train ride to become a bit depressing. I realize that I am now closer to the throne. Only my two brothers stand between me and the crown. Since I was a young boy, I have had periodic unsettling premonitions about being forced to assume the throne. Perhaps that is why I venture so deep into Russia, thousands of miles from London. There is always the hope that Dominic and Mathilde will start a family soon and I will fall farther behind in the line of succession.

There is something else I must share with you. I sent Prince Dominic's good friend, Lord Ramsey, back to England a month ago. He is inspecting the work I ordered done on the very first train I designed almost ten years ago. I am having it completely refitted and upgraded. My designers and engineers will have vastly improved the comfort and equipment throughout the train. It will be waiting for me when I disembark in Dover. This extravagance will ensure that my staff will be close at hand regardless of where I am while in England.

And of course, there is the comfort and privacy it affords. I wish you could be with me to share that privacy.

One topic I am avoiding is that of not seeing you on my way to London. Yes, I know I promised. I am a cad and a victim of circumstances. You deserve better.

We are both wretched, torn in opposite directions. I had hoped you would have come to father's coronation, but alas, as you said, your duties as regent deny you and me our time together. I understand but languish in tortured sorrow.

It is a wonder you love me as you do; a miracle you allow me to love you. Sitting on this train with no disaster or pending emergencies in the offing gives me too much time to think of you. My sweet Valentina, you have been on my mind every one of the thousands of miles I have traveled as we now approach Calais.

I will write again soon. We must have time together when I return to Russia.

All my love, Braxton

2

THE BRITISH ISLES INTERLUDE

With the combination of inclement weather, terrain, and unreliable continental track, the journey to Calais took three weeks. Braxton dispatched his tired and overworked train to Germany for a refit and overhaul. His father, now King Richard following the death of Braxton's grandfather, had sent the Royal Yacht, HMY Elfin, to ferry him across the English Channel from Calais to Dover.

The prince boarded the yacht reminiscing how this very same vessel had been the one on which he had sat with his Uncle Cosimo, cousin

Count Aramis, his brother Prince John, and his brother's former lover, Viscount Ramsey. These men had been present when Braxton cobbled together the agreement that made him part owner of a railroad in England, controlling fifty-one percent of the voting shares. That was five years ago. Now Braxton was expanding his rail ownership by laying track across the vast continent of Russia.

Disembarking the yacht in Dover, the prince made his way to the station. His private, freshly painted train gleamed in the sunlight and dark smoke curled out the top of the engine's stack. Visibly enamored with the refurbished train, his countenance was that of one who had long been separated from a lover. His head felt a tad light and his chest soon puffed up.

Oh, how I love this train, my train, my first train.

Hours later, the weary traveler arrived at London Bridge Station. Standing on the plaform were Princes Dominic and John, and the Princesses Diedre and Carmen. All four stood mesmerized by the impending arrival of their youngest brother, Braxton; their storied sibling.

The third son of the king was now perhaps the wealthiest man in England. As London had drawn closer, he wondered, what will be different? Will they still see me as their beloved little brother, or will my wealth and notoriety have created a distance between us?

Braxton's worry disappeared as soon as he spied his four siblings lined up to welcome him. He paused, gazing out over them as he approached the steps leading from his car down to the plaform. His heart swelled, comforted with the love emanating from them.

They appeared not to have changed. Carmen had perhaps grown even more beautiful. Braxton held her in awe, innately aware of the intellectual and emotional capacity far beyond her years. The young prince winced at the thought that his beautiful and talented sister would one day be taken away from him and his family when she married Maxim and became the next Empress of Russia.

His siblings looked up and saw a man they could barely recognize.

His six foot, two-inch height, his athletic build and commanding countenance caused them all pause. He was no longer just the strikingly handsome, youthful prince they remembered. His presence was now commanding and authoritative. Braxton had become a man of the world.

The prince jumped down from the train and rushed to his brothers and sisters, unceremoniously embracing each one of them.

"Really, Braxton," Diedre grinned, suffocating within his enthusiastic embrace. Some things never change; of which I am very glad."

"I love you, Diedre," Braxton chortled, also taking hold of Carmen.

The young aristocrats departed the train station plaform arm in arm and climbed into a large open landau. The carriage did not quite have the capacity to comfortably hold all five of them. However, not one would be left out!

It was a bright crisp day. Braxton had not anticipated the enthusiastic public welcome he was about to receive. Crowds lined the streets along the route to Buckingham Palace. His father had arranged an 18-gun salute to welcome him home. The streets were lined with hundreds of flags. The red, white, and blue Union Jack flapped in the breeze, heralding his arrival and his parent's upcoming coronation. Braxton, mindful of his frightening experience as a young boy when the worshipful crowd had pulled him from his carriage while arriving at the Queen Anne Stakes, stood in the center of the carriage waving to well-wishers.

The returning prince's travels had been the source of a voluminous series of articles and publicity. He appeared to be, at that moment, the most beloved man in England.

Their Imperial Majesties, King and Emperor Richard and Queen and Empress Mercedes, did not stand on ceremony to welcome their youngest son, meeting him and his siblings at the porte- cochere in the Buckingham Palace quadrangle.

Braxton leaped out of the carriage and into their arms. The courtiers looking on were stunned but uniformly agreed this would undoubtedly be a very different imperial court, at least as long as HRH Prince Braxton was in residence! Braxton's arrival added a levity and gaiety that would define and bring warmth to coronation week.

———

The family was left to themselves that evening and most of the following day. John and his German wife, Viktoria Louise, resided at Kensington Palace. Dominic lived with Mathilde at Clarence House. Diedre and Braxton had rooms overlooking the front of Buckingham Palace and the Mall. Following their parents' coronation, Diedre would return to Berlin and the prince would decamp to Renaissance House.

Braxton had anticipated it would be impossible for him to conduct his affairs at the palace. Weeks before his arrival he had initiated inquiries with his Uncle Cosimo regarding taking over the lease of Renaissance House in London. As Renaissance House belonged to his mother's family, the Chiacontellas, he was not surprised to learn his uncle and cousin Aramis were staying there during their coronation visit. This pleased Braxton greatly. He had not seen either of them in over a year.

The prince spent the following week enjoying the festivities that led up to the coronation.

———

"Father, I still do not understand why the wait. Your coronation is still days away, and it has been a year since

Grandpapa passed away, may he rest in peace," said Prince John at a private family dinner.

Braxton responded in an enthusiastic tone, "Why John, it is all for me!"

Dominic quickly quipped. "You dare not say, little brother?"

Braxton returned the volley, "Yes, Pappa and I had an understanding that it was unlikely I could be of much help in assisting.

Grandfather's demise, but I would surely be of great service for Pappa's and Mamma's coronation." Carmen muffled a laugh.

Mercedes set down her fork and knife and drew her dinner napkin to her mouth.

"How rude, Braxton!" Diedre exclaimed.

Carmen, failing to completely contain her laughter said, "That is our little brother, always conjuring up ways to throw us off center."

"You do not really mean that, do you, son?" Mercedes asked feigning alarm.

"He only means to entertain us, as usual," grunted the king and then continued, "As to John's question, you know from your study of history we have had several kings who were crowned immediately following the death of the previous king. That usually occurred during war or when the succession was to be contested. You all are, of course, familiar with the adage, 'Possession is nine- tenths of the law?'"

The young royals and Mercedes sat in silence, focusing on what Richard had to say.

"King Harold II was crowned the day following Edward the Confessor's death. William the Conqueror was crowned the day he became king. Those were times long past. The security that comes with a thousand years of laws and traditions have made a difference as to how things are done today. Keep in mind, the empire did not exist. We lived in a medieval land, having several kings and fluid borders. Only 700 hundred years ago, the line of succession was not necessarily observed by everyone. As in the War of the Roses, the Lancasters and the Yorks extinguished each other's male line of succession over the course of 30 years while fighting for the crown. Remember, it is during this time it was thought the two princes, Edward V and his brother.

Richard, were murdered in the Tower of London by Richard III." "How morbid," Diedre interrupted.

"Morbid indeed," John said.

"Shall we once again return to your question, John?" the king asked. "As you well know, we have dignitaries from all over the world attending. Over thirty Indian princes have arrived. Rather impressive, yes?"

"Pappa," Carmen said, "I noted the other day that the route from

Westminster Abbey to Buckingham Palace is lined with stepped wooden platforms. I have been told they are to hold people desiring to watch the royal procession."

Dominic volunteered, "That is true, and you will see the same in the abbey. There are temporary risers being constructed as well. Over six thousand people will be in attendance."

Braxton added, "You know, I inspected them the other day. They are not dissimilar to Potemkin-like structures. They appear luxurious when covered in silks and bunting, but underneath is all rough wood. Quite shoddy and temporary. I'm pleased to know the chairs will be of some quality. They were being brought in as I departed the abbey and I understand they are from some significant palace or some such."

"In any event," Queen Mercedes interjected, "Tomorrow we will all be present at the abbey for rehearsal."

"Why rehearse, Mamma?" John asked. "It is all just a matter of Pappa and you putting on the crowns and then parading back here for the celebration."

"You, brother, have perfected and elevated simplicity to new heights," Braxton teased. "The coronation of the new king and queen of England is a time-honored tradition and of great import to the people."

Mercedes, indignant at John's comment, said, "I do not think you shall be in possession of that harum-scarum disposition following tomorrow's rehearsal. Allow four hours in your schedules." She smiled mischievously and raised her glass in a toast.

Braxton, Dominic, John, Diedre, and Carmen exchanged alarmed glances.

———

The five royal siblings sat on one of the temporary plaforms overlooking their parents standing below on the royal dais. It had been constructed recently for the ceremony. The abbey was festooned in brilliant banners, bunting, cascading tapestries and a forest of potted topiary and what must have been fields of vibrant colored flowers.

Dominic said, "That was very clever of you, Braxton, to ask Diedre's husband, the future kaiser, to take Maxim out to the country for hunting these last couple of days. Mathilde has the 'motherhood' excuse at the ready whenever she does not care to attend one function or the other.

So here we sit, the five of us, stranded at this interminable rehearsal.

John pulled out a flask and five small silver cups. "Bravo, brother," Diedre whispered loudly." The king and queen looked up from ten feet below, both wearing quizzical, bored looks.

"Pity Mamma and Pappa," Braxton whispered. "They are sure to know we are up to something. Receiving a cup from his brother John, he said, "Thank you ever so much."

"Yes, thank you, John," Carmen and Diedre repeated in unison.

John turned to Dominic who was sipping his whiskey, and said, "Dom, when you become king would you kindly just trot on down to the House of Lords in the Cinderella Carriage ..."

"You mean the State Carriage, do you not, John?" Diedre interrupted.

"Yes, the fabulous one," he said, waving her off and continued. "Have one of those stuffy old peers plop the crown on your head and then return to the palace. We will all be waiting there for you at the extravagant ball and dinner you will be hosting in your own honor."

"John, now that is where simplicity is actually a boon. I will second the motion. It is a capital idea!"

The siblings laughed aloud, echoing throughout the somber cathedral; catching the attention of the very sober officiates and their parents.

John leaned back, placing his feet on the railing so the soles of his boots greeted those looking in the direction of the revelers.

Mercedes threw a daunting evil-eye at John, which he missed as he was partaking of the flask.

Despite the denigrations of the actual event put forward by the unruly royal siblings, the coronation of

King Richard and Queen Mercedes was attended by royalty and nobles from throughout Europe, the empire's dominions, as well as a multitude of cheering subjects. England, and its traditions, remained intact and revered.

———

Following the coronation, as he was preparing to move to Renaissance House, Braxton was summoned to the weekly meeting between the king and the prime minister. The prince was announced as he entered the reception room. As had been the custom with predecessors, the prime minister was standing, and the king was seated. This had been the custom instituted by a previous monarch who desired to keep weekly audiences with the prime minister short, assuming the minister would keep his remarks briefer if he were standing.

Braxton bowed to his father and the prime minister bowed to the prince.

King Richard had aged during the years Braxton was on the continent. The gleam remained in his eyes but was now framed with greying hair and a beard.

The king opened the conversation, "Braxton, the prime minister and I have been discussing your role as envoy. We are very pleased with how you have comported yourself. While you were away, your late grandfather, the prime minister and I were impressed and grateful for the reports you provided. Decidedly, your accounts have made an invaluable contribution to the government understanding what is transpiring on the continent."

The prime minister spoke after the king appeared to have finished, saying, "Your Royal Highness, the king's ministers echo his majesty's sentiments."

His father informed Braxton he would be created

"Prince Royal" and was on the honors list for The Order of the Garter. Braxton bowed and thanked the king.

"Now, to another matter. The prime minister and my government have a significant request." King Richard looked to his minister and said, "My Lord Prime Minister, please elaborate."

Speaking to the prince, the prime minister said, "Your Royal Highness, the government is not being well served in the Far East, particularly not in Imperial Japan."

This unanticipated and surprising statement caught Braxton's attention.

The king rang a small bell on the table next to him. The double doors by which Braxton had entered were opened. Master Seiko Higoshino entered to room.

Prince Braxton made no effort to hide his own look of incredulity catching sight of his friend and teacher.

Seiko, lips pressed together in a tight grimace, looked directly at Braxton. He then bowed to the king, Braxton, and the prime minister. King Richard rose and asked the men to follow him to a table sitting away from the doors at the far end of the room.

The king took a deep breath, saying, "Braxton, please accept my apologies for not forewarning you of this meeting."

The prime minister continued, "The government reached out to Master Seiko when he arrived in England last month. You have spoken so highly of Master Seiko Higsohino in your reports, we believed he could be integral to our plan regarding the Far East, and in particular, Japan. Please note that Master Higoshino had been forbidden to speak with anyone regarding our discussions."

Seiko sat upright and expressionless.

Braxton had felt personally close to Seiko for years. Their spiritual connection was a bond. He sensed his teacher's embarrassment, bordering on feelings of dishonor.

The prime minister began again. "We have asked Master Seiko Higashino to assist the government on a sensitive matter. We are aware you are both close professionally and personally. We could not have imagined a more perfect team for this assignment.

"Imperial Japan is a sleeping giant that has been involuntarily placed on the international stage with little or no knowledge or experience as to how to protect its own interests. Stability is paramount in Asia. Russia, China, India, Southwest Asia, and possibly the United States are vying, along with Great Britain, to gain influence and trade concessions from Japan."

Braxton knew he had said as much in his reports. The prince suddenly felt a sense of unease. He was planning on returning to Russia. He suspected he was going to be advised to do something that did not fit within his plans.

King Richard elaborated on the purpose of the meeting. "We desire you to continue in your capacity as royal envoy. It is our hope that in this capacity, you will expand your role and go to Japan, interceding with the Imperial Japanese government to secure our interests."

Braxton looked at Seiko, who sat stone-faced, his attention directed toward the king.

His majesty continued, "We will, of course, continue to require the same useful information you have provided while in Europe and Russia. You speak the Japanese language. You have studied all things Japanese with Master Higoshino. You know as much about the Japanese culture and the people as does any Englishman. We would anticipate your assignment in Japan to last at least one year, maybe two."

The prince clenched his jaw, drawing a furtive look from Seiko.

The king, in a tenuous tone, continued, "My son, we do not expect an answer today. Please take your time to consider our proposition."

Braxton stood. "Thank you, father." He bowed and turned to the prime minister. "Thank you, Prime Minister, for your consideration. I appreciate your generosity allowing me time to consider this opportunity to continue to serve the empire." He paused. "I am reticent to accept, but I will consider it. In the meantime, I will be in London for the following two weeks and again for a fortnight at Aurelio Palace."

The young prince continued, "Prime Minister, I would like to take this occasion to invite you to come to our country home three weeks hence. Plan on being my guest for at least one or two days, should we need to discuss matters further, dependent of course, on how matters develop."

Braxton was about to ask his father's permission to leave when he turned back to the prime minister and said, "Oh yes, and may I suggest you signal the cabinet to be available to attend us at the palace should we plan to move forward?"

The king and prime minister exchanged surprised glances, caught off-guard by Braxton's apparently quick acquiescence and chess-like strategy.

Seiko let a small smirk escape his lips, knowing Braxton's methods so well.

"Yes, Your Royal Highness. With his majesty's permission, the cabinet and I, if requested, will attend you at the Aurelio Palace."

"Yes, of course. You have my permission and full

support, both of you," his majesty replied, almost chuckling, eyes sparkling with pride in his son.

"Oh, and one more thing."

"Yes, what is it Braxton," his father asked, impatience underlying his tone.

"Your Majesty, Prime Minister, Master Higashino, if I accept this proposal which requires my absence from England for at least two years, I am compelled to ask for eight months to complete my business in Europe and Russia. There are arrangements that must be made." Braxton rose and asked the king's permission to withdraw.

Exiting the room, Braxton left word with the king's private secretary positioned in the adjoining room to have Master Higaoshino attend him at Renaissance House at his earliest convenience.

———

When Braxton arrived at Renaissance House, he found his uncle Cosimo and Aramis were away, having left word they planned on joining him at Renaissance House in ten days. He retired to the part of the château that had served as his nursery as a child and then became his private rooms as he grew into a young man. The first thing he did was write a letter to Valentina.

My dearest Valentina,

I am in London and have moved my things from Buckingham Palace to Renaissance House. It is one of my favorite places. This is where, as a mere boy, I began formulating my future life. I started with my horses and still lived here when I purchased the railroad. I am delighted to see nothing has changed these past few years, although there have been some improvements to the furnishings, no doubt, thanks to Mother. This is a very special place. I hope to share it with you one day.

One of the purposes for relocating here from the palace was to work with Cosimo and Aramis while we are all in London. It appears they were called away on business. They are to return in ten days.

In the meantime, they have left me a mountain of paperwork to review. Of course, our dear Viscount Ramsey sent a trunk full of work from Russia. It arrived yesterday. I am so happy! I have my rooms and the house to myself and no interruptions, which allows me to make great progress slogging through all of it. You know how anxious I get when there is no work to be done. I thought I would die eleven days into the trek across Russia and Europe. But I made good use of my time. Just wait until Ramsey and Aramis see what I have put together for them. They so hate it when I have time to plan and strategize. My efforts always create mountains of work for them. I find that devilishly amusing!

As I have the house to myself, I have invited the staff accompanying me on my trip to quarter here. It will be much more convenient to get work done efficiently. I am sure they will enjoy the accommodations. It shall certainly prove to be great fun having people around with whom to share my home.

Tomorrow evening, I am hosting my family for an informal private dinner. Next week I am planning a garden party for the members of the House of Lords. Two days later the members of the House of Commons have been invited to a similar fête. Arrangements have been made for entertainment at both. The lords will enjoy an orchestra set up on the loggia overlooking the gardens. Members of the House of Commons will be treated to a full orchestra featuring the West End's most popular music of the day. I look forward to the second event. I may set up a race or two on the Renaissance House track. That could be jolly good fun.

The purpose of these events is to reacquaint myself with members of the government, and they with me. Having been absent from England for so long, it works in my favor for everyone to feel confident I am "au courante."

It is all politics and yes, as a member of the royal family, we are not permitted to be involved in such. But, as an entrepreneur and the king's envoy, it is imperative I have a comprehensive understanding of national and international politics and world economies. I will entertain smaller groups here and at Aurelio Palace once I ascertain where and on whom I need focus my attentions. We are encouraging select business leaders from across the country to attend these fêtes. They are the people with whom I have more in common and would prefer to spend my time.

Most importantly, understanding more about my country and its needs will facilitate my evaluating a new assignment offered by the government. This assignment could complicate both your and my immediate futures. Pray take no offense at my not detailing the offer. That must remain confidential. Should I decline the proposal, knowledge of my refusal would embarrass the government and my father, the king. Rest assured; I will endeavor to do nothing that will keep us apart.

I will telegraph a "Yes" or "No" indicating whether or not I have accepted the offer. The details will have to wait until we meet.

All my love, Braxton

———

Braxton had another matter to address: Carlo Ratini. Carlo had been in Braxton's service leading his Intelligence Operation, or I.O., for almost two years. He had done very well and had been his director of the Mars project in Venice and throughout Europe. The Mars project had operated clandestinely to identify and eliminate Braxton's enemies and potential threats.

Carlo successfully supervised the six agents commissioned to carry out Braxton's orders. Lord Ramsey had served as liaison between Carlo and Braxton. It was now time to lay the groundwork to duplicate the Mars project in England.

The prince had been made aware of threats he needed to quash before they grew into problems. His encounters with his upcoming house guests would shed light on new potential dangers. Braxton would enlist Carlo via Lord Ramsey, to assist him with this matter while at the Aurelio Palace.

———

The busy prince, having completed his business in London and Renaissance House, departed for the Aurelio Palace. He was happy to be returning to another one of his childhood homes. Riding his own train on the track his railroad had built through the land he had developed into a thriving industrial enclave brought great satisfaction.

The landau ride from the train to Aurelio Palace was brief but provided him an opportunity to take in the surrounding countryside where he had spent most of his childhood. The palace staff turned out in formation to welcome him. He thanked them for being there, for faithfully serving his family and made a point to tell them how much he had missed his Aurelio Palace family.

Nowhere else on earth was he more loved than at the palace. Braxton was the boy who had entertained them with his youthful precocious pranks and genuinely kind human nature. The boy had become a man who spent his own money creating the Aurelio Palace Academy that educated their children in a public school, providing them a quality education. He had always made an effort, even as a boy, to do what he could to look after the welfare of the household and the estate workers.

Ever dreaming and scheming as a child, the young

man had set his mind to one day owning the Aurelio Palace. His grandparents, the deceased Duke and Duchess de Chiacontella, had given the palace to his parents as a wedding gift. It was highly improbable their majesties would be returning to the Aurelio Palace now they had assumed the throne.

His travels through Europe having exposed him to the most exquisite residences in the world, the prince had determined that Aurelio Palace was worthy of a renovation and the expense to maintain it. The palace had the potential to rival anything he had seen in his travels. Renovation and updating would take years to complete. Should his parents allow him to purchase the palace from them, he would make changes that would not only reflect his station and wealth but would serve as headquarters for his growing economic empire.

Braxton had been disappointed that Josh, his former stable boy and now the head trainer for his stables, was not at the house to greet him. Josh, with whom he regularly corresponded, had written the prince that he wanted to be there when Braxton arrived. But unfortunately, one of their most prized mares was having difficulty foaling, necessitating Josh be present to assist.

After addressing the household staff, Braxton made his way directly to the stables. He was gratified and impressed to find Josh examining the newborn foal.

Josh's dependability and business acumen had made the former stable boy successful and wealthy. Braxton, observing Josh's handling of the young animal, thought back to their simpler days of long ago. I remember the first time I saw him, when he looked up at me after he had put out the fire in the stable yard. Josh has always been a good friend and the best business partner a man could have. We built a racing team together and won the Queen Anne Stakes.

Now look at him. He runs an internationally renowned racing stable and breeding facility.

The prince kept out of Josh's sight, waiting for him to complete his examination. The task completed; Braxton stepped into the stall.

"Josh, my dear friend."

Josh's eyes lit up and his familiar toothy grin danced across his face. "Brax! You have arrived!"

The men embraced, roundly slapping each other on their backs. "Yes, I am here, just in time to see my business partner hard at work bringing new life into the world."

Josh turned to the veterinarian and said, "Thank you for your help here. Our new charge seems quite healthy. I will be back later to check on the foal."

He then turned to his friend and said, "Come Braxton, let me wash up and we can spend some time together. I have so much to share with you."

Braxton and Josh left the stable and spent the remainder of the afternoon and evening reminiscing. The conversation soon turned to their current business of racing and breeding.

The prince's stables had prospered. Their reputation had spread throughout Europe and now the Americas, with wealthy breeders sending their mares to the stable to strengthen and improve their bloodlines. The revenues could have easily supported Braxton and his lifestyle, however, he had taken the largest part of his gains from this venture and invested them in the Aurelio Palace Academy and its students. He continued to give back to the community he loved. The Academy was ably run by its headmaster under the supervision of a Board of Governors and continued to graduate capable students, both male and female. Braxton embraced the Academy as an investment in England's future and that of his businesses, which were prospering with the addition of his graduates as employees.

Braxton spent a great deal of time during his stay at the Aurelio Palace monitoring classes and reviewing the subject matter being taught. His experiences in Europe and Russia had equipped him with the knowledge of how to effectively revise and update the Aurelio Academy curriculum. He increased their emphasis on mechanical engineering and geology. The teaching of math and science were elevated at minor expense to classical literature and languages. He was positioning the Academy to pioneer civil engineering.

At significant personal expense, he hired instructors and professionals who had firsthand, practical work experience. He designated a portion of the estate to function as an outdoor laboratory and training area for the design and building of structures, bridges, and roads. His students would enter the world with genuine experience in their fields. Academic and practical challenges were designed to test knowledge, problem-solving, and creativity.

The Academy had begun attracting students from outside the estate and surrounding counties. Braxton wanted to educate those who desired the Academy education, but the Academy now required larger facilities to house and educate this influx of students. The impetuous prince decided it was more expeditious to act first and beg forgiveness later. It was, after all, not his property, but that of his parents, the king and queen.

He took hold of unused or underutilized portions of the vast palace and renovated these structures to accommodate the Academy. Once again, it occurred to him he did not own the palace yet but continued on with his projects.

Forcing himself to face the reality that he must broach the subject of purchasing the palace from his parents, he wrote them a letter.

Dearest Mamma and Pappa,

I am so enjoying being back at Aurelio. It is truly my favorite place on earth. The Academy is flourishing and the stables thriving. All is good here.

Regretfully, I owe you an apology. I have taken it upon myself, and at my own expense, to make repairs on the palace and renovate several of the outbuildings. Forgive me, but presumptuously I have started adding on to the Academy. It has grown so much that more buildings are required to accommodate the expanding curriculum and increase in the number of students.

Then there are the stables. I have all but taken over the entire facility. Again, things are going well, and space is needed. Of course, there was much to be done in repairing roofs and fencing. All that has been tended to. The paddocks have been dug up and new clay laid.

I have craftsmen arriving from London to attend to the cupula.

Some of the lead has fallen away from the lattice causing water from rain to damage the frescos and darken part of several interior columns. Of course, this should not be news to you, as that has always been a major concern of yours when residing here.

Which brings me to my point. I know you must miss this paradise. I certainly have. But as our new king and queen, I cannot anticipate your spending time at Aurelio. It would seem impossible. You have Buckingham Palace, Windsor, the castle in Scotland, and five more residences. I do not imagine you relish the thought of keeping up a home in which you cannot reside. With the Aurelio Palace in little use, it is subject to inevitable decay. Surely, none of us would care to see that occur.

I would like to purchase the Aurelio Palace. By the mere existence of the Academy and stables, the palace has taken on a new life and purpose. It is in truth only partly our family's home now. Dominic, John, and Diedre are married and living elsewhere. Carmen, when married, would certainly live with her husband. Importantly, neither of my brothers, whom I love and adore, can afford the upkeep.

Think of the future of the Aurelio Palace Academy. The graduates have the potential to make valuable contributions to national and international affairs, both in government service and business. The Academy's prestige is growing and is a credit to our family.

And of course, the racing and breeding stable have become renowned. That, too, is a credit to the family. It also provides the income that underwrites the Academy. Then there are my business interests. I would like to headquarter my staff in the west wing. It has not been utilized since before it was gifted by Mamma's parents, the Duke and Duchess de Chiacontella. I will restore it and put it to good use. Perhaps most importantly, one day I hope to make it my family seat when married and to raise my children here.

I hope you can see your way clear to consider this rather audacious request to purchase Aurelio Palace.

Your loving son, Braxton

3

QUEEN MERCEDES AND THE AURELIO PALACE

Her Imperial Majesty, Queen Mercedes, arrived at the Aurelio Palace unannounced one week after Braxton posted his letter. As her arrival caught the palace household, along with Braxton, completely off guard, no preparations had been made. The palace was disheveled and crawling with laborers.

Braxton lived simply, so the kitchens were half staffed and some of its personnel employed on other projects on the estate. The informality congruent with refurbishment and building amused Mercedes. She grew more confident she had made the correct decision to personally deliver Richard's and her reply to Braxton's letter.

Prince Braxton was standing at a lectern in the Academy lecture hall speaking of civil engineering and its place in the future of the developed and undeveloped world. He was explaining what he had seen and what he saw as real possibilities in Eastern Europe and most of Russia.

Mercedes had insisted her arrival not be announced. She stood just out of sight of the podium from which

Braxton spoke. She had attended many university lectures in her time, but none was ever so relevant and interesting. Two hours later, Braxton completed his talk and was receiving a standing ovation from over one hundred students. As the applause began to die down, she nodded to the majordomo who had accompanied her.

"Her Imperial Majesty, the Queen!"

There was shuffling, murmuring and then silence as heads turned toward the voice that had announced Mercedes' presence. The queen, still clothed in her traveling attire, made her way to the plaform on which the podium stood. The crowd had risen to their feet when she was announced. They bowed and curtsied as she passed.

There was total silence. Braxton, still dazed by his mother's surprise visit, bowed to her as she approached. He extended his hand to assist her up the four steps to the plaform. His mother then offered him her cheeks, in the French style. He gently kissed both.

Mercedes turned to the audience and asked that they take their seats.

She smiled and turned to Braxton. "Please find a chair my dear."

Braxton did as he was told, settling into the one chair on the plaform.

Returning her attention to the gathered assembly, Queen Mercedes stood at the podium and addressed the students.

"I hope you will forgive me this impromptu visit and indulge a mother who has come to revel in the success of her beloved son. "Today I am not here as your queen. I am here as a mother who loves her children, and here to dote on my son Braxton." She paused, her voice betraying her emotions.

"You all know firsthand how hard your prince has

worked, and hopefully have given some thought to the financial investment that he has made towards your education."

The assembled faculty and students sat in rapt attention.

"His active interest in your education is well deserved. I want to thank you, as his mother, for validating his efforts. You, and those who have already graduated, are the best our empire has to offer the world. Your dedication to your education and your future professional lives is, and will be, my son's legacy."

Mercedes then took a moment to look around the auditorium, leaving the motherly tone behind. She stood a little taller and assumed her regal stature.

"What will be your legacy? What will you do with your lives?

Will you be good sons and daughters? Will you be good husbands and wives? What kind of parents will you be to your children, your grandchildren? Will you strengthen and empower the empire?

"My dear Braxton has given you the tools and the opportunity. Your actions will evidence your decision. I, for one, believe in you. His Royal Highness Prince Braxton believes in you. God bless you, and God Save the King!"

She turned toward Braxton and blew him a kiss. He stood in frozen amazement.

Mercedes descended the plaform and proceeded out of the room accompanied by thunderous applause, hurrahs and shouts of "God save the King!"

Braxton had not moved an inch as his mother disappeared through the door. The audience then turned and looked directly at the still immobile prince. Moments later he bowed to the crowd and exited through the rear of the auditorium.

———

Braxton returned to his rooms to bathe and dress for dinner. He had asked a footman to inform his mother he hoped she would join him on the west terrace a half hour before the dinner gong sounded.

They each realized this would be the first time they had dined alone together since Braxton was but six or seven years old. They had much on which to reminisce and also a future to contemplate.

———

Mercedes entered the Japanese salon. The radiant queen filled the room with her tall, mystical figure, gowned in the latest Parisienne couture. Wearing a tiara and jewels, in Braxton's eyes she took on the appearance of a goddess. Lady Randolph Churchill, the reigning beauty of the day, could not match her effervescent beauty. She was indeed an empress and his mother, whom he adored.

Braxton instantly felt like the young boy who, years ago, would hide behind curtains or under furniture striving to catch a glimpse of his mother departing or returning from many spectacular events.

He strode up to his mother, bowed and kissed her gloved hand. She pulled him close, as any mother would her dearest child. "Hello Mamma. Are you not full of surprises!"

"Yes, my dear. Finally, I have achieved something I have always desired."

Braxton looking at her quizzically asked, "And what is that?"

"To surprise you."

His mother released him and removed two glasses of champagne from a silver tray held by a footman standing nearby. Handing one to Braxton she took his hand and drew him across the room onto the terrace and into the gardens.

Mercedes impishly asked, "Do you recall the night following the inferno in the rotunda?" Hearing those words, Braxton coughed and almost dropped his glass.

He stuttered, "Well I, uh, suppose somewhat vaguely, I might remember."

She responded lightly, "Ah, try not to be silly Braxton. Everyone knows you have a perfect memory and recall events exactly as they occurred. I decline to further bait or tease you, so let me now share something with you of which you know nothing."

They continued their measured walk, sipping their champagne as the sun began to set, its rays gently reflecting off Mercedes' tiara and jewels.

"I came into the nursery on the night of the fire to see if you were sleeping and to steal a kiss. You had worried me greatly. On that night, I realized it was you who were involved in the mess. You frightened me beyond belief. I found you filthy and exhausted in your bed. I also noticed the hidden panel to the secret passageway ajar. I quickly closed the panel and put a chair in front of it. Nanny arrived shortly. We bathed you, changed the linens and put you back to bed."

"You spoke to me in Italian that night, asking my forgiveness and for my help. There was no question I would grant both requests. The following night as I came to check on you, I found you were not in your bed. Also, the candlestick from the previous night was missing. I suspected it had once again accompanied you through the passages."

Absorbing these words, Prince Braxton swallowed the contents of his glass.

His mother smiled inwardly and continued, "Earlier that day I had inspected the secret passages, the same passages your Uncle Cosimo and I had discovered in our childhood. I found the tools of your misdeeds.

"Instantly, upon seeing you had left your bed, I suspected you were trying to cover your trail from the previous evening. Had I correctly surmised the situation?"

Looking down at his empty glass, Braxton replied, "Yes, Mother." "Of course, I was right. The last thing I wanted to do was impede your efforts. So, I retreated to the corner of your room and waited.

Eventually, you returned. The following day I explained everything to your father."

Coming to an abrupt stop, her turned to his mother and asked, "You told Father?"

"Yes. I tell him almost everything. He has a right and the privilege as father and sovereign to know just what I want him to know," she chuckled.

They continued their walk in silence for a few minutes longer. "Well, Mamma, it appears you have succeeded. This entire afternoon and evening have been full of surprises."

Braxton gazed about the sprawling gardens hoping to spy a footman carrying a tray containing more glasses of champagne. He yearned for a change of subject.

In a somewhat impatient and tired tone, he asked, "Now tell me, Mamma, are you here in response to my letter?"

"Impertinence does not become you, Braxton. Remember, I am still your mother. Let us stroll a while longer before addressing the purpose of my visit."

Passing through the garden's rose quadrangle, a

liveried footman finally approached with two more glasses of champagne on a silver tray. Accepting them, Braxton and Mercedes continued their walk, filling their banter with light talk and gossip, making their way back to the palace.

Braxton had instructed the servants to prepare the Japanese Salon for their dinner. The meal was presented on precious Japanese china and exquisite ivory flatware. The oriental lanterns had been lit and the room scented with light hints of smoked cherry incense. It was an elegant, yet cozy ambiance.

Mercedes and Braxton made light conversation as the footmen presented the meal. She asked the servants to leave the salon upon completing their tasks.

"So, tell me about the family. What is the latest news?" Braxton inquired.

"I suspect Mathilde is with child but is keeping it to herself until the pregnancy is further along. Out of respect for her, I too am keeping her secret."

The prince exhaled, sensing the ever-present fear of succession nestled in the back of his brain had lessened.

Concern in her voice, his mother queried, "Are you well, Braxton?"

"Yes, of course, Mother. This is such an unexpected surprise. I am so happy for them both."

Mercedes fixed a look on her son and said, "Why is it so unexpected? They are married. Married people tend to have children. Your existence attests to that."

"Yes, mother," Braxton said, feeling ridiculous.

She continued, "Your brother John is another matter. His role in the succession is problematic, due to his sexual proclivities. But there is no point in discussing it."

Braxton, taken aback by his mother's openness in addressing John's "never-to-be-mentioned" habits, averted his gaze. His own dalliances gave way to feelings of disingenuousness. "I understand Mother," he said.

"And Dierdre, somehow, with that husband of hers and the misery that is her marriage, has succeeded in producing two sons and a daughter."

Braxton offered what he thought might be news to his mother. "You may or may not know this. I hope it pleases you. It appears that Maxim and Carmen are secretly engaged."

"That is no secret to me, Braxton. I am her mother. The moment I saw her I knew she was in love. It was only a matter of time before I pried it out of her. Both her father and I are concerned she would have to live in Russia. She did not like the idea when she was about to be betrothed to the late czarevich, but she seems quite fond of Maxim.

"We have discussed her living in Russia, and she is concerned about it. I suppose she has shared this with you. Regardless, we are not going to stand in her way."

Braxton asked his mother, "And the government? What do they say?"

"Well, as you know, it is the church that is the issue here. She will have to renounce her and her children's claim to the English throne if she converts to Russian Orthodoxy and marries Maxim. We both know her conversion is required if she is to be crowned czarina."

The prince volunteered, "My conversations with Carmen do not cause me to believe that is a concern for her."

"Frankly, Braxton, it is not a concern of ours either." She paused and looked Braxton directly in the eyes, "Your father's and my concern is when are you going to start producing your own legitimate children?"

Braxton was once again taken off-guard. "Mother, I am sure I do not know of what you speak."

"Really Braxton? From what I have heard of your travels you have been getting quite a lot of practice in the act of breeding." Her tone and countenance betrayed nothing. It was as if she had asked about the weather.

"Mother, stop!"

"My son, what is it you want out of life? You have accomplished much in your short time on earth. My dear, are you content? Are you happy? What more do you seek? You hold your future in your own hands. What life course do you plan to navigate?"

"Mamma, I am very content with my life. I am so very grateful you and Pappa have given me leave to pursue it on my own terms. I have been allowed to do exactly as I wish. I have traveled. I have seen much of the world. I have had many challenges and have met them full on.

"Long before coming under the tutelage of Master Seiko, I have known I wanted to play a significant role in the world, outside the royal family. I have always desired to accomplish things on my own. I felt impelled to run from my responsibilities as a royal and earn my place as king of my own economic empire, one in which I rule, not reign. Now I mean for my empire to touch every corner of the world. I will one day be a leader of men and industry."

Projecting a renewed confidence, Braxton leaned over and refilled their champagne flutes.

"I do not look for fame, but I do look for fortune. I abhor notoriety. I must make a difference and have a positive impact on all that I touch. With my wealth, I can confront evil and provide for the less fortunate. With my wealth, I can help protect our family and the nation.

"Mother, when I realized I was earning and keeping more money than the Russian Imperial Treasury, I knew I would one day be the richest man in the world. I am achieving my wildest dreams!

"Now it is time for me to indulge my greatest wish, that of having a family of my own."

The queen stared at her son as she had during the duration of his revealing discourse. Her eyes moistened.

Mercedes then lifted her glass, and said, "My dear Braxton, I lift this glass in tribute to all you have accomplished, to all you will accomplish in the future, and to your new family." Braxton acknowledged the toast.

"Well, regarding starting a family, I am very taken with the Grand Duchess Valentina."

"Do you mean Maxim's cousin, the czar's daughter?" "Yes."

"Good, I was hoping those rumors were true." "What rumors, Mother?"

"Don't be silly or play games with me, Braxton. You and I know there is little that happens here or on the continent to which I am not privy. For your information, I have read your reports, and unlike the men who have read them, I read 'between the lines.'

"Oh Braxton, it is often difficult to find opportunities to keep you grounded. So, on this occasion, I would like to do just that and give you a little advice."

Braxton quizzically turned his head, not knowing where this conversation might lead.

"That liaison between you and my nephew, Aramis, was a gamble. I hope you have had your fill and will either be more discreet in the future or put an end to such behavior. It is up to you. You know the possible consequences. That is all I have to say about that."

"Aramis?" the prince mumbled. His mind raced wildly; his face blanched. He once again drained his glass of champagne.

"Of course, Aramis. Are there more?" Mercedes asked. Braxton refused to look at his mother as he whispered, "Does Pappa know?"

"Of course not," his mother replied, removing the bottle of champagne from the ice bucket, and refilling their glasses. "As I said before, he knows only what I need him to know as your father and sovereign."

Mercedes let the conversation settle as she picked at the food remaining on her plate. Moments later, she caught Braxton's attention with a relaxed smile and patted his hand resting on the table.

"Now, concerning this fabulous palace." She rang a small translucent jade bell resting beside her. The salon's doors opened, and a servant arrived carrying a porfolio. She motioned for it to be given to the prince. The servant then left the room.

Braxton held the porfolio in both hands. He looked at his mother with incredulity, then down at the porfolio.

"Your father and I have signed the Aurelio Palace and its one hundred thousand acres over to you. The Aurelio Palace is yours. It is our gift to you."

Braxton swallowed hard and braced himself, placing one hand on the table.

Mercedes floated up and out of her chair. She knelt beside him as he quietly collected himself. "Braxton, your father and I are so honored to be your parents. I know that your Chiacontella ancestors who built this palace would want you to have it. The Academy, the horses, the businesses, they are all wondrous undertakings. It is our way of reminding you of our unconditional love and support in all that you do.

"Braxton, it is with love and humility that we bestow upon you our favorite possession. We know you will honor it."

She rose, kissed his forehead and gracefully walked out of the room, closing the door behind her.

Braxton wrapped his arms around the porfolio. Leaning over it, his tears slid slowly down his face.

———

The prime minister arrived three days later. Braxton had not bothered to curtail the renovations and construction occurring in various places throughout the palace, outbuildings, and the estate. He felt it would do the prime minister and the cabinet good to see progress in so many areas of the palatial estate that represented the many things that defined his life

The prime minister was impressed with the activity. He had always admired the prince and was delighted to witness the young man's undertakings meeting with success. He was mildly concerned Braxton was perhaps over-investing so much of himself and his fortune in these projects. Was this activity around the chateau a signal Braxton might turn down his proposal?

The prime minister was escorted up the grand flying staircase to the second floor. They soon passed beneath the infamous rotunda, crossing beneath the dome to the doors standing on the south side.

Two footmen stood beside the twenty-foot double doors. As they opened the doors, the prime minister stepped forward and froze.

The room was enormous. The doors opened onto a 200-foot long, 30-foot-wide center promenade, flanked on both sides by 30- foot columns. The Romanesque columns were fashioned of auburn marble veined in gold spidering the glistening columns. The ceilings were of ornately carved, recessed marble tile.

Extravagant mythological carvings on mahogany walls lined the entire room.

Huge Romanesque chandeliers, lit by gas, illuminated the center of the room. Roman-style torches served as over sized sconces, also gas lit. The flames were not subtle, nor were they obtrusive.

Exquisite marble inlay decorated the floors stretching before the prime minister. At the far end stood a twenty-five-foot tall statue atop a five-foot pedestal. The figure was the original Cardinal Duke de Chiacontella, dressed as a Roman Emperor. A skylight from above lit the god-like icon.

To the right, on the other side of the first colonnade, was a large table, 30-feet in length and surrounded by high-backed chairs.

Centered behind the table was a massive fireplace carved of what appeared to be the same marble making up the columns. Three large French windows completed the wall on both sides of the monstrous ornate fireplace. The eastern exposure revealed the refurbishment of the wing that would serve as the headquarters for Braxton's business interests. The southern wall contained a door that led to the future offices. If he could have observed the western exposure, the prime minister would have seen the renovation and expansion of the wing that was to be part of The Academy.

The columns to the left partially shielded the space that resembled the one on the right. On the center of that wall was a duplicate fireplace of the one directly across from it. The three French doors on both sides of the fireplace led to a full terrace and presented a view of the palace gardens and park.

Braxton appeared from behind the large desk placed in front of the fireplace. To the left of the desk was a large, low-level table surrounded by eight comfortable chairs. To his left stood a higher table, a worktable that accommodated four to six people.

Walking briskly toward the prime minister who remained standing dumbstruck, Braxton said, "Prime Minister, thank you for honoring the Aurelio Palace with your presence."

"The pleasure is all mine, your Royal Highness. I have long heard of the treasure the Chiacontella's had hidden in the country. Never could I have imagined a palace so grand, and certainly worthy of the most imperial Roman emperor!"

"Thank you, my Lord. Interestingly, nothing had been altered before I came along, other than adding gas, as the palace was constructed almost 300 years ago. As you know, my Chiacontella ancestors lived relatively modestly on the continent but indulged themselves with a Medici-like existence here in England."

More pleasantries were exchanged. The fireplaces ablaze, Braxton showed the prime minister around the room, pointing out busts and paintings of his ancestors. The plush, strategically-placed Oriental rugs brought a warmth to the space that would have escaped any other room this size. The chamber effused power and gravitas.

Noticing a large oil painting of the present king and queen on their wedding day above one fireplace's mantle, the prime minister said, "My Lord Braxton, what are you going to do with that empty space above the mantle behind the large table on the opposite side?"

"I am so glad you asked Prime Minister. I have recently commissioned a painting of my parents in their coronation robes. As you know, they do not aspire to sit for hours and hours for any portrait. It will be a challenge getting them to cooperate. I am going to coerce them to sit for the painting by donating money to a hospital and naming it after them, making the task more palatable!"

Braxton stepped toward the end of the fireplace mantle and gave three tugs on an ornate servant's pull suspended from the ceiling. A footman entered carrying a tray bearing a decanter of Cognac and crystal snifters which he placed on an oval table.

Aurelio's new owner and the minister sat across from one another.

Once having presented the two men with cigars, leaving one of the French doors opening onto the terrace ajar, the footman left the room.

"Prime Minister, I would like to take this opportunity to thank you for allowing me to be of service to the empire. My role as envoy has provided me with experiences of which one could only dream. It has been my most sincere honor and pleasure to have served the king, the empire, and you, in that capacity."

The prime minister was grateful to hear the hearfelt and humble remarks coming from a man he had come to revere, a man of high birth and a humble heart. A man of immense talents and a grateful soul. He valued Braxton's contributions to the realm, known to him through the prince's minutely-detailed reports. The reports had not just provided numbers and statistics but contained accurate and perceptive insights. Braxton's accounts while traveling throughout Europe and Russia had helped lay the foundation for preserving the British Empire's place on the world stage.

"Prime Minister, I did not ask you to come here to provide you with my answer. I believe you know me well enough to have ascertained my decision. For years you have been kind to me. I think of you as a father figure and

with that, I would and could never refuse you. I am yours
to command!"

They stood and shook hands, then sat down, side by
side, not across from one another.

"Minister, it pains me to say I require two additional
months in England to attend to my affairs. You are, of
course, aware through my report that absenting myself
from our isle has placed a great burden on me. A good deal
remains to be done."

Braxton presented a new proposal. "Should the
government think it worthwhile following my anticipated
successes in Japan, why not have me continue along the
coast of China and Singapore and on to India?

These colonies have never been properly represented
by the crown. It makes sense to take advantage of my
being in that part of the world. With our challenges in
trade along the route and the hellish time we are having in
India, perhaps my travels could provide value.

"That, Prime Minister, is why I asked you to have the
cabinet attend us here."

The leader of parliament's initial reaction was
cautious. As they continued their conversation into the
early morning hours, they came to an agreement and
mutual understanding of the value and significance the
prince's offer represented.

At 2:00 in the morning, the prince summoned a footman. The prime minister handed the servant instructions
to be forwarded to 10 Downing Street, directing the
cabinet to assemble at the Aurelio Palace two days hence
for a "cabinet weekend."

The following day, the prince instructed the household
to prepare for the arrival of the 15-member cabinet. Plans
were hastily made for formal dinners, hunts, shooting, and
many hours of meetings.

The cabinet weekend would last five days.

The week proved to be particularly productive. Many of the jealousies and empty rivalries were mediated. There was noticeable excitement in the government. The ministers felt their efforts were more purposeful and they were growing stronger together.

Oddly, they also felt a kinship for a royal: Prince Braxton. The young entrepreneur had treated them with his customary respect. He had known many of them and their families from his youth. Now they could see he had become a man.

He communicated his respect for their talents and selfless contribution to the empire. Their acknowledgment of his abilities would pay huge dividends later. Braxton's reputation as a gifted entrepreneur and statesman traveled quickly through the government and the ruling classes' families.

―――――

During the following weeks, Braxton detailed his instructions for how his business interests were to be administered while he was on the other side of the world. Lord Ramsey was his senior director. The viscount had left the railroad to work exclusively for Braxton. The prince trusted his judgment and relied on him to make decisions in his stead. For this, Ramsey was awarded a percentage of the profits.

Ramsey had long been reticent to be involved with the Intelligence Operation, although he was in fact its head. Braxton and the viscount set about strengthening and streamlining the operation. Prince Braxton and Ramsey had come to the realization they must protect their interests at any cost. They reluctantly stepped deeper into the gray world of espionage.

The prince headed to London to make social rounds with his family and attend to business interests. He spent a great deal of time at the railroad and initiated discussions about moving his manufacturing interests in rail from Germany to Manchester.

Braxton was keen on using English engineering and manufacturing to support his interests.

While Ramsey and the prince were in Manchester, Braxton endowed a trust that would construct a hospital for children. He named the hospital after his parents, "Their Royal Majesties Richard & Mercedes Children's Hospital."

During his stay in Manchester while accompanying the prince, Lord Ramsey met with Carlo Ratini to solidify the evolving London Mars project. Signore Ratini also insisted Lord Ramsey be made aware of another delicate matter, one that threatened Braxton's reputation and that of the royal family.

"Mademoiselle Hélène, Comtesse de Bèrengar, is ruffling some feathers," Ratini said to Lord Ramsey. "Due to her inappropriate ranting in social settings, her relatives have found themselves in several rather embarrassing situations. In an attempt to calm her down, they have confined her to the family estate in Manchester, far from society."

"Signore, do you feel her isolation is sufficient? Is it having the desired effect on her?" Ramsey asked.

"I do not. And what is worse, she will come into her majority soon, attaining her freedom and a vast inheritance. What are now nasty rumors could soon become an international scandal for the royals."

Ramsey thought for a moment, then in a whisper said, "Let her guardian know that if she is not kept under control, we will take matters into our own hands."

"Yes, my lord."

Braxton returned to London to learn of two Buckingham Palace proclamations. The first was to announce that Prince Dominic's wife, Princess Mathilde, was with child. The recognition of her pregnancy was welcomed by Braxton as he would soon be one step further removed from the succession. He prayed the birth would go well and that the line would be secure in one other than his own.

The second announcement from the palace was the betrothal of his sister, Princess Carmen, to the Grand Duke Prince Maxim.

Another triumph for the empire and a move that, hopefully, would secure a peaceful Europe. The decision had been expedited in lieu of the czar's health. It was long past time Maxim should have married. He required a wife to produce an heir and stabilize the Russian throne.

Two weeks into his stay in London Braxton was summoned to the palace to meet with his parents. He found them with Carmen, waiting for him in the White Drawing Room. The conversation, of course, started with the impending birth of their majesties' first grandchild. The chatter was light and hopeful.

As he had anticipated, the topic then turned to Carmen's engagement.

"Braxton, what are your plans for returning to your business interests on the continent?" the king asked.

Carmen fidgeted and shifted her weight.

Mercedes reached over and patted her daughter's forearm. "What is on your mind, Carmen?" Braxton asked.

Carmen shook her head.

Mercedes smiled and said, "We were wondering

because the family is of course planning to go to Moscow for the wedding."

"When is the marriage scheduled to take place?" Braxton queried.

The king sat silent, observing the conversation.

"It is in two months," Carmen said, adjusting her skirt then fidgeting with her necklace.

Mercedes directed the conversation to the preparations, "We think we will take the entire family. Though Mathilde, being with child, and the younger cousins will not be in attendance."

"What Mamma and Pappa are saying, dear brother, is that we would like you to consider providing us passage on your train and making all the arrangements."

The room stood tortuously silent.

Feeling trapped, Braxton thought, this will further delay my return to the oil fields. It will require no less than ten additional cars. There are the obligatory stops at every major capital along the way. Balls and galas. No doubt the trip will take a month. Then the weeks in Moscow. Damn!

In the end, Braxton resolved himself to the fact that all he had anticipated was true. She was his sister; it was his family. Maxim was his friend. Russia held his future in its hands.

Upon leaving the audience, he rallied to their cause and immediately set about making arrangements for railway cars to be transported to Calais in advance of the family's sailing for France. The train would be ready and waiting for the royal family's arrival on the French coast.

———

Following this conversation, Braxton, ever quick to spot an opportunity, requested a meeting with the prime minister and the minister of war.

"Gentlemen, thank you for taking time out of your busy schedules to meet with me." The three men sat on the loggia overlooking the Renaissance House gardens.

"It is our pleasure, Your Royal Highness," the prime minister said. The portly minister of war nodded in agreement.

"The reason I have asked you here is I would like you to consider

assigning the guard escorting my sister to Moscow to my entourage once she is married. She will have no need of the men, but I shall." "Prince Braxton, of course we are here to support you and the royal family. May I ask why you think you will have need of a military contingent? His majesty's ambassador to Japan has men who could be of service."

Braxton turned to the prime minister and said, "Perhaps you should take that question, my lord."

The prime ministered covered his mouth and coughed, not at all inclined to come to the prince's aid.

Braxton, sensing the prime minister's reticence, continued, "Following our meetings at Aurelio, it came to my attention there are many unknowns that might present themselves during the upcoming travels. Hong Kong and Singapore are melting pots of many cultures. Cultures not inclined to share our same interests. And then there is India, a veritable viper's den of intrigue and discontent. It is vital my entourage be able to defend themselves should we find ourselves in untenable situations."

The matter was discussed at some length. Both ministers were eventually won over by Braxton's argument.

"Excellent," Braxton said. "Now I have another

requirement. I insist the men immediately begin learning Japanese and taking instruction in

Japanese culture and martial arts. I recommend Master Seiko Higashino be put in charge of this effort and be authorized to hire additional tutors and practitioners of Japanese martial arts. This will allow six to eight months to learn as much as they can absorb regarding all things Japanese. The success of my mission is dependent on all members of the party knowing as much as possible about this strange land before arriving on its shores."

As Braxton was leaving the meeting he turned and said, "Gentlemen, has it ever occurred to you while serving as the royal envoy these last years, I have received no remuneration whatsoever? Do you realize that, unlike all other members of the imperial family, I do not receive a stipend from parliament? Does it strike you as interesting that I have personally born all the costs?

Fortunately for all, I would have it no other way."

The two ministers shifted uncomfortably in their chairs.

"Your argument has merit, my lord," acknowledged the minister of war.

"I would agree," the prime minster said.

"Thank you, gentlemen." Knowing he had made his point, Braxton executed a shallow bow and left the room.

4

AN IMPERIAL MARRIAGE AND A
SECRET ROMANCE

Every member of the royal family, except for the pregnant Mathilde, sailed for France three weeks following the coronation. The trip through Europe and various stops lasted a month. Braxton took steps to protect his privacy, his time and his productivity. He was the only traveler with a private car. He discouraged his family from frequenting the cars dedicated to his staff.

As was often the case when royals traveled to Moscow, most would lay over at the Catherine Palace in Tver while the train's coal and water were replenished. The stop was also useful in providing a respite for the royals and the upcoming rigors of Moscow, a city caught in medieval times. Even though it was nominally the imperial capital, Moscow held no allure for those preferring the more western culture of St. Petersburg.

The imperial capital served to maintain power through observing ancient traditions, appealing to the more rural peoples populating the greater part of the vast land mass spreading out to the east and Far East. Moscow was known to be endured by the visiting western nobles.

Arriving in Moscow, the marriage of Maxim and Carmen consisted of ancient religious observances, intriguing yet mystifying ceremonies and centuries-old traditions rivaling any western Europe had to offer.

Every major royal house and principality in Europe was represented. The wedding was held at the Cathedral of the Assumption, the same cathedral where an attempted assassination had been made on Maxim's life.

———

Maxim and Braxton, finding what time together they could, reviewed and strategized their efforts in mining, forestry, and oil exploration. The prince and his team received news confirming oil deposits in Siberia. The reports did not speculate on how much oil might lie beneath the Russian soil. The most promising deposits lay beneath the tundra.

Few roads and no railroads existed in Eastern Siberia nor in the tundra. The concept of exploration and drilling in a land that offered no shelter, and was frozen most of the year, required expertise and experience neither they nor their engineers possessed. It appeared no one had ever drilled for oil in such a harsh environment. Braxton intensified his efforts to acquire experienced drillers by searching for experts on the North American continent.

Profits from mining, forestry, and the sale of the art confiscated from the traitorous Russian nobles enriched the Russian treasury. Braxton's accumulated wealth from his business and personal transactions exceeded his expectations. A significant difference between Braxton and the Russians was he did not need to support an expensive imperial court, government, or military with his profits. For the Russians, the rubles flowed out almost as fast as they flowed in.

Prince Braxton did not have the burden of financing debt. He had more financial resources than he could put to productive use. And so, he continued to personally finance the Russian mining and

logging, oil development and exploration. The interest earned on the money he loaned the Russian consortium was an unencumbered source of income.

———

Prior to Braxton and the royal family arriving in Moscow, Braxton's appointment as the Royal Envoy to Japan had been announced first by a Buckingham Palace proclamation followed by headlines across Europe and North America. To Braxton's distress, he had not had an opportunity to forewarn Valentina of his decision to accept the appointment.

He could see the hurt in Valentina's eyes when they first saw each other upon his arrival in Moscow.

"Valentina, I meant to..."

"Don't bother. What is done is done," she replied, placing her arm in his. "These are matters beyond our control; ones which we must accept."

"Valentina, truly you are patient, loving and understanding." He leaned over and kissed her cheek. "You are God's gift. I love you."

They then walked arm-in-arm into the dining room, joining their families for an informal dinner at the Grand Kremlin Palace.

———

The following evening, Valentina, disguised in a full-length, hooded black cloak, made her way to the train and Braxton's private car. The rail yard was dark and silent. She arrived unaccompanied in a closed coach drawn by a team of two horses. The coachman waited for Valentina to alight from the carriage.

"Return in three hours," Valentina quietly instructed the driver.

He nodded, tipping his hat. Snapping the reins, the coach lumbered off, the horses' hooves crunching in the gravel.

Braxton jumped off the car's plaform and took her in his arms, placing his lips on hers.

"Valentina." Their kiss was deep and passionate.

"Come," he said, ushering her toward the steps leading to the car.

They entered the luxurious compartment where wood-paneled walls reflected the low light from several elegant sconces. A table was set for two in the center of the forward compartment. White linen, crystal, china and one silver candle stick had been set. Two large silver cloches concealed their dinner.

Facing Valentina, Braxton placed his hands on either side of her hood, slowly lowering it to her shoulders. She smiled up at him, her winsome eyes gleaming. Taking her face in his hands he brought their lips together again, whispering, "I love you."

She wrapped her arms around him and laid her head on his shoulder. "I love you with all my heart, Braxton." She lifted her head and said, "I feel a bit like Cinderella."

"Why is that my love?"

"The coachman returns at midnight," she replied with a twinkle in her eye.

"And the glass slipper, will you leave it behind so I may come to you and take you to be my own?"

Her mouth gently parted. She looked to the floor while opening her cloak and raising the hem of her gown several inches. The room's light ignited thousands of tiny diamonds covering her slippers.

The dazzled prince's eyes and mouth opened in wonder. He looked up at Valentina then down at her shoes before returning his gaze to hers. "Indeed, you are my Cinderella."

Valentina turned her back to Braxton. He removed her cloak, unveiling all of the rose-colored taffeta gown. She turned and faced her lover.

"And a rose you are, my Cinderella."

Leading her to the table, Braxton drew back her chair. Once Valentina was seated, he leaned down and kissed the back of her neck.

Braxton then served them champagne from the silver ice bucket resting on a stand beside the table. He raised his glass and said, "To my Cinderella."

"And to my Prince Charming."

They looked into each other's eyes while sipping the sparkling liquid, the tiny effervescent bubbles streaming to the top.

Braxton thought to himself, I must marry her. I could not possibly love another. She loves me with every ounce of her being. Valentina is the one I must share my life with. She is the only woman who has the desire and connaissance to help me achieve my dreams of whom I might become.

Following dinner and their exquisite lovemaking,

Braxton helped Valentina into the carriage. As he stood alongside the carriage, Valentina bent over and removed one of her glittering slippers. She handed it to Braxton saying, "Here, keep this and return it on our wedding day."

———

Since the renewal of the Intelligence Operation, Signore Ratini's men had delivered Mars letters intermittently throughout Europe to those Braxton learned were an impending threat to his interests.

These were people and organizations his agents reported were working in one form or another against England, the Chiacontella Banks, or Braxton's business pursuits.

Letters had also been delivered to recipients engaged in activities that had nothing to do with matters of concern to Braxton, but harmful to others. This was done to ward off a connection anyone might have deduced connecting Braxton to the Mars letters.

The letters were brief and ambiguous:

The Eyes of Mars Are Watching You.
Be Careful What You Do.
I Am the God of War.

Just as they had in Venice during Carnivale, these letters had a chilling effect on their recipients. Addressees could not know precisely to what the letters referred, but information gathered from diverse sources confirmed these messages had an impact. Fear disarmed and limited actions thwarting conspiracies that when consummated, could have caused much damage. It was a dangerous game. Braxton and Ramsey could only hope they were not discovered.

Ramsey, not wanting to distract Braxton unnecessarily, decided not to bring the concern he felt for the festering problem that was the Comtesse Hélène de Bérengar. He shuddered to think how her behavior might compromise Braxton.

5

SIBERIAN TUNDRA

After his family had returned to England, Braxton bade farewell to Valentina and boarded his train for Siberia.

Russian mining and foresting flourished. Braxton increased the number of engineers and supervisors. More mines were upgraded and new mines opened.

Braxton and Ramsey sat in the staff's train car alone. Freezing wind accompanying the harsh Russian winter battered the rail carriage, rocking it from side to side.

Both men wore heavy coats. The coal-fired stoves at either end of the car refused to supply adequate heat. Ice covered the windows inside and out, providing the illusion that they were inside an ice cave.

"I shall be glad when the supply train arrives with those cockle stoves," Ramsey said. "They are so much more efficient and warmer. Christ!" He rubbed his gloved hands together.

Braxton said, "My sister swears they produce the most heat while using little fuel. It was her idea to order them. As you know, they are used widely in Germany and Austria. Some are exquisitely decorated.

I have no idea why we do not have them in England."

Ramsey explained why the stoves were so effective. "They provide more warmth because they do not let all the heat out the top of the chimney." Lord Ramsey again rubbed his gloved hands together and continued, "The fire burns much hotter and faster.

Once the fuel is completely burned, the damper is shut, retaining heat radiating from the tile's surfaces."

"I suppose we should do our best to forget the cold and address the unanticipated financial crisis we are facing," Braxton said.

"I am afraid you are right. Despite our original calculations and unforeseen circumstances, our ledgers confirm we are running short on capital," Ramsey groaned.

Braxton shivered, saying, "I underestimated what it would take to build the infrastructure needed to support the workers and their families. The population growth is out-pacing our ability to finance the building of roads, telegraph, railroad tracks, and worker's camps." Viscount Ramsey added, "The more mines we open and the further east we go, the more our resources are stretched. We may have to curtail some of our expansion."

"The hell we will!" Braxton said, slamming his gloved fist on the table.

Lord Ramsey jumped.

With a determined fire in his eyes, Braxton yelled, "We will not slow down. We will not curtail operations. I know where the money is and I will get it!"

———

Following Carmen and Maxim's three-month honeymoon, Maxim, the Russian heir apparent, had not returned to

Eastern Russia and the burgeoning mining and forestry activities. His absence did not go unnoticed. The heir's duties demanded his presence in St. Petersburg in anticipation of his uncle's imminent death. But the Russian workers only understood power. Power in the person they could see, regardless of whether it was authoritarian or benevolent. They needed to see their leader to inspire the hard work required of them. In waiting for his uncle, the czar, to pass away, Maxim's prolonged absence from the tundra created a psychological downturn throughout the workforce in the mines and forested lands.

Prince Braxton knew he had to find a personality other than his own for the Russian laborers to rally round. He sent an insighful communiqué to Maxim and Valentina.

The message read in part:

Maxim, you, the future "Father" of the Russian people, have returned to the west. Your children are forlorn and saddened. Their spirits have been weakened by your departure.

Valentina, I believe you are the parent who needs to assuage your subjects. Come. Show yourself to your people and inspire them to work happily and productively.

What better plan than to have the czar's daughter tour the mines, forests, and territories of Eastern Siberia? Valentina saw the significance of Braxton's request, and relished the opportunity to be with him again.

The Grand Duchess Valentina left St. Petersburg on a small train Braxton sent to gather her for the journey. She embraced her mission, inspecting mines and lumber sites between St. Petersburg and beyond Moscow. The co-regent toured the mining facilities and areas where trees were being cut and loaded for shipments. She visited hospitals, villages, and schools.

The grand duchess extolled the virtue and necessity of all Russians working together to bring their country into the industrial revolution so all Russian citizens would prosper. Her greatest impact was felt at the schools that were training her dedicated subjects for jobs in the expanding mines, forestry and potential oil reserves. She reignited an almost spiritual commitment to the fatherland and the people. It was an appeal much in tune with the more progressive thinking of the day. Her message took hold. Valentina was hailed as the "Mother" of Russia as her cousin Maxim was soon to be the "Father."

Before Valentina arrived at each stop along her journey, her words of inspiration and encouragement preceded her. There was an air of anticipation and excitement. Productivity increased long before her arrival. Her magic inspired her people, raising their spirits.

Two months into her trip, Valentina arrived in the stark terrain that was Eastern Russia– Siberia. She was a vision of beauty. Her rich dark hair and aquamarine eyes mesmerized Braxton. He took her hand gently as she descended from the train onto the plaform, assembled quickly for her arrival on the barren tundra. Her grace and elegance contrasted with the bleak land. Together again, the warmth of their love continued to grow, even in this frozen wilderness.

———

One very cold evening as the snow was gently falling on the tundra, Valentina asked Braxton to dress warmly. She had made arrangements to borrow a small Russian sleigh.

It was much smaller than the traditional troika, the large sleigh pulled by three horses.

This brightly painted miniature sleigh was attached to one horse with room for only two people.

The horse and sleigh stood alongside the train between temporary buildings and the massive iron horse. Valentina stood holding the animal's bridle, stroking its snout as steam hissed and escaped the train intermittently, vaporizing into the cold night air.

"Valentina!" Braxton called out from his private car's plaform. "Are we going out in that?"

Valentina looked up and smiled. She exuded beauty and confidence in her luxurious full-length crown sable fur coat and matching close-fitting sable hat. The center of the round hat was adorned with a brilliant diamond broach. The diamonds captured light from the surrounding buildings and refracted multicolored rays in every direction.

"My dear Braxton, unbeknownst to you, I am an accomplished troika driver. This little sleigh will require no effort. Now, please come down off your perch and get in," she said as she released the horse's bridle, took her seat in the sleigh and took hold of the reins.

Braxton wore a full-length jet-black Russian mink coat and an ushanka atop his head, covering his ears. His smile radiated joy as he bounded off the train and climbed aboard, settling himself beside his exquisite companion.

Arranging blankets across their laps, he said, "Ah, this is so much more comfortable and warmer than I thought it might be."

Valentina snapped the reins and the sleigh lurched forward, the horse eagerly reacting to Valentina's skillful handling.

The night was bright and crisp. Stars and a full moon competed as to which could shine the brightest on the young couple. Subzero temperatures went unnoticed, as they were covered in blankets made of exotic furs. The horse trotted for twenty minutes. The entire time, Braxton remained beguiled by his beautiful, strong, and mysterious Valentina.

She slowed the horse's pace to a walk and loosely wrapped the reins around the sleigh's hitch. Pulling a large, elaborately decorated silver flask from the folds of her coat, she handed it to Braxton. Soon she held two silver goblets of the same matching decorative motif as that of the flask.

"Braxton, would you please pour?"

Caught a bit off-guard, he sat a little straighter and poured the hot sbiten, a traditional mix of honey and vodka, into the still-warm goblets. He closed the flask and placed it to the side as Valentina handed him a goblet.

"It is my wish to toast you, Braxton. I would like to drink to your successes and successes yet to come."

He smiled and kissed her gently on her cheek. "Thank you, my dearest Valentina."

They looked with longing at each other as they downed their drinks.

"Valentina, I too would like to present a toast, a different kind of toast. While you know I value you above all other women..."

Valentina interrupted him, "Do you not think we should have our goblets refilled before the salute?"

Goblets filled, Braxton continued, "I love you Valentina, and I hope you love me too."

He reached into his pocket and withdrew a rectangular black velvet ring box.

Surprise in her voice, Valentina asked, "What? What have you done?"

"Soon we will be apart, once again, for a very long time." He paused and looked into her eyes, "I love you. I have here a token of my heart's desire to spend the rest of my life with you. I love you for all that you are and will become. I will always love you unconditionally, regardless of what might befall us."

Valentina leaned over and kissed Braxton and said, "I do and will always love you unconditionally, no matter what might come our way."

Braxton grinned a tight smile and lifted the box's cover, revealing two rings sitting side by side. Red inset diamonds circled the smaller gold band of one. The second was a gold signet ring set with a solitary red diamond.

Valentina gasped, "Oh Braxton, they are beautiful. So perfect.

Red diamonds, that night together, dinner, the two of us, my apartments in the Grand Kremlin Palace." She removed the glove on her right hand.

"Yes, Valentina, that night." He took the ring circled in red diamonds and slipped it on her index finger. She held it up, waving it a bit back and forth hoping to catch the heaven's vibrant lights.

"Now you," Valentina said, beaming at Braxton.

Braxton removed his right glove as Valentina took the signet ring and placed it on his little finger.

"There, that looks so handsome on you!" She leaned over and placed her lips on his. Braxton wrapped his arms around her and embraced her with a passion that consumed them both. Valentina gently pulled away and gazed into his eyes, smiling slightly and laid against his shoulder. They snuggled close side by side admiring their rings.

Their hands soon feeling the cold night air, Braxton exclaimed, "Gloves!" They both laughed and returned their gloves to their hands.

Valentina, hanging her head, appeared to withdraw.

Braxton, confused by this sudden change in her, attempted to look into her eyes. She focused on her goblet, refusing to acknowledge his gaze. Only the sound of the horse's hooves and the rubbing of the sleigh's runners atop the snow broke the deafening silence. "Braxton, yes we do love one another, unconditionally. But I fear you have mistresses with whom I cannot compete."

Braxton recoiled, "I do not know what you mean! We just promised ourselves to each other!"

"By mistresses, I refer to your ambitions and your dreams. I am not certain there is a place for me in your life as a wife, for I cannot abide forever these mistresses who constantly seduce you away from me."

Braxton looked around not seeing anything, but feeling every snowflake striking his face. Bitter cold and an emptiness permeated his body. He could not think, much less speak. The prince took the reins from Valentina's hands and urged the horses forward again, then quickly again brought the sleigh to a stop.

Trembling from his emotions and the frigid air, the forlorn prince turned to face Valentina. He removed the goblet from her hands and tossed the now near frozen contents into the snow. He drew her hand in one of his and used the other to raise her chin, revealing her tear filled eyes.

"Valentina, you are my world. You mean everything to me. I want you. Most of all, I need you."

Valentina interrupted him again. "My love, you may think that I am your world, your everything, and tonight, maybe I am. But tomorrow I may not be needed in your world. You will once again be off, embracing a new challenge, another world."

She thought for a moment. "I know I too have

mistresses that demand my time. But I shall never put them before you or allow them to seduce me."

Braxton pulled Valentina close, embracing her. He held her as she cried softly, her tears turning to ice as they fell on the fur of Braxton's coat.

"I love you, Valentina. I want to make you my wife." As he held her in his arms, she appeared to relax. After a while, he settled Valentina back against the seat and rearranged the blankets. Braxton positioned himself beside his beloved princess, took hold of the reins and for the first time, drove the sleigh.

Braxton looked up towards the heavens ablaze with stars and the moon, quietly praying, "God, please find a place, a time, a way for Valentina and me to be together."

He knew his impending trip to Japan could destroy any possibility of their union. It was Braxton's turn to cry as he drove them back to the train and a shapeless, unknown tomorrow.

Suddenly, a meteor exploded across the sky brandishing an overwhelming light outshining any midday sun and lighting up the tundra! Braxton instinctively pulled back on the reins. The horse, shrieking and neighing, reared back on its hind legs, its forelegs flailing. Valentina jolted up in her seat and lunged forward, clawing for the reins to help Braxton gain control.

"Braxton!"

"Valentina, I cannot hold on!"

The fierce, unyielding pull of the reins cut through their gloves. Valentina screamed, "The horse! It is getting away from us!"

Clawing at the sky, the animal thrust itself into the air and pulled the sleigh off the ground. Braxton and Valentina lost their grip and were slammed against the high leather back of the seat.

The wooden sleigh's shell fell crashing onto the ground, shattering the runners and bottoming out the wooden sleigh's carcass. Straining to escape the confines of its harness, the horse wildly pummeled the sleigh with both hind hooves, crushing the bulkhead and throwing Braxton and Valentina into the air.

"Ahhhhhhh!" Valentina screamed.

Braxton hollered, "I have you!" He held her tightly within their heavy coats and blankets.

They hit the ground. The sound of cracking bones and the lovers' groans cut through the freezing night.

The horse, still attached to the ravaged sleigh, vanished onto the tundra.

Then there was total silence.

The light from the meteor receded. The stars and moon were once again the only lights reigning over the still land.

Cold winds brushed the furs holding Braxton and Valentina together.

A pained, whimpering cry emanated from Valentina's lips. "Braxton, help me."

Her cry went unanswered.

6

DARKNESS

Why is it so dark?

He shifted uncomfortably, the odd numbness in his legs perplexing him. His toes were cold. Biting his lower lip, he struggled to feel his leg with his left hand. "Ah!" he groaned.

My shoulder is terribly stiff.

He reached up with his right arm, attempting to rub out the soreness.

Why are my legs so heavy? I cannot move them. He shuddered, fumbling with his covers.

Why am I in bed? He moved his hand sporadically atop the bed cover, feeling for something; anything.

Why is it so dark?

His lungs felt constricted, limiting his breathing. He moved his head rapidly from side to side. The immense effort caused him to sweat. Gasping and throwing his arms down hard on the bed clothing, he arched his back and blurted out in a shrill voice, "For God' sake! Please make this a dream!"

Ramsey awoke to the sound of Braxton's voice.

Shooting out of his chair he startled the panicked prince, his chair crashing to the floor.

"Braxton!"

The writhing nobleman raised his disheveled head, searching for his friend in the darkness. His voice quivered with alarm.

"Ramsey, where are you?"

He extended both arms, groping for anything he might understand. Once again, pain coursed through his left shoulder. With both arms he reached forward, wincing in agony.

"I cannot see you!" His heart raced and his chest tightened as he cried, "What is it? What is wrong? I cannot see! I cannot see!"

———

In the dreary sixteen-hour blackness that makes up the winter nights of Siberia, a locomotive and string of empty freight cars sat ghostlike. Frozen and seemingly abandoned, they awaited their yet-to-be-found cargo: oil. Silent passenger cars sat alone on an adjacent siding, some more luxurious than others. Smoke streamed out the top of the tubular metal chimneys from the coal fires within. Slivers of light escaped from the heavy curtains blanketing the interiors.

Strong winds ripped through the rail yard as people moved in and about the temporary buildings, sending supplies and drilling equipment to the surrounding rigs exploring for oil. Warehouses and living quarters dotted the bleak frozen encampment.

Two well-dressed men in their mid-twenties sat in the most opulent car at the rear of the train. Prince Braxton was attended by Viscount Ramsey, reading Valentina's letter to her lover aloud.

Dearest Braxton,

It is with a heavy heart that I leave you. My "mistresses" are making demands. Father is close to death and cousin Maxim has commanded my return. The imperial succession weighs in the balance.

I dreaded leaving you and abhor the thought of returning to Moscow alone, yet I must fulfill my own duties. It all seems so wrong. Yet, when this task is complete, I will have satisfied one more of my mistresses. Who knows where that shall find us?

The doctors say you cannot be moved. I spent the last six weeks at your bedside as you drifted in and out of consciousness, talking to you and affirming my love and commitment to you. It pains me so to have had to leave you. Please know that I will return as soon as possible.

Observing your body's struggle to regain consciousness hours, days, and nights on end, my eyes and heart were opened to who you are and how much you mean to me. I have come to realize I can love and accept your mistresses. I am ready to share you and my life with them. I embrace this as I do our heartfelt commitment to one another.

With all my love, Valentina

Braxton's heart swelled with hope that there did indeed exist a chance he and Valentina might spend the rest of their lives together. But listening to her letter had exhausted him. His eyes, though wide open, were sunken and his face sallow. Every limb ached. His golden hair falling about his forehead had lost its luster. The tall, once vibrant man lay broken. He cared not to move or speak.

When she truly knows how broken I am, will she still have me?

The prince turned his head to the wall and murmured, "Ramsey, how long have you been here?" His body felt hollow; a week chill coursed through his bones. "My memory fails me. What happened?"

Ramsey pulled the heavy Russian furs up around Braxton's shoulders.

"Here, drink some water," he said, holding a crystal tumbler to the invalid's dry lips.

"No."

"Yes, Braxton. Valentina has given me strict orders to have you drink five glasses of water every day."

"And I bloody hell will...later," Braxton moaned.

Propping up his friend's head with a hand behind his neck, Ramsey said, "You said that hours ago. Now you have two of these to drink."

He paused. "Just one now. Can you do this, Braxton?"

Braxton propped himself up on one arm and leaned his head forward. Ramsey placed the glass against the prince's lips. Tilting it, he allowed water to gently flow into Braxton's mouth.

"Thank you. Now you may rest. We shall give it another go later." "What happened? Tell me," the weak prince panted.

"I think you should rest first, then I shall tell you all. Sleep now."

Braxton's voice, barely audible whispered, "Tell me. Tell me until I fall asleep. Please."

The steam escaping from the train and distant clanging from the drilling stations interrupted the heavy silence. A dim light fought to find its way inside the compartment. The winter day's sunlight lasted but a moment. The sun, far removed from the arctic rim, appeared for an instant then quickly disappeared.

"As you may remember, I was not here when you and Valentina had the accident. Or you may not be aware of the sequence of events. I left the German factories on my way here only days after you and Valentina had shared the sleigh ride out onto the tundra. The message about your terrible experience did not reach me before I had departed Germany.

"From what I have been told, the horse returned late that evening, dragging the mangled sleigh into the yards. A search party was sent out immediately, following the tracks left in the snow. The party found you and Valentina unconscious under a mass of blankets and furs. Thank goodness the furs came with you into the snow. Had that not been the case, you both would have frozen to death.

"They dared not move either of you. You were both unconscious, but thankfully, alive." Ramsey paused, not knowing if Braxton's closed eyes and shallow breathing meant he was sleeping.

"Keep going."

"They sent for a wagon to transport you both back to the encampment. Valentina was badly bruised and had a dislocated shoulder and fractured wrist. Fortunately, she soon gained her senses and was ambulatory within days. You, on the other hand... well let us just say you were a bit undone."

Braxton appeared oddly amused, lifting his head, a slight grin struggling to emerge, "Hah, I guess so," he whispered.

Ramsey continued, "When I arrived two weeks later, you had a cast on both legs and one arm in a sling. Bandages had just been removed from your head and you sported an ugly scar across your scalp. It was the first time I had ever seen you unshaven. You had weeks of growth on that handsome face. You were quite a sight."

Ramsey paused sensing a stillness. He walked over to the reclining prince and placed a hand on his arm, saying "Braxton?"

Ramsey waited for an answer that did not come.

Two more weeks passed. Braxton sat in a wheel chair in his private car, dressed in an elaborate wool and silk dressing gown concealing the casts binding his legs. Ramsey, at a nearby table, took dictation from the prince.

Dearest Valentina,

I have lost over two months of my life, almost six weeks of which you were by my side, caring for me. More than 40 days of what should have been days of happiness but were lost to us, as I was truly not aware or awake to live it. It grieves my heart.

Ramsey shared how you cared for me, my own nurse Nightingale; how you watched over me every moment of every day.

I am dictating this letter. Ramsey indulges me, as I have not the strength.

"Did you know that Ramsey shaves me? He will not let my manservant do it. He said you insisted he take over where you left off. You shaved me? I am intrigued. I must admit it is a bit awkward having him help as much as he does, but I am grateful. He is a true friend. It motivates me to get well and become self-reliant again.

Should you be the one nursing me, I would be less inclined to recover so quickly. You cannot possibly imagine the healing effect your profession of love has had on me. I hope I heal sufficiently to once again be the man you remember and love. I am tired now and must rest. Please write.

Truly yours in every way, Braxton

P.S. Please give my best to Maxim. I have had no news. Is he now the czar? When can you return to me?

Ramsey placed his pen in the inkwell and looking at his friend, asked, "When are you going to tell her?"

"In my own time."

Resting his head on the back of the chair, Braxton mumbled, "Thank you for writing the letter. I trust you have informed everyone that news of my condition is not to leave the camp." Braxton shifted in his chair, reaching down to rub his casts as if his legs could feel the relief he so longed for. "God how my legs chafe."

"You are welcome, and yes. They have been informed. Soon, the casts will be removed."

"Please take me back to my compartment."

Fatigued, Braxton's fruitless search for a comfortable position in his bed exhausted him. Drained yet wide awake, he thought back two weeks to when he remembered first coming to consciousness from his semi-comatose state, recalling awaking and experiencing his blindness.

I know I must tell her, but I fear I may lose her. She deserves a whole man. Though I cannot gaze upon her beauty, it is forever imprinted on my mind. Her fragrance, her heavenly voice, and her kisses. Yes, her kisses.

———

Weeks dragged by for Braxton. His strength returned as he continued to work while stranded in his chair. Clerks read reports and handled correspondence. The Siberian winter was surrendering to spring as the days rapidly lengthened.

"Ramsey, would you please make arrangements to get me out of this prison? Help me find some way to venture outside and enjoy the short spring and summer before winter sets in once again."

"Certainly, as soon as you decide to get out of that chair." "What the hell are you talking about? Get out of the chair?" "I want out more than you know!"

Ramsey stood facing Braxton; his arms folded. "Well, then, get up!"

"Damn you, Ramsey! How in God's name do you propose I do that?"

"Well, my prince, shall we just see about that?"

The viscount reached over and grabbed the table in front of Braxton and pulled it out of his reach.

The prince lifted his arms up in shock and defiance, his face draining of color, his torso shaking.

"I cannot!"

"You can and you will," the aristocratic nurse said.

"Take these," Ramsey said, placing two crutches in Braxton's hands.

"What, pray tell, am I supposed to do with these?"

"Hold on to them. I have two men coming to lift you out of that chair."

"But the cast. I cannot possibly walk in it."

"You have to. You should have been walking days ago, ever since the other cast was cut off."

"Damn!"

———

Days later, Braxton had mastered maneuvering around on the crutches, feeling his way about the two rail cars that were his home and work environment.

A week later, assisted by Ramsey and his clerks, Braxton spent more and more time shuffling about the yards, his helpers at the ready to come to his aid should he fall. As Braxton increased his exercise, his energy improved.

———

In the period prior to her leaving, Valentina had worked on various projects as she sat alongside the unconscious Braxton. She had left him a large porfolio detailing her efforts.

Her chief concern upon arriving in Siberia months before the accident had been how to drill in the winter.

Summer drilling was fine. But how were they to drill in sub-zero temperatures?

She had read and consulted with experts via correspondence and journals on the subject. The Americans had what little knowledge and experience there was in this environment.

Braxton and Valentina had poured over the studies. Valentina sorted out who had specific expertise in different areas related to functioning in tundra-like conditions.

The enterprising grand duchess had also located and sent for engineers with experience in drilling tunnels in the middle of winter in the Swiss Alps. The list of experts in specific fields was catalogued and promulgated to members of the consortium.

While Braxton slept, she had initiated the installation of telegraph wires to allow communication between the camps throughout the Russo Consortium, the loosely held entity encompassing their mining, drilling and lumbering enterprises. She was instrumental in consolidating efforts building and equipping the laborers' camps.

Her innate understanding of families and their needs, just like Braxton's, qualified her to move forward with his plans to provide healthy working and living conditions for the laborers.

———

One day, while hobbling around the yards, Braxton heard a shout from one of the distant wells.

"Oil! Oil! Oil!"

My Dearest Valentina,

Today was the day we have been waiting for. If only the telegraph you so wisely set into motion was in place. If that were so, you would know long before receiving this letter that our prayers have been answered.

At first it was only a trickle, but a week later the flow increased. It was as if we were close, but not close enough. The engineers and I recalculated and modified our strategy. This time, we met with success, and a gush of oil spewed high into the air.

Of course, we had no idea what to do with the black mass as it flooded everywhere. Much oil was lost. I have closed down all drilling until this situation can be resolved. What a lovely problem to have!

Write soon and tell me when you shall return. All my love,
Braxton

P.S. Ramsey is so kind to continue to take my dictation. He drives me to distraction demanding I get up and about. Both casts have been removed. However, my legs appear to be suffering from amnesia. They are reluctant to support my walking. But I am improving.

All drilling ceased for two months while safeguards for tapping into the sites were put in place. The search for more oil deposits, however, moved forward.

The engineers worked diligently configuring systems that could pump the raw crude into tanks that held the oil until it could be transferred into barrels and loaded onto freight cars.

Drilling commenced again. Five gushers soon followed and were contained.

Braxton's next concern was that they might produce more oil than there was a demand for. Embracing yet another challenge, he set about finding the solution.

"Ramsey, by my calculations it is evening and the sun should have set. Is that true?"

"Yes, Brax. Why do you ask?"

"Well, I seem to have some sort of sensation of faint light. You know, just before the sun rises on a cloudy winter morning."

Ramsey, reading aloud, looked up from the paper, folded it, and placed it in his lap.

Braxton's head slowly moved up and down, then left to right, as if looking for an object floating in the air.

"Really? Are you sure? I have heard the blind sometimes experience phantom light."

"Of course, I am certain!" an annoyed Braxton exclaimed. "I was afraid to mention it earlier, but I have been having these intermittent sensations for the last week or so. I thought it might be wishful thinking. What light do you have on in here?"

Ramsey leaned forward; his eyes fiercely attentive. "One lamp on a table directly in front of you and one overhead a foot forward from where you are sitting."

"Dim them, please."

Ramsey decreased the light emanating from the kerosene lamp in front of his friend. The light was all but extinguished.

"Dim both of them."

Ramsey smiled, mirroring the slight grin crossing his friend's face.

The viscount's hands shook as he rose out of his chair and extinguished the lamp.

"Has anything changed?" "Yes, in both instances!"

Braxton's heart pounded and his head spun. He gripped the chair's arms, "Ramsey, I am on the mend!"

"Praise be to God almighty!" Ramsey blurted out as he stepped over to Braxton, reaching down to hug the jubilant prince, pulling their heads together. "Braxton, this is a miracle."

———

Lord Ramsey had purchased options on behalf of Braxton on facilities refining oil into kerosene in Europe.

"Ramsey, I want you to exercise the options. With these oil strikes we must make a market. What are we going to do with an ocean of oil if we are unable to sell it? I believe a market exists in Europe, Russia, the Middle East and Africa."

Looking nervously out the railroad car window, Ramsey said, "I agree, but it will require a significant amount of money to underwrite the costs associated not only with increasing our participation in the market, but in developing new markets as well." Icy rain pelting the glass added to the chill created by Ramsey's comments.

"I know. There must be a way. Our plans do not require our capturing the entire market, but I do desire a large piece of it."

Ramsey protested, "Very well. Again, the cost? Liquidity?"

Braxton avoided the question. "Also, as the oil will be sold to the refineries and other entities outside the Russian Consortium, ensure the title is held at the Chiacontella Bank."

Ramsey asked, "Have you told our Russian associates you are personally buying their oil? Does this create a conflict?"

"Of course, I have told them. All they asked me to do was create a market for their oil, which I am doing. There is no conflict."

Ramsey, with a sideways glance, asked, "Are they aware you are having difficulty raising capital?" Irritated with Braxton's refusal to address the financial issues, Ramsey lay his forehead on his desk and mumbled, "Braxton, you may not be able to see well enough to read, but your hearing is keener than ever. Answer my question."

Braxton focused on Ramsey while adjusting himself in his chair, pulling the large fur blanket up around his waist. "Why do you have your head on the table?"

"You can see me from where you are?" Ramsey inquired, his head still on the table.

"I actually can see well enough to write again," Braxton chuckled.

The viscount raised his head and glared at his prince. "What?" He paused and swallowed. "For how long?"

"Um, long enough. Long enough to see you have been wearing yourself out looking after me. I am going to provide some respite. I have things that I must attend to."

"What on earth are you talking about?"

"We are running out of cash and the situation requires I raise a considerable sum."

Ramsey sat up straight but bleary eyed, pushing his hair away from his face.

"You are correct in stating the obvious. I am quite tired and frustrated. We go on spending and expanding and expecting money to appear from thin air. Now, out of the blue, you tell me you can see. It is too much. Your health and recovery are of the greatest import, yet you drive yourself and others beyond limits."

"Relax, my friend. I have a scheme."

"You usually do," Ramsey replied, sarcastically. "As you are going to regale me with your scheme regardless of what I have tried to impress upon you, go on."

"Interested, eh?" Braxton laughed, exercising his newfound sight as he observed Ramsey squirming, literally and figuratively.

"Just tell me. Out with it my most royal friend," Ramsey said in a resigned, exasperated tone.

"Well, as you know, millions are tied up in capital expenditures and we have had little return. Thank God the lumber and mining interests are capitalizing themselves and are helping finance our oil operations here. But my expenditures on the kerosene refineries have depleted most of my financial reserves."

""I am quite familiar with the situation. You know I know this," Ramsey replied.

Braxton ran two fingers between his collar and his neck, saying, "All that remains are the paintings the Grand Duchess Ekaterina, may she rest in peace, gave me. I was hoping collateralizing them for the railroad and then the properties would have been the last time I would suffer that indignity.'

Ramsey sat back in his chair and steepled his fingers. "I thought you said your Uncle Cosimo's bank would not lend on them as you are almost over-extended."

"That is true, but I had hoped there might be a solution. The Chiacontella Bank branches are somewhat autonomous. I thought, perhaps, in the worst of circumstances, several branches would consider coming to my aid. That has proven not to be the case. I recently asked them to reconsider their decision regarding advancing me funds. My uncle Cosimo and cousin Aramis declined my request.

"As duke and head of the Chiacontella banks, Cosimo was reluctant to press his bank directors. I had offered him Ekaterina's paintings, my Paris collection, and the Aurelio Palace."

"What terms did they offer?"

Braxton took a deep breath and exclaimed, "The syndicate, those bastards, refused to negotiate an acceptable formula."

Ramsey asked, "Acceptable to whom?" "Why me, of course."

Braxton lifted himself out of his chair and hobbled about the compartment.

The viscount asked, "Why could they not find a solution?" "They demanded unreasonable collateral and guarantees."

"Those properties and assets you offered would more than cover any anticipated loss." Ramsey looked at Braxton with a knowing look. "And weren't you and your cousin Aramis extremely close? I seem to remember you two spending a month together alone in Capri."

Braxton turned away from Ramsey and took a deep breath, remembering the sojourn on the Mediterranean isle. He said, "Because money is thicker than blood and they think they can bring me to my knees and demand an interest in my concerns."

The prince pounded the wall with a fist. "That will never happen!"

Braxton grew more and more angry. "Those ungrateful swine! It is my successes that have quadrupled the bank's assets! And to think they are family! Standing beside his writing table, Braxton swiped his arm across the surface, scattering papers, the inkwell, and ledgers into the air and across the train compartment.

Ramsey observed this uncharacteristic behavior with alarm. Have all the years of Braxton's driven, unrelenting focus on charting his own life, building his economic empire and furthering his humanitarian interests finally taken a toll on his physiological wellbeing, exacerbated by the accident?

7

KREMLIN CONFRONTATION

Dear Valentina,

I am leaving for Moscow in about a week. A rather delicate situation has arisen and requires my immediate attention. I have been severely disappointed by Cosimo, Aramis, and their bank. I must attend to matters at hand.

The matter is of such grave import that your cousin Maxim, and your father the czar, are hosting a meeting between the Chiacontella Bank and myself at the Grand Kremlin Palace. Perhaps you are aware of the details of my plan. If not, please feel free to query Maxim.

Is there a chance we will have an opportunity to spend time together? Will you be in St. Petersburg or Moscow? I need to hold you and kiss you. I love you.

The upcoming trip to Japan looms large as my health slowly improves. Preparing for the journey, confronting the bank, and limitations placed on me by my health has vexed me beyond belief. My hope is my judgment and thinking are not impaired by the weight of my burdens. I find myself being uncharacteristically short with those I respect and care about.

Challenges come at me from the very four corners of the earth.

Having you here with me would provide great comfort. For the first time I am contemplating the reality of my own mortality. It is something with which I have never before concerned myself.

Please forgive me in that the first letter I have personally written to you is not more ebullient and triumphant in spirit. I miss and long for you and wish to be free of life's complications.

All my love, Braxton

————

The Grand Kremlin Palace had no difficulty hosting its guests within its 700 rooms. Once all had arrived and been situated, the czar, Grand Duke Prince Maxim and Prince Braxton were to receive them in the Hall of the Order of St. Andrew.

The Duke de Chiacontella and his son, Count Aramis, led the procession of twenty bankers into the cavernous hall. All were dressed in black wool pants and long frock coats. Their high-collared white shirts were secured with black cravats and stick pins. The bankers, gaping in awe, were momentarily distracted by the gilded marble chamber's magnificence, its vaulted ceilings crowned in gold, white and blue.

The czar had lined the room with 100 members of his Imperial Guard. The Guard was festooned in high-collared grey coats, decorated in rows of silver buttons. The tall men wore shiny knee- high black leather boots. Black bear skin hats, resting barely above their brows, gave them a fierce countenance. Rifles were born at the ready.

Catching site of the guard, the bankers shuddered and moved closer to one another as they continued toward the throne.

His Imperial Majesty sat on the gilded, red velvet high-backed throne with the Grand Duke to his right. Braxton stood to his left. The guard closed in behind the bankers as they neared the czar.

The Chiacontella bankers had arrived in Moscow convinced of their superiority and unmitigated financial power. They reveled in the fact that not many years earlier, they had been a secondary European bank. The peacocks now strutted, confident in their status as major players in the continent's finances.

The directors assumed they had enough power and influence to dominate and control the aging Russian monarch. They had fallen prey to Western ridicule and misnomer that the czar was not really a Western monarch, but one mired in the medieval ages.

Never before had any of the foreigners laid eyes on the czar. His bone blade nose divided his sunken cheeks. A tangled grey beard contrasted with what was surely a bald head covered by a colorless woolen cap. A massive, muted mosaic-patterned robe depicting iconic byzantine folklore covered him from his shoulders to his feet.

The czar, making every effort to mask his compromised health, gathered himself and rose from the throne, peering down through piercing coal black eyes.

The bank dignitaries puffed up their chests, making little attempt to hide their arrogance, barely nodding their heads in respect. Their feigned deference and blatant insolence infuriated the czar. People bowed to the czar! This was an insult not to be tolerated.

His face reddened as his eyes widened with uncontrolled fire.

Commanding in an unexpectedly loud and crushing voice, he roared, "Get to your knees!"

The Imperial Guard raised their rifles. The sound of rounds being chambered and metal clashing against metal shook the bankers.

They all turned to see the hundred-man guard looking directly at them down the length of their rifles.

The men, including Cosimo and Aramis, fell to their knees. "You have been summoned here because you have greatly displeased us. You have dishonored our agents and thus shown disdain and contempt for Imperial Russia. We are disgusted and condemn you for it." He thrust out his arm pointing vigorously across the visibly shaken foreigners. "We are prepared to destroy the Chiacontella Bank!"

Cosimo and Aramis, their heads bowed, did not dare move. Braxton took some delight in the theatre he had masterminded.

He felt pained by what his willful uncle and cousin were experiencing. At the same time, he embraced a chilling sense of victory for having orchestrated this confrontation. Braxton had been prepared to leverage all he had to secure a loan, but Cosimo and Aramis had failed to facilitate a very reasonable and mutually profitable arrangement. Worse, through demanding part ownership in his ventures, they had attempted to take advantage of him. Him; a Chiacontella; their blood.

They had not cared to leverage their control of the bank's branches to assist Braxton, their largest client. A client who had been responsible for their sudden rise to prominence. A client who had the ear of the czar.

He would not allow his uncle and cousin's lack of leadership and loyalty stand in his way. This had been one of the more difficult, but most courageous decisions of his life. Looking out upon his uncle, cousin and kneeling bankers he mused to himself, my dear Uncle Cosimo, obviously I read the Machiavelli volume you so kindly left for me on the beach in Capri. Braxton fought the smug look fighting to play across his face.

The czar remained standing. Lowering his stern and commanding voice, he said, "There is not one of you in this hall who does not know of the matter of which we speak. When you depart this sacred ground, you will accept the equitable proposition that will be presented to you."

The shocked men, heads downcast, exchanged fearful glances. "Now, you will be escorted to the Hall of the Order of St George where you will finalize the agreement."

The bankers, aware the Imperial Guards had surrounded them, dared not move or look up.

Waving his right arm, the czar exclaimed, "Remove these vermin from our sight!"

The Guard angled their rifles across their chests as they encircled the frightened men. The Chiacontella bankers rose, holding even closer to one another as the Guard marched them from the hall.

The czar, Grand Duke Prince Maxim, and Prince Braxton exited the room behind the dais.

———

Heads down, the bankers followed the Imperial Guard out of the throne room. Entering another magnificent chamber, they remained cowed. Heavy chandeliers lit the hall, illuminating the inlaid floors of red, gold, amber and bronze.

The bankers traversed the space to tables lined with precisely enough chairs to seat each of them. Each table contained ornately carved, onyx inkwells with matching quills. They were placed alongside red leather porfolios embossed with the imperial two- headed eagle. Therein lay a revised loan contract. The papers contained no requirement for collateral from the borrower. It appeared the czar was offering collateral.

The imperial crown and jewels were displayed inside a large, gilded framed glass case placed opposite them. Intimidated by the unending display of untold magnificent jewels, their imperial palatial surroundings and the day's previous events, it required several minutes for the financiers to understand their position and attend to their task.

The Chiacontella men, stunned by the terms, looked to one another for unspoken support. The men knew the czar had, in effect, placed a target on the bank and on them personally, should they consummate the agreement by accepting the crown jewels as collateral for the loan.

The Chiacontella bankers knew they could never accept the crown jewels as collateral. It would dishonor the czar and position the Chiacontella Bank and its bankers as vulnerable targets. The European crowned heads and their governments, having seen what had happened to the czar, would feel their ability to borrow threatened and would take measures to ensure the Chiacontella banking houses were censured. The Chiacontella would become pariahs in the world's financial markets. Loans would be called, collateral removed from their vaults, and their business concerns devalued.

As Cosimo stood, preparing to ask the commander of the guard to allow him to speak to the czar, footmen opened two large doors. All eyes locked on the doors.

Braxton entered. He was followed by clerks carrying bound papers. These were duplicates of Braxton's original offer of his own property and paintings as collateral.

Cosimo signaled the red leather folders on the table be removed.

They were replaced with Braxton's contracts. Still, not

a word was spoken. Cosimo, Aramis, and the bankers all signed the documents. Braxton's secretary handed Cosimo the collateral certification documents.

"Uncle, please come with me."

Cosimo followed Braxton to a nearby salon.

"Uncle, you and the Chiacontella Bank have perhaps irreparably embarrassed me, my family, and the Chiacontella. I am disappointed in the short-sightedness shown by those who could have acted otherwise. Because of the bank's folly I had no choice but to consider searching out alternative banks. Your leadership has brought this upon us. I fear that if you continue in this direction your banks will not survive the nineteenth century."

Braxton looked directly into his uncle's eyes. "I read the book you left me on the beach in Capri. I found it largely irrelevant, but in this instance, I suggest you reread it. I feel I should direct you to two passages I have taken liberal license to condense: *'Many more princes are seen to have lost their lives and states through plots than by open war...for being able to make open war on a prince is granted to few; to be able to conspire against them is granted to everyone.'*"

Cosimo shuddered and dropped his head.

Braxton continued, "You have left me desolate in disappointment and shame, Uncle. My heart aches that you could not have foreseen the consequences of your director's blatant avarice and your mismanagement."

Cosimo reflected on how he had allowed his greedy bankers to control the negotiations. His traditional family arms-length management style would no longer suffice in the world of the industrial revolution. Geography could no longer insulate regions from parochial interests. Local decisions made today, unlike in the past, often reverberated across borders.

The duke was at a loss as to how to apologize to Prince

Braxton. He did not know if his nephew would ever trust him again. The next day, Cosimo petitioned Braxton for an audience. He had in hand a new proposal.

The prince made himself unavailable. His secretary, under his instructions, met with Cosimo. Cosimo, Duke de Chiacontella, bowed to the minor noble of lesser rank. He then asked the secretary to present the porfolio he had prepared for His Royal Highness, Prince Braxton.

The prince's man took the documents to Braxton while Cosimo waited.

All requirements for collateral had been removed. Cosimo, Aramis, and the branch directors had signed and personally guaranteed the note.

One hour later, Braxton met with Cosimo.

"Uncle, I would like to thank you for the very generous changes you have made to the agreement. I hope this ends a most unfortunate chapter."

Cosimo felt relieved that Braxton had not further admonished him and appeared to be somewhat amenable to forgiving this horrible infraction of trust and family loyalty.

"Thank you, my prince. Nephew. I look forward to the possibility of repairing our personal and professional relationship."

"I as well, Uncle."

The documents in hand, Cosimo bowed and left the palace.

Braxton mused: I am as much a Chiacontella as Cosimo. What possessed him to pursue such folly? I now own him and the bank.

Ante ruinam avaritia germinabit.

Before the fall greed doth flourish.

8

THE LAND OF THE RISING SUN

Braxton lost no time returning to Siberia. He calculated he had lost four months entangled in family commitments, politics in London, St. Petersburg and recovering from his and Valentina's accident. The dawning awareness of his own mortality and his ever- present sense of urgency drove him to work even harder.

In his role as royal envoy, Braxton felt it imprudent to ask the prime minister to give him more time in Russia to tend to his personal affairs. He was therefore committed to working more efficiently on his own enterprises before leaving for Japan.

At heart, he was Britain's Prince Royal. His highest purpose in life was to prosper and preserve the empire. Securing a vast network of natural resources and trade in the Orient would enhance the economic security of the empire. Braxton was equally driven to serve the crown. Braxton and Seiko had been spending hours every day perfecting his Japanese. Their time together included the study of Japanese history and culture. The student immersed himself in the economy and politics of Japan.

He was intrigued and captivated by Japan's rich history. The prince pondered how best to show the Japanese the value of increasing trade with the British. Their cultures were vastly different.

Human nature was not. He would find a way to marry the two.

Braxton's trusted military adjutant, Major Barrett, and his company of Royal Guards, were assigned to protect Braxton and his entourage. The contingent that had initially accompanied Braxton's party as royal envoy was folded into the major's unit. These men had also been studying Japanese and participating in Martial Arts training. This training had commenced following Braxton's meeting with the prime minister and the minister of war in London many months earlier.

Seiko's linguistics team instructed clerks and managers accompanying Braxton to Japan in the language and customs of his country. With the entourage working towards the same goal, an enhanced productivity and esprit de corps emerged.

———

"Ramsey, I am instituting an immersion program."
"Immersion into what?" Ramsey chortled. "Are you going to teach everyone how to swim?"

"One that will require all conversations be conducted in Japanese."

"Oh, I see. Do you not think that a bit ambitious, Braxton?"

"Yes, I do," the prince replied imperiously. Gazing out the train car window he continued, "Not more than a month into it, it will become commonplace that all correspondence and record- keeping within the organization be completed in English and Japanese, side-by-side."

"Side-by-side?"

"Exactly. That will allow for making corrections and not losing efficiency in our daily affairs."

Ramsey shook his head, "And? Is there more?"

The prince grinned mischievously, folding his arms across his chest. "After six months, all conversations, internal documentation and record keeping will be conducted only in Japanese." "My God, you will drive us all to drink!"

Braxton smiled wryly and said, "Sake." Then winked.

———

One month later the door to Braxton's rail car opened. "Most honorable prince, may I interrupt?" Seiko said, bowing deeply.

"Of course, Master Seiko. Please come in. How may I help you? Seiko stood opposite the prince's desk, his head downcast. "It is with great sadness and humility that I come with news. News that betrays my failure. For this I am greatly shamed for having dishonored you, my prince."

Braxton rose from his chair behind the desk. "Surely, Master Seiko, you are not capable of such." He paused. In a gentle voice he said, "Please, look at me, for I am your friend, your student, and I honor you among all men."

Seiko obeyed, revealing deeply sorrowful eyes.

Stunned at what he saw, Braxton came from behind his desk and placed his hands on his teacher's shoulders. "Tell me, what pains you far beyond anything I can imagine? Am I the cause? Is there anyone else who could have engendered the abject pain I see?"

In a soft, cadenced voice the teacher answered, "We

are not making the required progress teaching the men Japanese. I fear I have failed you, Your Royal Highness. Many do not have the aptitude for linguistics. I have failed you." Seiko's body seemed to shrink in stature.

Alarmed, Braxton took hold of Seiko's arm and ushered him to a large divan. "Come, teacher. Come sit here with me." Braxton took both Seiko's hands in his.

"It is not you who have failed me. It is the would-be students who have failed themselves. No one is dishonored. Your expectations are driven by mine. It is I who have failed you, for my demands exceeded the men's abilities. It is me who owes both you and the men an apology. I am truly sorry."

Following several moments of silence, Braxton rose and yanked the servants pull. A footman entered the car. Braxton ordered hot sake, which appeared in minutes. The servant set a round bamboo tray with simple white porcelain cups and a matching carafe on a nearby table. The prince invited Seiko to join him. Both men drank their first, then second cups in silence.

"What do you think we should do?"

"Honorable prince, we must find other students."

Braxton pondered Seiko's solution. "I agree. We do have time," Braxton responded. "Have you any idea where we might find these students?"

"Vladivostok has a consulate with Japanese-speaking British soldiers, soldiers who escort men back and forth to Japan. They also have clerks who are fluent in English and Japanese. If we could engage them in our enterprise, we would greatly benefit from their skills."

"Well, as Ambassador at Large and Royal Envoy I have the authority to do whatever is necessary."

For the first time during their meeting, hope glimmered

from Seiko's eyes. "I can travel to Vladivostok and draft them for you, honorable sir."

"I shall write a communiqué to the British consul and military commander. Major Barrett will accompany you. You will need him to deal with the consul and such."

"Thank you, my prince. You do me great honor."

"No, it is I who must thank you. Rest assured; you have my every confidence."

Braxton lifted his elegant Japanese cup to toast Seiko, "Here's to you, my dear and most honorable friend, and to our journey!"

———

Within five months the team and men recruited from Vladivostok had coalesced into a Japanese speaking, reading, writing, and thinking organization.

As the date for their departure approached, Braxton assembled a party to precede his arrival in Japan while he and his delegation would arrive a month later.

Following Seiko's departure to Japan, Braxton wrote a letter to the British prime minister.

Dear Prime Minister,

I hope this letter finds you well. First, I must thank you for allowing me to extend my stay in Siberia. At last, we are almost ready to embark for Imperial Japan.

Recently, while studying a map, my mind was struck by the coincidence of one island nation, Britain, and the other island nation, Japan, working together. I may make use of this coincidence at a later time. Interesting comparison, do you not agree?

I have sent Master Seiko on ahead with my adjutant, lieutenant Norton. They are augmented by six administrative personnel and eight Royal Guards. The party will coordinate transportation for the main party on two English Man of War. That completed, they will remove themselves to Japan. Per your instructions, upon arrival they will make their way to Tokyo and my father's embassy.

It is my understanding the ambassador has inquired about a large compound on the outskirts of the imperial capital. In previous correspondence, I have petitioned his excellency to solicit the Japanese prime minister for consular status.

I thank you and my father, the king, for granting me the rank of Ambassador at Large, Royal Envoy. I have forwarded the credentials to our ambassador. Interestingly, on good authority it is said he is somewhat mercurial and self-possessed. It will make things so much more civilized for all concerned should he resolve himself to the fact I am the Crown's principal diplomat.

Securing the trade agreements you have outlined requires diplomacy and perceived power. I am in no doubt, you would agree. My rank notwithstanding, we must manifest the empire's power, i.e., our military strength. With that in mind, I shall put on quite the show.

God Save the King! Braxton of Wales

———

Seiko sent a letter to Prince Braxton following his arrival in Japan.

Most Honorable Prince,

We arrived in my country ten days ago. Our journey was uneventful.

By now, you will have received my previous letter affirming our securing the British ships for transport from Vladivostok less than one month hence.

Japan has changed. The Japan of the 1880s is almost unrecognizable to me. Arriving in Tokyo, we witnessed a phenomenon only seen in the West. My country has been decimated by foreign traders. Steamships ply the waters and harbors, polluting them with garbage and waste thrown overboard. The once sacred waters are defiled. Mountains of smoke and ash spew from ship stacks only to fall on our holy lands. It pains me greatly to see the filth and degradation that affects the Land of the Rising Sun.

My honored customs and culture are disappearing. My people, once proud, seem trampled by Western customs, mannerisms, language, and clothing. The mighty Shoguns are defeated. The Samurai are relegated to being of little consequence. The underclasses challenge spiritual leaders. All of this has been instigated by foreigners. These are bad times for a disappearing ancient Nippon. My heart weeps.

I must caution you. The Dutch, Americans, and other nations have an immense presence here. I am fearful the British are isolated.

Other nations conspire and combine influence to push the British from favor. Rumors of deceit and malice run rampant. You must take care.

The Imperial Household and the government are at odds. This does not bode well. The Samurai lay in wait, grasping at anything that might restore them. Bad omens abound.

Your quarters have been secured. The compound has been purchased in your name, leased back to the British government, and designated a consulate.

A copy of your credentials has been presented to the Crown's ambassador, Lord Nestry. They are to be forwarded to the Japanese government and His Imperial Majesty, the Emperor.

Our reception at the British Embassy was lukewarm. I do not feel we are welcome here. The English prime minister's portfolio certifying your rank as a senior British diplomat is rumored to have rankled his excellency.

I am recommending you alter your plans for your arrival. We are experiencing roadblocks securing birthing for our ships in Tokyo Harbor. At this time, you must wait at anchor offshore. I do not know when access to the harbor will be granted. You cannot disembark without approval. It escapes me whether the obstruction rests with our embassy or the Japanese government. Strange forces are at work in my beloved country.

I humbly entreat Your Royal Highness consider making port in Yokohama in order to circumvent the issues at hand. I can arrange for you to disembark in this provincial city as opposed to the imperial city.

Accept my unworthy apology for not having already secured clearance.

Your humble servant Seiko Higoshino

———

One-month later, Braxton arrived in Vladivostok. He and his men boarded two British warships for Japan. Reaching Yokohama three days later, he was met by Seiko and Lord Nestry.

"Your Royal Highness, it is an honor to have you and your contingent visit this pagan land," the ambassador said, as he bowed, bobbing excessively.

Moving slightly backwards, the prince paused then reached back to take the sycophant's hand. "Thank you, your excellency." Braxton released the hand and folded his arms. Taking a harder tone, with lips pressed together he looked down at the rotund man. "Pagan?"

The British diplomat, caught off guard, swallowed hard. His eyes widened as the prince dressed him down.

"In whose eyes Lord Nestry? Are we the pagans or heathens in their land? I believe they call us gaijin, or rather outsider, foreigner." Braxton inhaled through his nose. "Nevertheless, we are their guests. I, for one, think we should honor our hosts and not disparage them. Would you not agree that as guests and diplomats it would be the preferred form of behavior?"

"My apologies," groveled the diplomat.

Braxton contemplated his surroundings. What an amazing land. It is bustling with an intensity I could never have imagined. No one is sitting idle. Every movement seems to have a purpose. The cleanliness is remarkable.

The ambassador interrupted Braxton's thoughts. "May I ask why you have chosen to land in Yokohama? It would have been so much easier for you to disembark in the imperial city, Tokyo."

"Surely, ambassador, you know that was impossible, or rather highly improbable, as my representative, Master Seiko, was unable to persuade His Majesty's embassy to obtain permission from the host government to land in Tokyo Harbor. Would you rather have my men be tossed about at anchor?"

"There must be a misunderstanding, my prince."

"A misunderstanding, Ambassador?" Braxton tightened his jaw and hardened his stare. "I assure you the misunderstanding is anything but that." Distancing himself from Lord Nestry, he raised his voice, "Regardless, once my men and supplies are offloaded, we will march to the capital."

"But, Highness," the ambassador stuttered, "That might give offense. I mean, foreign soldiers marching through the countryside."

"The offense was the insulting manner in which my father, the king's, royal envoy and entourage, have, or shall we say, have not been received." Braxton waived off the ambassador.

Hours later, Braxton, uniformed in full regalia, positioned himself at the head of the Royal Guard. All were mounted on magnificent steeds brought with them from Russia.

Marching his men toward the capital city in a show of strength displayed the power of the English Empire. This action would force Imperial Japan's government to take note of the royal envoy's penchant for inventive and aggressive decision making.

Arriving in Tokyo, the prince took a circuitous route through the center of the city. "Let the Japanese people see the representatives of the Crown in all their majestic glory," he said to the ambassador.

The drummers beat a rhythmic cadence accented by the drone of bagpipes. Small children scattered, hiding under carts and behind their parents, protecting their ears from the screeching bagpipes, a blaring noise that for centuries had been used by the Scottish to frighten their adversaries in battle. The horses' metal-shod hooves clanged against the stone pavers. The noise of highly polished ceremonial armor clanging against itself accompanied the ringing stomp of 300 boots marching along the hard-surfaced streets.

The Japanese people had never seen such a large number of Englishmen, much less the extravagant uniforms and plethora of flying banners held high by soldiers on horseback. Braxton entered the city with the aura of a conqueror. He was, after all, a son of the most powerful emperor on earth.

The military display approaching the capital alarmed the government. The Japanese Emperor, informed of their presence, insisted on witnessing the gaijin arrival at a discreet distance. It was rare for a member of the imperial family to leave the vast Imperial Palace and its grounds. The Japanese people were forbidden to gaze upon their "god-emperor."

Arriving at a hilltop far removed from the progressing English force, the emperor witnessed British military power on display. It was the first time he had seen armed forces of a foreign power. This impromptu foray into the real world alarmed him and forced him to hide his nerves beneath a stone-cold expressionless exterior.

———

Arriving at his newly acquired compound, Braxton sent for Major Barrett and Lieutenant Norton. "Gentlemen, having spied the emperor's colors in the distance on arrival to the city, I feel it is important we assuage any insult we might have visited upon our hosts.

"Lieutenant Norton, you will take my gift to the Imperial Palace immediately.

"Major, you will assign two platoons to the lieutenant to accompany him and the gift."

The two platoons were quickly dispatched to the Imperial Palace.

A foot soldier led one of Braxton's magnificent jet-black racing stallions. Robed in a silk and a wool horse blanket embroidered with the Japanese Emperor's Imperial Insignia, the 17-hand steed pranced and snorted, nostrils flaring, parading through the streets. The sun danced off the animal's shiny, satin-like coat.

The emperor was reported to have been well pleased with the gift.

The following day, his imperial majesty acknowledged Braxton's gift with one of his own. He sent Braxton an entourage of one thousand elaborately dressed courtiers accompanied by a gilded rosewood chest containing a trousseau of traditional Japanese Court Dress.

———

After the exchanging of gifts, a fortnight passed before Braxton was to meet with Japan's first prime minister, Prince Ito Hirobumi.

Hirobumi, a monarchist, was impressed with the imperial display Braxton had engineered. He was also sensible and had grand ambitions for his country. The Japanese nobleman was conflicted as to how to deal with the European powers vying for a foothold in Japan. Previous treaties with various countries, particularly the Dutch, had proven not to be to Japan's advantage and had created divisions between the imperial household and the government.

Hirobumi was eager to devise a solution.

When studying at University College in London in his youth, Hirobumi had briefly seen the three-year-old Braxton in the company of his grandfather, the king. The ensuing years had not been particularly kind to the middle-aged politician. This once well- dressed, man-about-town had kept his sense of style but had obtained a wide girth in the interim. He noted that Braxton was in his prime; tall, slender, and strong.

The Japanese were well known for their abilities to duplicate any item, from clothing to armaments. This served them well in their race toward westernization.

Courtesy of the fine Japanese tailors, Prince Hirobumi, like all wealthy progressives of his day, dressed in the latest English fashion.

The minister was an advocate for Japanese westernization. He wondered if Braxton would prove to be an ally or a foe. He had spent hours pacing his office wondering if he could enlist the royal envoy in his quest to bring the imperial household in line with his goal of modernizing Japan. He looked forward to their meeting.

Braxton was escorted from the royal compound under

the protection of a company of Royal Guards. Exiting the residence, they were taken unaware when intercepted by a regiment of the emperor's Imperial Guard, meant to dwarf and intimidate the English.

Responding to the large Japanese military presence, Braxton's guard immediately surrounded the prince and his adjutant.

Comprehending the awkwardness of their situation, Braxton signaled Major Barrett that he would allow the Imperial Guard to escort him and his party.

Along the route, Braxton was cheered by a spontaneous throng of young Japanese lining the streets. Dressed primarily in traditional garb, many waved miniature British flags. The size and enthusiasm of this assemblage alarmed Japanese government officials monitoring their progress.

Surprising the officials, the onlookers threw flowers, clapped their hands and waved. Braxton and his men returned the warm reception with their own smiles and waves.

The prince turned to his adjutant, smiling broadly "I see you were successful in distributing the Union Jack about."

"Yes, Sir. Rather, Master Seiko accomplished that task. I must say, Sir, he did a fine job of it."

"I understand each flag had a coin attached to it." "Sir, I venture to say that may be true."

Both men gazed forward atop their mounts, brandishing amused smiles.

Word was sent quickly to the prime minister and the imperial household recounting the passionate reception afforded the English.

For years, the younger generations had struggled under the stifling control of the powerful isolationist elite.

Japanese youth yearned for westernization. The old guard interpreted this as an attempt to wrest power from them. It was a threat to their existence.

Prince Hirobumi interpreted the people's favorable reception as a positive development, perhaps strengthening his position. The prime minister's adversaries, including the old guard, had immense influence at the palace. He had recently begun to ponder a strategy encouraging citizen support for his position on westernization.

Braxton was perhaps the catalyst that would move the minister's interests forward.

Hirobumi, having heard multiple reports of the people's ardor for the English prince, considered actively promoting western-style parades and exhibitions.

Arriving at the government's compound, Braxton was received with great fanfare. An honor guard, in traditional Samurai armor, lined the stairs three-men deep on each side leading to the ceremonial entrance. An 18-gun salute sounded in the background. Trumpets blared as Braxton dismounted and climbed the stairs. A military band played the British National Anthem. Although Braxton had been well received and honored many times throughout Europe, this display dwarfed any of his previous receptions. He wondered if this appeal to one's ego was an attempt to manipulate him. Could they possibly believe it would affect his negotiations?

Hirobumi, speaking in English, graciously welcomed Braxton to his office. "Your Royal Highness, it is indeed a pleasure to meet you. You do my nation great honor by gracing us with your presence." He bowed to Braxton. The royal envoy returned the gesture.

Braxton had instructed members of his entourage and soldiers not to converse with the Japanese in their native tongue until he told them otherwise. He was certain he could learn more from listening to what the translators interpreted while at the same time listening to the tone and context.

Braxton knew he must maximize this first encounter. The Japanese were known for moving slowly, rarely revealing their hand, often leaving matters hanging for months on end. He must learn as much as he could from this first meeting.

The prime minister had heard rumors Prince Braxton's entourage spoke the language. When pressed on this, Braxton said, replying in English, "Your Highness, please do not take my reluctance to speak your honorable language as a sign of reticence to engage with you. It is true I have had some training, but alas that training does not honor you, my most generous host. I beg you not to dishonor this assembly with my unpolished tongue. Let us please speak in English. So much would be lost should I attempt to converse in Japanese." Hirobumi then assumed the prince understood little Japanese and the rumors had greatly exaggerated his fluency.

After exchanging further pleasantries, Prince Braxton presented the prime minister with the complete works of Shakespeare and a large painting of University College, London, the Japanese prince's alma mater. In addition, he gave Hirobumi a framed lithograph of the Houses of Parliament and Westminster Palace.

"Prince Braxton, you have touched my heart with these wonderful gifts. My time in your country holds many special memories. Three of which you have rekindled today. Thank you."

The minister, wasting little time, asked Braxton the purpose of the visit and how the Japanese government could accommodate him.

Braxton was also direct.

"Minister, the British Empire is the greatest nation the world has ever seen. The advances of my country, a small island nation like yours, has come through courage, ferocity, inventiveness, and persistence. I see all these elements present in the Japanese people, a noble people.

"Such is my father, the king's, belief in this island's people that his government has tasked me with exploring opportunities to help your honored nation attain its righful place on the world stage. This advancement could only lead to great things for both our countries. His Majesty envisions our governments working together to facilitate economic growth between our empires."

Braxton's remarks embodied precisely what Prince Hirobumi wanted and needed to hear. In an aside, and in his native tongue, the prime minister asked a senior minister how he thought that would be received at the Imperial Palace. Overhearing and understanding the Japanese banter, Braxton had his and Master Seiko's suspicions confirmed. There was disagreement and perhaps animosity between the imperial household and the prime minister's government.

The prime minister, not mincing words, went on to address Braxton, stating he assumed the purpose of the delegation was to secure preferred trade status.

"Yes, my lord," Braxton replied, "You are correct. But it is not certain the Japanese could obtain preferred status with the English Empire." Braxton purposely paused.

A look of incredulity crossed the prime minister's face. "Please forgive me, Prince Braxton, but I must clarify. It is you, not the Japanese, who seek preferred trading status."

Braxton chuckled inwardly, replying "Why would you say that minister? Does it not make sense to have equality in trade? If you, my Lord Prime Minister, assume we want preferred status, it would stand to reason you too should have equal status. I fear, Prince Hirobumi, that you under-estimate your country's current position. Your country deserves the same honor you would bestow upon us."

The Prime Minister, inwardly flustered and impressed with this royal envoy said, "Well, of course, your royal highness. We agree. How then do we justify and mutually benefit from this proposed arrangement?"

Braxton directed the minister's attention to an elegantly bound leather porfolio embossed with the English Royal Coat of Arms and held by the English ambassador. Lord Nestry handed the volume to Prince Braxton who in turn presented it to Prince Hirobumi.

"In this porfolio, Excellency, my government has laid out a proposition detailing trade. An agreement elevating status between both countries. Essentially, it regulates and equalizes all tariffs and fees on goods traded between our countries, territories and colonies for a period of ten years. It recommends all barter be monitored by officials from both our countries. A council made up of members from both nations would oversee the administration of the agreement contained therein. It goes on to detail a military treaty designed to promote trade and safe passage of all ships plying the seas between our countries and vassal states."

The portly Japanese minister put his hands on his hips. "Excuse me, but what you say here is far more extensive than expected."

"Why is that Prince Hirobumi? Certainly, for us to honor the agreement we must do all we can to ensure continuity and success.

This, after all, is not just about trade. It is about the glory of the Japanese Empire."

"I see," Hirobumi said, motioning the English prince to join him at a table nearby. Both men sat.

"Please continue."

"As the British Empire has the most extensive fleet in the world sailing the world's oceans, you will see that the cost of maintaining the fleet at the expense of the British crown works in Japan's favor. It is the position of my father, the king emperor, that Japan, a country with a growing young trade, should benefit from its friend the British Empire, which desires to see it prosper."

Hirobumi turned to his ministers and commented in Japanese on the unanticipated generosity and foresightedness of the proposal.

He also alluded to a concern he had that there must be something extra in the proposal that would benefit the English. They must uncover what it was. Braxton showed no indication he had understood what was said.

The ministers were incredulous. Braxton knew he still had much work to do. He made note of each minister's comments to the prime minister. The underlying tone of the minister's muffled exchanges further validated conflict between the government and the palace.

Hirobumi turned from his ministers and addressed Prince Braxton.

"The emperor has commanded you present your credentials at the Imperial Palace on a yet undetermined date. There are certain customs and formalities that are unique to our country. As you know, our emperor is a deity, a god.

"When I was in your country, I had an opportunity to see the ways of your people. We are different. I respect and honor your traditions and I am grateful you will honor ours. I have assigned a court protocol official to help you understand our customs as they pertain to being presented to His Imperial Majesty. Please know that it is a singular honor to be presented to our Emperor God. Most of our people will never have the opportunity to lay their eyes upon him. It is considered a crime to look upon his person. An exception has been granted to you out of respect for your rank and your father, the king emperor."

Braxton rose from the chair. He nodded in respect and said, "I am truly honored and send my deepest appreciation to his Imperial Majesty for his kind invitation."

"Prince Braxton, my ministers and I will review your proposal. We will then forward it to the emperor.

"Things move slowly here. Perhaps we will be able to meet on this matter in a month or two."

"Prime Minister, I look forward to our next meeting."

9

SON OF HEAVEN

"Master Seiko," Braxton said later that day after returning to the consulate, "I suppose you have heard the Imperial Household is providing me with one of their functionaries for instruction on Japanese court etiquette?" Braxton said, stifling a small laugh.

Seiko shot the nobleman a knowing look. "Yes, my prince, much along the lines of how I received instruction on how to conduct myself at your grandfather's court." He paused for a moment and continued, "I remember well the overwhelming trepidation when first employed by your family."

"I never thought about it like that. I understand the significance and I am quite sorry to not have comprehended what you were going through at the time."

The prince's Japanese teacher and confidant was hard at work refurbishing a piece of Japanese art but had risen from his workbench when Braxton entered unannounced.

"Master Seiko, when we are in private, all this formality is not necessary. I do not require it."

"I do, my lord prince." Seiko bowed his head.

"I suppose your traditions and who you are will not permit us to be informal," Braxton said, smiling softly.

Seiko returned to his seat and smiled up at Braxton, his ebony eyes dancing, "Thank you for your indulgence, my lord."

"As you wish, Master Seiko," Braxton said, resigning himself to the protocols Seiko would always adhere to.

Rubbing an ancient woodblock with a rag soaked in an oily, milky colored solution, he asked, "How may I be of service, my prince?"

"Oh, yes. I trust my interrupting is not too much of an inconvenience?"

"If it were, you know I would never let on, my lord."

"Undoubtedly." Braxton stood still for a moment then said in a mocking tone, "You know, your ability to be respecful and condescending at the same time is rather confounding."

"It is rare to see you confounded, prince," Seiko said, as he continued to patiently restore the artifact.

"Well, I am a bit perplexed at the moment," Braxton said, scratching his chin and taking a seat opposite Seiko.

"How is that my lord?"

"Well, you see, it is taxing, understanding cultural differences.

Nuances and the like are difficult. For instance, this palace and the way the emperor conducts affairs of state. It is quite unlike the West. It is suffocatingly formal. How does anyone survive in such a world, much less accomplish anything?"

Seiko looked up at Braxton, his eyes lit with an amused winkle.

"What on earth can you mean, my lord?" Seiko asked.

Braxton continued, "From my reading and study, I understand that the emperor is popularly depicted as having complete autocratic control over Japan's laws, taxation, military, and ultimate spiritual authority. His rule is absolute."

Seiko remained at his work. "On the surface, what you say is true, Sir. Power is wielded by members of the Imperial Household and the prime minister and his cabinet. The control held by these entities is fluid and fleeting. Perhaps you could equate it to the House of Commons, the House of Lords, and the Crown vying for power.

"In my country, most honorable prince, it is difficult to know who wields power at any given moment," Seiko explained.

Braxton leaned forward, placing his elbows on the desk and his chin resting on his fists, observing Seiko bring life to what had been a dark and filthy block of wood. Detailed lines emerged as the craftsman's restorative efforts unveiled intricate figures.

Braxton thought to himself, the details of the ages-old piece of art are slowly unmasked with every swipe of Master Higoshino's hand.

Such is the painstaking labor of understanding this island nation.

"Master Seiko, Lord Hirobumi is an architect of the Japanese constitution; a constitution recently adopted by the Japanese nobles. What intrigues me is the rules seem to change, rather than follow the dictates of the document."

"Yes, that is true. Yet there is more to it, my prince."

"Do you speak of the infighting between the Imperial Household and the government?"

"Yes, but that is just what you see on the surface. I entreat you to venture below and observe. It is much like the waterfowl that gracefully and seemingly effortlessly glide atop the water. Look below and you will find their webbed feet working furiously. That is part of the mystery of our culture. Not unlike an iceberg, what is in plain sight is not representative of what lurks below."

Braxton interrupted Seiko as he got out of his chair. "Please share with me what you know." Doubt and frustration replaced his quizzical smile. "It is vital to the negotiations I understand wherein the power lies. I can be of no service to England or Japan should I be chasing windmills. Blast, if I don't feel like one of Cervantes' characters." In a soothing voice, Seiko attempted to assuage his prince's angst.

"Unlike your country and America, our constitution is young. Its value and integrity are beholden to those wielding the reins of power. The Japanese culture is ancient and embedded deeply in its people's traditions. Japan has adopted a Western form of government, while never having experienced Western culture.

Governing within this foreign form of rule is unfamiliar to us. It is not unlike someone who has never ridden a horse attempting to do so with no training.

"Today the Imperial Household controls the balance of power.

Only months ago, Minister Hirobumi held the reins." Braxton sighed and sat back.

Seiko refreshed his cloth with the mysterious concoction and continued about his work.

The prince stared at the woodblock and mused, "Power seems evanescent here, not as permanent or clear as it is in England.

Perhaps it is our cultures' differences that make life here so difficult for me to comprehend."

The artisan ceased rubbing the wooden block and placed his cleaning rag in a shallow, undecorated wooden bowl. Reaching into a porcelain jar, he scooped out a dollop of paste and applied it to his hands. Moistening the paste, he scrubbed his hands with a porous stone the size of a plum. His action released the fragrance of peach blossoms. The refreshing scent filled Braxton's nostrils. He inhaled deeply, breathing in the perfumed air.

Seiko continued to scrub his hands. "It is far more costly here to transfer power. Factions and alliances whiplash back and forth, much like the partisans in your parliament. The difference here is when opposing factions fight for power, many lives are lost."

Washing your hands, Masker Seiko. Is that symbolic of something?

Are you washing your hands of your country's politics?" "No, my prince. I am merely cleaning my hands."

Drying his hands, the somber teacher lowered his voice. "Soon, power will swing back to the prime minister and his government or, perhaps, another unseen power."

———

Braxton was often impatient with his self-imposed timetables. In this instance, his timetable was irrelevant. The Japanese had their hands on the clock. He remained frustrated.

The invitation to present credentials to the emperor had not arrived. The impatient envoy chaffed at being unable to move forward with his diplomatic agenda.

One of his tactics for maintaining some semblance of control was to keep his entourage's linguistic talents hidden. If the Japanese discovered their secret prior to gaining access to the emperor and presenting his credentials, Braxton would lose his negotiating advantage.

The Imperial Household stood in the way of his making progress in what he hoped would be preferred trade status and the military cooperation that came with protecting Japanese trade. Once the alliance was signed, British warships would have the right to search any ship carrying cargo to and from Japan, including Japanese vessels. Access to all shipping would serve as a conduit for gathering intelligence and keeping tabs on Japan, a country that had significant ambitions to expand its empire throughout Asia, and perhaps beyond.

Braxton, having been one of the architects of the treaty, had his own personal motive. His Intelligence Operation would benefit from information gathered monitoring Japanese trade.

Additionally, the British government had the foresight to see the recently tamed Shogun class as a hotbed of Japanese imperialism. Their quest for regaining power, fueled by centuries-old nationalism, could catapult the Shogunate back into power. Their isolationism would end all international trade.

———

The emperor had first learned of Braxton when the internationally acclaimed royal's horses had won the Queen Anne Stakes years ago. The young prince's success at racing had fascinated him. The Japanese autocrat desired to improve his stables by breeding some of his stock with the Aurelio Palace Stables. He had been frustrated by Japan's infighting. His attention being drawn to the internecine conflicts left little time for him to satiate his desire to improve his equine stock.

The emperor had thus been overwhelmed with the unexpected gift of the stallion. It was a dream come true. If the animal belonged to His Royal Highness, Prince Braxton, it had to be of the best lines; sound, and fast!

The emperor was eager to meet the Englishman, the

gaijin who had entered his realm unannounced, then paraded his soldiers across the countryside. The same interloper who had brought him an extravagant gift that had been his heart's desire.

Who was this man charming his kingdom's youth? Breaking with long tradition? In his impatience to receive Prince Braxton, his imperial majesty sped up the timetable for commanding the English prince to appear at court.

Ten days following the meeting with Prince Hirobumi, Lord Nestry made an unannounced appearance at Prince Braxton's compound.

The royal envoy had yet to receive his first "lesson" in Imperial Court etiquette when the ambassador handed him an ornate package. The item was the size of a large book and two inches thick. It was festooned in exotic colorful papers and ribbons, a "portefeuille extravagant en soie et fleurs." Untying the first ribbon led to folded pages and more of the same. The arful maze ended in an "invitation" commanding Braxton to attend his imperial majesty at the Imperial Palace the following day.

"Well, Lord Ambassador, it appears his Imperial Majesty would like to make my acquaintance sooner rather than later!"

"Yes, your Royal Highness, it appears so. It is also interesting to note that our contacts in the palace inform us he is more interested in discussing horse racing than trade."

"Actually, Ambassador, so would I!" The prince chuckled, noting a smile from the ambassador. "So, what are your thoughts, Ambassador? How has my arrival and our entourage been received by the people?"

The ambassador rubbed his chin for a moment, then replied, "Your arrival in Yokohama and ensuing march through the countryside and on to Tokyo caught everyone by surprise. As you know, the Imperial Court expected you to arrive in Tokyo. When your ships did not appear in Tokyo Bay, the government sent several small, fast boats to look for the British Man of War battleships.

Losing sight of two large British warships in those confined waters confounded the search parties and was cause for alarm.

"No one thought to look for the ships in Yokohama Harbor. This is why your men had adequate time to offload their cargo and assemble for your march."

Prince Braxton interrupted, "So you think this is news to me? You could not possibly fathom that had been my plan all along, Ambassador?"

Lord Nestry swallowed and continued with a less confident tone, "You were halfway to Tokyo before the government knew you had landed!"

"How did they take the news of our arrival in Yokohama?"

"I can assure you, Prince Hirobumi was a bit put off. He dressed down members of his staff for not having better command of the location of foreign ships in their waters. He was particularly vexed by the thought that should anything befall your royal person, it could have led to an international crisis. Trust me; they will be watching your every move from now on."

The Japanese reaction amused the prince. His precocious nature had worked to his advantage. He was now perceived to be unpredictable and inventive. Maybe the Japanese would come to respect the young prince as someone of immense stature in a role traditionally considered reserved for elder statemen. This would obviously play to Braxton's advantage, just as he had planned.

———

The following day, his majesty's royal envoy, Prince Braxton, emerged from the British consulate compound. He was seated inside an oversized sedan chair made of gilded wood, and thus, hidden from view. The palanquin, a boxlike, wheel-less vehicle was carried by four men costumed in robes complementing the ornate conveyance. Wood rails running through brackets along the upper sides of the box rested on the carrier's shoulders, suspending the chair a foot off the ground.

The Royal Guard in their most excellent red and gold uniforms, protected the palanquin from prying eyes and a curious Imperial Japanese guard sent to convey the royal envoy to the imperial palace.

The mounted Imperial Guard had arrived in ceremonial Samurai uniforms. Colorful banners and ribbons flew from pikes held by foot soldiers. A band played a blend of traditional Japanese and Western marching music.

Why had Braxton chosen to ride unseen inside the chair? Once again, the English stirred the onlookers as they looked on with curious stares, sometimes cheering, "English!" "Braxton!" "God save the king!" Other random words in broken English were shouted along the way. Clapping and cheers peppered the trip. Though he could not be seen by the Japanese crowds, they erupted in adulation as he passed. The English prince was perceived by many of the land of the Rising Sun's youth to be their path to westernization.

The entourage arrived at the Seimon Ishibashi Bridge, spanning the moat that encircled the 2.3 square miles of palace grounds. Only the sedan chair was allowed to traverse the bridge and enter the palace gate. Both the English and Japanese escorts remained on the opposite bank.

Braxton, alone in the chair, was, for the first time upon

leaving Vladivostok, not surrounded by guards loyal to him.

Passing through the palace gate he arrived at the imperial audience hall. Only the four Japanese men carrying his luxurious transport were to be seen. The vast stone-covered plaza exhibited no sign of life. The distant sound of nothingness prevailed.

The carriers lowered the chair to the ground. The creak of the palanquin's door opening echoed throughout the grounds. The prince stepped out of the chair, looked up and was awestruck by a towering hall constructed of rough-hewn stones. The monolithic structure was sparsely accented by dark wood framing the roof of gray, clay tiles.

The carriers remained standing, facing forward with their heads bowed.

Why is this place so empty? It has a peaceful but compassionless feel. Why does this culture intimidate with understatement?.

His majesty's imperial royal envoy, His Royal Highness, Prince Braxton, inhaled. He straightened his back, turned and climbed unescorted up the 25-footwide granite stairs. Large varnished decorative wood doors at the top of the steps creaked open, their handler's unseen.

The surrealness of the doors energized and lured him in. He instinctively widened his steps, propelling himself forward at a steady gate. The silence inside the building was interrupted by the sound of his footwear trodding the stone floor.

A vast bareness surrounded the prince. Undecorated, massive wood pillars supported a broad-beamed ceiling staring down upon him. He strode the length of the hall toward another set of towering wooden doors. As he approached the massive portal, he discerned seven fierce Samurai standing on either side, formidable in their ferocious ancient armor. Yet, they appeared in all their monstrosity to look past him. Braxton came to an abrupt stop 15 feet from the massive doors.

The Samurai did not move.

Waiting for the doors to open, his mind drifted. Valentina's visage played across his mind. He had not experienced this severe quiet since those silent nights on the Siberian plain, the evenings when he and Valentina would find themselves alone wrapped in sumptuous furs and entwined in each other's arms beneath a canopy of stars.

This was a very different stillness. Braxton momentarily yearned for Valentina and the quiet of the Siberian nights.

The prince was jarred back from his reminiscences by the low, thundering sound of a large gong being struck behind the closed doors.

The British ambassador and two translators appeared from behind a large shoji screen.

"Your Royal Highness, I almost did not recognize you," the ambassador stuttered.

"Is that so, my lord ambassador?"

Glancing around as if looking for answers, Lord Nestry continued,

"Your attire sir?"

"That is none of your concern."

Alongside the ambassador stood two Japanese men dressed in formal court attire with their heads bowed.

"Why are these men here?"

"Sir, I have provided each of us with a translator."

"Thank you, Lord Nestry, but they will not be necessary. Please dismiss them both."

"The emperor does not speak English," Lord Nestry protested. "Dismiss them, Ambassador," he said curtly.

The ambassador was opening his mouth to speak when

the gong sounded once again. Both translators, having overheard the conversation, snapped a bow to Braxton and the ambassador and scurried off. Lord Nestry faced the prince and said, "Sir, I do not understand."

"May I suggest, Ambassador, you take your position behind me before the doors open and knock you off your feet?"

I cannot believe this man is our ambassador. He must be replaced with a more capable person once the agreement is signed.

Still speechless, the ambassador stepped quickly to his assigned position, to the right of the prince and one step behind.

The doors opened wide.

10

EMPEROR AND ENVOY

Once again, Braxton noted the doors opened seemingly on their own.

Another large, high-ceilinged hall loomed. The expansive chamber evoked a softer feel than the hall Braxton had stood in before. Silk fabrics covered in embroidered figures of animals, flowers, trees and far-off mountains adorned the walls. Paper lanterns, suspended from brilliant, black-lacquered beams crossing the ceiling, provided a soft light, illuminating the chamber. At the far end of the room, a middle aged man dressed in formal Western attire – white tie, waist coat, and tails – sat upon the elevated "Chrysanthemum Throne." The throne was not unlike Western thrones. A deep, rich black carpet covered the plaform and two large silver sconces, each holding 20 lit candles, hung on the wall to either side. The dais was draped with a black canopy trimmed in gold. Beneath the awning stood a single large chair upholstered in black velvet, the legs and frame decorated with intricate gold patterns.

The royal envoy was disappointed to see the Japanese

court had abandoned more of its traditions, having adopted a Western-style throne room. For a moment, he felt aggrieved for the people and their eroding culture.

Braxton's visage startled the court. The customary silence was disrupted by uncharacteristic whispers and gasps arising from courtiers. The emperor sat up straighter to get a better view.

Braxton stood 6' 2", dwarfing everyone in the hall. The royal envoy was not wearing the traditional English court dress. He wore the traditional Japanese court dress the sovereign had gifted him upon his arrival. This was in stark contrast to the Japanese monarch and courtiers dressed in Western suits. Braxton was resplendently attired as a Shogun in Sokutai. His formal Japanese dress consisted of multiple silk robes, elaborately embroidered, layered one over the other with the outermost layer split in front and back to permit freer movement. He also wore a kanmuri ceremonial hat.

Appearing in ancient court dress, Braxton had implemented an insighful tactic, altering his hosts' perceptions. He had honored the emperor and his court by wearing the emperor's gift to their first meeting.

Braxton stepped forward with the ambassador following one step behind.

A flush crept across the British ambassador's ample cheeks. Never had he been without a translator. Lord Nestry spoke only enough Japanese to communicate on a rudimentary level with his servants at the residence.

The Englishmen approached the imperial dais. An awkward silence followed.

Braxton said under his breath, "My lord, introduce me."

The ambassador had no choice but to introduce him in

English. He cleared his throat and announced, "His Royal Highness, Prince Braxton of Wales, Royal Envoy of His Imperial Majesty King Richard, King of the United Kingdom of Great Britain and Emperor of India!"

The emperor, not fluent in English, exhibited no emotion. Braxton repeated the introduction in Japanese: "Kare no denka, u~ēruzu no Burakusuton Ōji, kōtei heika no ōritsu shisetsu, richādo kokuō, Igirisu kokuō, Indo kōtei!"

Stunned hearing the Englishman speak fluent Japanese, the emperor's countenance hardened. He turned to his right, and reproached Prince Hirobumi with an piercing angry stare.

A haunting silence resonated throughout the throne room.

The living god rose from his throne. The court had never seen their emperor rise for anyone. This act further excited audible whispering throughout what was strictly a conspicuous quiet assembly.

The emperor held up his hand to quiet the courtiers. Speaking in his native tongue, he smiled and welcomed Braxton to Japan.

Credentials were presented. The conversation grew more relaxed as the emperor and envoy familiarized themselves with the nuances of one another's Japanese.

Lord Nestry, surprised by the fact Braxton spoke any Japanese, much less fluently, felt a bit faint. He teetered but kept his balance.

The monarch was about 15 years older than Braxton. Yet he thought of the younger man a contemporary and desired to learn more about him.

"Your Royal Highness, would you please honor me by allowing me to share the palace gardens with you and host luncheon?"

Again, the surprised courtiers and alarmed ministers held their tongues, a look of panic crossing their faces. Their bodies stiffened and their eyes narrowed. What was His Imperial Majesty doing?mWho was this gaijin, interfering with their order and status quo?

The royal envoy's heart rate quickened, grasping the importance and extraordinary opportunity to spend time alone with the emperor. Softening his expressionless face, he answered, "It is indeed my honor and privilege, Your Imperial Majesty."

Braxton then bowed, careful not to lose the kanmuri from atop his head.

Prince Braxton sensed the animosity emanating from the courtiers and ministers. Apparently, the ruler hoped to plant a seed amongst his household. He desired, by his example of openness and curiosity, that they too should be receptive to new ideas.

His imperial majesty had not formulated or finalized his preferences for trade and westernization. He wanted to learn more about the English and their motivation. Ultimately, the emperor would choose what was in the best interests of his nation. The absolute ruler was committed to keeping the balance of power tilted in his favor.

The emperor descended from the throne and motioned Braxton to follow. They traversed the length of the throne room. Courtiers executed deep bows as the god-emperor passed. The gaijin thought it a bit bizarre, observing the Japanese courtiers dressed in western attire bowing to their monarch wearing western garb while Braxton was dressed in centuries-old Japanese regalia.

Braxton had a sixth sense these people might one day bow to him as they did to their ruler. He quickly dismissed the idea.

The Imperial Court's trappings evaporated as they

decamped the palace and entered the legendary, mystically elegant, yet understated gardens. The serenity of the gardens transcended the cultural space between Braxton and the emperor.

Cool early-morning air had warmed into a bright crisp midday.

The sky held a brilliant hue of blue and gold. Wind chimes tinkled in a light breeze. The fragrance of night-blooming jasmine filled the air.

"You know, young prince, our culture is ancient and complicated; even rigid. Our traditions are in deep contrast to your Christian world. Japan is an agnostically inspired nation. Surely, you can see the problems inherent in our dissimilarities."

Emperor and prince crossed over an arched wooden bridge. Braxton looked down and saw thousands of plump gold, yellow, white, and bronze koi gliding through the water.

"Your Imperial Majesty, the disparity of cultures can remain a barrier or transform into a crossing. I, for one, am here to bridge our cultures with mutual interests."

The older man stopped. He peered deeply into the Englishman's eyes. A moment later the emperor nodded in agreement. They resumed their thoughful pace; both having clenched their hands behind their backs.

Braxton, sensing the monarch had lowered his defenses, said, "My country is the most powerful nation the world has ever known." He paused to let his last statement resonate. "Your nation strives for power and security."

Braxton held up seven fingers. "There are seven seas. How many oceans can one nation dominate? Britain has all seven seas within its grasp. The burden is great."

The emperor, eyebrows raised and a smile building, responded, "Yes, it must be challenging carrying such a burden. A burden many in my court and government yearn to carry.

"My young prince, I must confess," the emperor said in a careful tone, "while I am not opposed to learning from the West, I fear my court and ministers may be moving too quickly in that direction."

His Imperial Majesty appeared to look inward and blinked rapidly.

Prince Braxton did not reveal his surprise at the monarch's confession and countenance.

Mimicking the emperor's tone, Braxton responded, "We seek a partner who will foster trade and commerce. We seek an ally who is willing to help shoulder that burden." The prince inhaled deeply.

"What, may I humbly ask, are your nations' ambitions?"

The older gentleman ignored the question. Instead, he gestured toward a simple building alongside a small lake. He bade his guest follow him there. They navigated the narrow roji garden path entering a smaller, intimate garden.

Braxton followed his host's example, rinsing his mouth and washing his hands in a stone basin outside the small, temple-like structure. The Japanese ruler removed his shoes. The Englishman slipped out of his geta sandals. They entered the building through the nijiriguchi, a two and a half-foot square entry. Lowering oneself while entering signified humility in preparation for the tea ceremony. The two men took their seats at a low table opposite one another on embroidered silk pillows atop tatami mats fashioned of rice straw. Shōji - sliding wooden lattice doors covered in translucent paper made up the four walls. The chashitsu, or tearoom, was comprised of a modest room reserved for the tea ceremony. A smaller room was used by the servants to prepare the tea.

The emperor valued the Prince Royal's transparency. "In your government's proposal delivered to my prime minister, you layed out a comprehensive trade agreement that would give preference to your country. Do you realize that in providing my country with safe passage to trade you are augmenting our trade and subsequent expansion?"

"Yes, your Imperial Majesty, we do. We do not condone, nor do we support military expansion or war. This is an agreement that has the potential to strengthen both nations economically with the assistance of our naval fleet poised to offer trade protection only."

"You must know, Prince Braxton, this proposal will take careful consideration and study by my government. It would be unfair for us to speak of this matter further at this time, for we are here to partake in the ancient tea ceremony."

The emperor signaled his servants to begin.

———

Following the ritual, the monarch walked with Braxton through the parks and gardens, sharing the expansive beauty and simplicity of his beloved Edo Castle.

"Prince Braxton, as a gift of hospitality, I will award you access to the Imperial Palace. You may visit the palace and grounds as an honorary member of my court. I encourage you to make yourself available to learn more about my people and our culture."

Bowing, the royal envoy said, "Thank you, Your Imperial Majesty. I look forward to learning much about this most ancient and sacred nation."

The absolute monarch presented his hand in the

European fashion. Prince Braxton grasped the hand, kissed it, backed away two steps, then bowed. The imperial retainers appeared from the shadows and escorted his imperial majesty towards the palace.

Braxton stared at the departing entourage disappearing into the maze of gardens.

11

PLOTS AND WARSHIPS

Word quickly spread through the capital that the English prince spoke excellent Japanese. Within days, another wave of information disseminated throughout Tokyo that everyone in the royal envoy's entourage spoke, read, and wrote Japanese. No previous delegation had ever had more than one or two people who spoke a smattering of the language, much less read and wrote it.

These were not the same English who had been vying with the other gaijin for trade and military concessions. Their young prince appeared powerful, organized, and genuinely interested in establishing a working relationship with the Japanese people.

Braxton initiated the second part of his plan. After almost a year of expense and training in Russia and Japan, he could now send his agents out among the people to familiarize themselves first hand with the Japanese culture and economy. He dispatched his team dressed in Japanese clothing to mingle with the people. He needed to test the waters and take the pulse of the populace. Braxton was generous with the time he gave his personnel and soldiers to leave the diplomatic compound and venture into the community.

Braxton's men were introduced to many aspects of the Japanese people, including those characteristics foreign to Europeans. Many in the entourage embraced and indulged themselves within the culture. The Geisha houses were frequented. In deference to his position as royal envoy, and with being compromised, Braxton did not participate in this experience. But the warmth, humility, and sincerity of the Japanese people became known and valued by him and all the Englishmen.

Braxton did not take advantage of the emperor's invitation to frequent the Imperial Palace. He spent the ensuing months focused on his business interests in Russia and Europe. Communication lines between Japan and England were stretched. Sporadic packets of correspondence, some weeks or months old, were delivered to the compound. Braxton felt like he was working with puzzles of information that needed to be pieced together. His clerks and managers were tasked with assimilating the incoming information as best they could. The entire entourage was free to venture into the city and out to the countryside to bring back news of all they discovered.

As was to be expected, the Japanese were initially wary. It took time and patience but after weeks of mingling with the population, significant tidbits began to flow in. Politics and trade were of chief interest to Braxton. However, he was also keenly interested in the viewpoint of the citizenry, particularly the younger generation. The Japanese youth were the future and were playing an increasingly important role in their society.

Braxton envisioned England, and his personal business interests, as a part of that future. The prince encouraged his men to dress in local attire when appropriate and to ingratiate themselves with the people.

The entrepreneur shared none of his private business dealings with the military men and diplomats. The Chiacontella Bank and Mars syndicate intelligence were seen only by Braxton. His secondary agenda would be kept private until the trade agreement had been ratified.

Soldiers and civilians were debriefed when they returned to the compound. Major Barrett's unspoken message was if you return with useful information, you may find yourself with more leave. This reward for services rendered worked well.

Braxton remained immersed in the foreign community in Tokyo and Yokohama. He was, of course, welcome to any event and received untold invitations. He included English officers and senior managers to facilitate building relationships. They fanned out into the trading community, which subsequently provided a treasure trove of information.

The relationships they built soon revealed a pervasive corruption throughout the trading community. The foreigners vying for trade agreements felt no shame in bribing Japanese clerks, bankers, government officials, and nobility. As bribes flowed from many different sources, there appeared to be no rationale behind them.

Many foreign traders inadvertently worked at cross purposes in their uncoordinated attempts to secure trade. The convoluted transactions were ephemeral and long-term profits often compromised.

It was clear the only way to secure the trade agreement Braxton's government desired was to boldly ask outright for the Japanese government to ratify the trade treaty.

During this time, the "Admiral Class" British warships dominated the seas. Braxton communicated to the British

Admiralty he wanted to invite the emperor and government for a ten-day excursion aboard three English warships. The trip would, upon leaving Japanese waters, cruise north along the southern Korean coast. The flotilla would then steam south along the Chinese coast subsequently returning to Tokyo. The Admiralty was incredulous that he would need three ships. The royal envoy explained he was not as much concerned for his guest's comfort as he was they should be impressed by the fact the British could spare three battleships to host them on an excursion that appeared to have no military purpose.

The English purpose was that of securing the trade agreement.

The voyage would whet the Nippon appetite for military expansion, expansion that must have increased trade to produce the revenue required to make it possible.

Japan had a vision of world power. Braxton knew once his guests spent days at sea observing the shores of their neighboring countries, a sense of urgency to expand their influence would be ignited. Who better than the British to help them accomplish their goals? They had already been presented with the English trade agreement; a proposal that would help them realize their ambitions.

As winter quickly approached, Braxton had to wait another five months before the cruise could take place.

———

Braxton asked for an informal audience with the Emperor and Prime Minister. The petition was granted three weeks later, the audience to be hosted at the ancient Suwanochaya Tea House.

The three men spent two hours in conversation. The topics spanned family, gossip, and international politics.

Nothing substantive regarding Japanese and British trade had surfaced.

Finally the emperor asked, "Prince Braxton, why is it you requested this audience?"

"Your Imperial Majesty, my government and I would like to extend an invitation to host your Imperial Majesty, members of the Imperial Court, his highness, the prime minister, and the cabinet as our guests aboard three of my father's battleships. We envision a ten-day cruise." The prime minister appeared stunned. "Why would you need to have more than one battleship? Are they not all quite similar? Quite large enough to accommodate any number of us?"

"Yes indeed, Prime Minister, they are very similar, but we feel our guests would be considerably more comfortable spreading out amongst the ships for the ten-day cruise."

Spending time on the greatest ships afloat piqued the emperor's interest. He turned to Braxton.

"Where do you suggest we go on this voyage?"

"I have chartered a course, Your Majesty, but the excursion can accommodate the wishes of the imperial household."

"Prince Braxton, we would be honored to be your guest, as I am sure would the prime minister and cabinet. Is that not so, Prince Hirobumi?" the monarch asked, gesturing towards the prime minister. An uncharacteristic imperial smile transformed the question into an imperial order.

"Yes, Your Majesty, of course."

Braxton went on to confirm that he and his staff would work closely with the imperial household and cabinet to solidify the plans.

The emperor and prime minister admired the young prince for his ability to draw people together. They saw him as a catalyst for a positive resolution between the imperial household and government. Would this gaijin be the one to set in motion the real unification of Japan? Extraordinary!

As winter descended on the archipelago, Braxton and his men further embedded themselves in the Japanese culture. They began to understand how to comport themselves in conducting business in Japan. They uncovered the real costs and potential profits to be made in Japanese exports and imports. The prince, focusing on his entrepreneurial interests, sought to ensure his conglomerate would make money at both ends, export and import. This study consumed most of their time during that winter.

———

A date promising a full moon was selected for the imperial tour's departure. When the day arrived, a thin orange line on the horizon foretold the rising sun.

Braxton and the ship's captain stood on one of the warship's quarter decks. Several steam-powered naval launches carried the imperial party to their respective ships. All were attired in formal western dress.

"I never thought I would see the emperor venture far from his palace without his retinue of hundreds, much less board a foreign vessel relatively unguarded," the captain remarked.

Braxton said, "The prime minister insisted this trip not be made public. An emperor rarely travels and has not, in over a thousand years, set foot off the main island of Japan. This is indeed a remarkable occasion."

"Your Royal Highness, rumor has it the prime minister has misgivings about this trip."

"Yes, he expressed his reticence a few days following the emperor's acceptance for both of them."

"May I ask if he said why?"

"In a way, he intimated he felt it unwise for his government and the emperor to be absent from Tokyo at the same time. The recent samurai challenge to his authority looms large in his mind, no doubt."

The captain changed the topic as the emperor climbed the stairs from the launch alongside the ship's steely hull. "He refused a 21- gun salute and declined our offer to raise the imperial insignia and their flag. He has requested that he not be piped aboard."

Braxton added, "And he has ordered his entire party to remain below deck until the ships have cleared the harbor."

Prince Braxton and the captain stood at attention and lowered their heads as the Japanese imperial party arrived on the quarterdeck and boarded the warship. No words were exchanged.

The launches were hauled aboard, and the anchors hoisted. All three ships shuddered as black, coal-fired smoke billowed from the vessels' stacks. Slowly, three massive battleships, the gray British Man of Wars, made for the open seas.

Now underway, the imperial guests emerged from below deck.

Braxton knew a successful trip could ensure the Japanese and British would work well together from here on out, with both sides achieving their international trade goals.

The emperor and Braxton sat side-by-side on deck chairs at the warship's bow. Braxton waited for the emperor to speak. The prince noticed the monarch's countenance soften as he removed his top hat and placed it in his lap. He inhaled, filling his lungs to capacity and extending his exhale. He repeated this several times. The prince noticed a bit of color emerge on emperor's typically pallid face.

The middle-aged monarch stared out over the ocean, and said, "I have never been at sea. I have never stepped off the shores of our island kingdom. The experience is simultaneously dizzying and humbling." The emperor smiled, and said, "In my palace I am a deity. On the ocean, I am nothing."

Prince Braxton reflected, a man who has been told all his life he is a god, has at this moment discovered, or at least has revealed, he is a mere mortal. As are we all.

"But you certainly knew that Sir?" Braxton probed.

"Knowing it, or suspecting it, is one thing. Having it confirmed on such a grand scale aboard a ship my nation can only dream of possessing; afloat on a limitless and merciless ocean, is overwhelming."

"Your Imperial Majesty, perhaps it is also a gift. One that will serve you well as you navigate your country's course in these changing times."

The emperor nodded his agreement. He raised his hat in the air. A servant appeared, bowed, and took the hat below deck.

"Ah, yes, prince. You are wise. You have not asked me why I had Prince Hirobumi placed on one of the other ships. You have good judgment to keep such questions to yourself." He inhaled the ocean air as he had done previously and began again. "I did not invite him on this ship for a reason. It has nothing to do with maintaining the continuity of the nation's leadership should something happen. If we were both to perish at sea, so be it. The nation would survive."

Braxton chose not to question the emperor's statement

at this time. Instead, he removed a medium-size leather case from a pocket inside his coat. He opened it and held it out to the emperor. The monarch smiled a toothy grin and took one of the offered cigars. The prince handed him a cutter. The emperor fumbled with it; a confused look crossed his face. A servant appeared, bowed, and stuck out his cupped hands. The emperor waived him off.

"Young prince, would you please show me how to use this?" "It would be an honor, Majesty." Braxton realized the emperor had stepped off the Chrysanthemum Throne for a moment and had stooped to ask him, a foreigner, how to perform a simple task.

"I remember the first time I used one of these, I lopped off too much of the end." Braxton laughed as he said, "I destroyed it! My older brother thought me an idiot. Well, I refused to give him the satisfaction of asking for another. I proceeded to smoke that mauled cigar. It was dreadful."

The emperor chuckled and said, "Please then, show me how to do it properly, as I would not want to experience that same misery!"

Braxton positioned his chair opposite the emperor and leaned over.

"This is the tricky part. It is very personal. One must ascertain how much to remove from the end. In time, Your Imperial Majesty will determine what works best for you. I shall take the liberty to cut it the way I prefer. On our next go-round, perhaps you may want to prepare it to better suit Your Majesty's liking."

The emperor looked at the prince and said, "Yes. Please."

The royal envoy sliced off a bit of the end and handed the cigar and cutter to the emperor. His majesty flipped the cutter over once or twice in his hand and looked back at Braxton.

"This is a gift?" "Yes, Your Majesty."

"Thank you," the emperor said, and placed it in his topcoat pocket. A servant appeared with a box of matches. The emperor waived him off.

"Royal Envoy, please light yours."

Braxton removed a small box of matches from his pocket. His back to the wind, he struck the match and slowly spun the cigar in his mouth using his two fingers and thumb, applying the match's flame to the far end. The emperor watched intently, oblivious to the prince's cigar's smoke enveloping his face.

The bright glow at the cigar's end caught the emperor's interest. "And now it is my turn!"

His Imperial Majesty and Prince Braxton sat back and enjoyed their cigars together.

———

The weather was perfect and the seas calm; the nights were balmy and bright. None of the passengers had previously been aboard a British warship. Waiting months after having received the invitation had fueled interest and opened the doors to friendly and open conversation with the English and the Japanese delegation.

Later that evening, meeting with Braxton, Lord Ramsey remarked, "There is nothing like a successful holiday to bond one's fellow travelers."

"Yes, that was part of the plan and another reason to schedule it months out. I, too, sense a growing camaraderie between our fellow passengers. One that should pay dividends, increasing prospects for a strong Anglo-Japanese trade agreement."

Several days into the cruise, the emperor and the prince were again enjoying their cigars at day's end.

"Your Majesty," the prince said, as a small table was set between them. It held a captain's decanter and two crystal tumblers.

The appearance of the decanter intrigued the emperor. "May I?" Prince Braxton asked, removing the faceted crystal

stopper from atop the bottle, shaped not unlike an inverted shallow- topped mushroom. "The odd shape provides stability while at sea."

The emperor nodded and asked, "Is that your famous Scotch Whiskey?"

"It is, indeed, Your Majesty. Under normal circumstances, we British use the decanter for serving wine, but today, we shall decant whiskey. You see, if the bottle is not sealed, one would lose the aroma, flavor, to evaporation. The glass top cannot seal the decanter. Fear not, I have a cork below deck that will do the job nicely."

Chuckling, the emperor nodding his head, smiling, said, "It is good to know that you English have thought of everything.

The prince handed the emperor a glass.

"To Your Majesty, Japan, and our nations' friendship." The men toasted.

"And to you, my young prince. And our friendship." The men savored the Scotch.

"Prince Braxton, as a sign of respect for you and to show my appreciation for hosting us on this cruise, I would like to share some of my thoughts, in confidence." Not bothering to look in the direction of his entourage standing ten feet away along the taffrail, he made a dismissive wave.

Braxton nodded at the ship's captain and the officers who were gathered around. Moments later, the forecastle deck was cleared, leaving the emperor and the prince alone.

The setting sun lit up the orange sky, shooting specs of red and yellow into the heavens. Calm seas offered little resistance to the vessel's bow driving though the ocean. The sound of water rushing past the ship's hull was the only sound disturbing the symphony of color cascading across the sky.

The men sat savoring their cigars, their Scotch, and the quiet.

I apologize for interrupting the serenity, "the emperor said softly. Braxton offered a quizzical look.

"My prince, Japan has a long history of internal warfare. It has only been in the last 250 years we have seen relative peace. In a thousand years of emperors, Japan has survived strong emperors, weak emperors, and yes, even puppets. But many times, throughout the centuries, it has been strongmen, nobles, samurai, and even low-born leaders wielding the power, all in the name of the emperor."

The longer the emperor spoke, Braxton leaned ever closer. He now sat on the edge of his chair, a cigar in one hand and a tumbler in the other.

"I am in a unique position, unlike many of my prede-cessors. I am emperor and I wield the power. I will use it for as long as I am able, as power will soon, once again, pass to a strong leader or government.

"To maintain the reins of power, one must keep his opponents at bay, guessing which direction they may take. While I respect and honor Prince Hirobumi and his government, who encouraged me to reign, I chose not to reign. Unlike your father, I chose to rule."

Braxton thought to interrupt and explained how the British Constitution would not allow his father to rule, but chose not to sacrifice the future of the trade agreement to his own hubris.

"I must therefore chart my own course. My course will not be dictated by the prime minister."

Braxton swallowed, waiting for what might come next.

"I meant no insult to your honorable father, His Majesty, King Richard."

"None taken, Sir."

The emperor continued, "To explain my earlier statement, this is why I have placed the prime minister aboard another ship. He has his course to chart. I shall chart mine with the assistance of your counsel, one son of an emperor to another."

12

A LIFE SAVED

One week following the cruise, the emperor invited Braxton to the Imperial Palace. They spent the day talking casually about everything but British and Japanese trade. For the next two months, they met on an informal basis, weekly. During this time, Braxton formed friendships with the empress and the four royal children.

The children ranged in age from age 6 to 15. They lived in the Imperial Palace, a life filled with wealth and luxury but isolated from the evolution of Japan's emergence into the modern world.

Prince Braxton felt a connection with the imperial family, having spent years as a young boy living in the Aurelio Palace, Renaissance House and within the social, economic and political constraints imposed on the royal family by the British Constitution.

The newspapers and Western books Braxton smuggled into the palace were the emperor's children's only contacts beyond their cloistered world. They yearned to learn everything they could about things on the other side of the palace walls and beyond its moat.

Braxton became their window to the world. He spent hours with them, recounting stories of his early life and travels. He placed much effort into informing them about diverse cultures. Like their father, they wanted to hear everything about horse racing.

The emperor's children were free to roam and play in the palace park, as it was far from the bustling city bordering the expansive palace grounds. Several small boats rested on the shore of a large lake. The children were forbidden to go out on the boats without an adult capable of swimming.

None of the family had learned how to swim. Swimming was thought inappropriate for members of the royal family. One afternoon, the children and Braxton were engaged in a game of "hide and seek" when screaming erupted, shattering the serenity of the palace gardens.

Turning towards the large lake, Braxton saw what he thought was the 13-year-old crown prince flailing in the water. Braxton ran to the shore, threw off his jacket, ripped off his boots and dove into the frigid lake water. He swam in the direction where he thought he had last seen the prince. He paused and scanned the waterline to realign his course. The prince was still bobbing in the water, but he had stopped screaming. The imperial heir sank below the water's surface. Ten feet from where he had last seen the prince, Braxton dove down and angled toward the prince's descent. Braxton could discern little in the dark water. He grabbed in the direction where he thought the prince might be. All he felt was decayed plants, mud, and slimy rocks.

His oxygen-depleted and his lungs demanding respite, Braxton shot to the surface. His head barely above the water, he gulped in three deep breaths and plunged back into the icy, murky darkness. His arms and legs ached, the cold water sucking the energy and heat from his body. Reaching the bottom, he felt what must be fabric, perhaps clothing. He grabbed ahold and, exploring with his other hand, he felt an arm. Confirming he did indeed have the prince's body in his grasp, he propelled himself to the surface.

Breaching the surface, Braxton realized the Japanese prince was not breathing. Keeping the young prince's head above water, he kicked furiously while swimming vigorously to the shore with one arm. Exiting the water, Braxton laid the boy across his lap and soundly slapped his back with his open hand. He was not sure why he was doing this - perhaps he had read about drowning in a book or had heard a story - but suddenly the prince lurched up, propelling a fountain of lake water out of his mouth that landed squarely on his little sisters, completely covering them in regurgitated pond water.

Screaming, they did not know if it was in horror of being drenched in mucky water or stunned, yet thrilled, their big brother was alive.

Braxton stood up and stepped away as the family and the palace physician examined the young heir.

Numb with cold and shock, the royal envoy felt a warm comfort envelop him as two palace servants draped a heavy, richly embroidered robe around his shoulders. A servant girl, head turned downward, tied the garment's belt at his waist. One female servant bade him hold his head down so they could reach his head to dry his hair with the towels they had at the ready.

Braxton's heart was still racing, and his body shivered as he withdrew from the yammering crowd and motioned his servants to follow him. The prince returned to his compound.

Braxton was rattled by the event. Although he had

instinctively dived into the freezing water and rescued the prince, he now was unable to comprehend how he had been able to do it. How had he been able to replace his own trepidation with an explosion of energy as he plowed through the water to save the crown prince?

The royal envoy realized had he not raced and played games in the water as a young man, the Japanese prince would have drowned. And so too would have the yet-to-be-ratified trade agreement.

Braxton would forever be grateful to his boyhood friend, Josh, for having taught him to swim when they would sneak off to cavort with his stable friends in the Aurelio Palace lake.

———

Days later, the world's newspapers shouted headlines similar to that of the London Times:

"HRH Braxton, Prince Royal, Saves Life of Japanese Crown Prince!"

King Richard and Queen Mercedes, breakfasting at Buckingham Palace, could not believe what they were reading.

"Well, my dear," said the king, "It appears our Braxton will seal the deal with Hirobumi sooner than we had anticipated!"

13

A TREATY BORN

In one of the many letters Braxton wrote to Valentina, he said:

Dearest Valentina,

Over a year has come and gone since I have gazed upon your lovely face. It seems an eternity, for I long to hold you. Ever since that fateful night before our tragic accident, when you were nestled in my arms, your visage has remained constant. Sadly, it fades a bit with every passing day. To have the real you here, with me, is my greatest and most heartfelt desire.

We have been remiss in our letters; they are too few and too brief.

What is taking place between us? What can be done to return the intimacy we so recently shared? I perceive our "mistresses" of duty and responsibility are walls that continue to separate us.

As for my mistresses, they fill me with impatience and frustration.

I have been in Japan for a year, and we nonetheless have no trade agreement. I feel as if the gods are playing us as a Stradivarius. I resent the music unfolding. It does not extend a romantic melody, one that would carry us into one another's arms.

Surely, there is a way for us to bridge the gulf that exists between us. In my isolated misery, without you my love, there is much that keeps me occupied. Without my work I could not survive our separation.

There is yet another frustration in my life, though it does not compare to my not having you by my side. I am constrained by protocol and cannot overtly pursue my own commercial affairs. When the treaty is signed and I am free of my royal duties, I can then consolidate and execute my own trading ventures. Until then, I remain immobilized, forced to busy myself by redrawing and refining my plans.

I meet with potential trading partners, but alas, my position constrains my interaction and any thought of finalizing agreements.

By the time you hold this letter in your porcelain hands, you will have undoubtedly heard of my plucking the crown prince out of the lake. I think I shivered for days after having emerged from the frigid, gloomy water. Truthfully, why the crown prince and I did not drown is beyond me. What is truly odd, it has been a week and I have yet to hear from the imperial household or the prime minister. Have I dishonored the emperor in some way? There really is no way of knowing.

I do wish, my love, we could be together and that my arms could hold you, caress you, and love you.

Give my regards to Maxim and your father.

Yours, truly and eternally,

Brax

———

The next day, the emperor, senior imperial household staff, the prime minister, and the cabinet arrived unannounced at the royal envoy's compound.

The prince was meeting with his top management staff in the large hall in the compound's primary building. Well into the meeting, one of the guards burst into the room, exclaiming, "Sir! I beg your pardon, Sir! The sergeant said to tell you we think the Imperial Guard or the emperor himself is coming this way! Sir!" The soldier collected himself, saluted and exited the room, closing the door behind him.

"You would think he might have waited for an answer," mused Major Barrett.

The imperial contingent growing closer, the sound of blaring horns and marching men slowly filling the room. Braxton jumped from his seat, saying, "I've only heard that once before, and it was the day the emperor watched us from afar when we entered Tokyo for the first time. It is indeed the emperor. Make ready!"

"Everyone, out into the courtyard. Master Seiko, instruct the staff to prepare this room for our imperial guests," ordered the prince.

The gates of the compound were opened as the imperial party approached. The British guard formed up to receive their guests. The men were dressed in their brilliant red uniforms, helmets glittering in the sun. They stood at attention with their rifles shouldered.

The emperor and prime minister arrived on horseback. The military entourage was dressed in traditional Japanese court attire. Aware of the emperor's approach, the Japanese people had prostrated themselves on the street. They dared not look at their emperor-god.

The gates closed once the party had passed into the courtyard. This move had been executed to hide the imperial entourage and the emperor from public view to perpetuate the emperor's mystique. For the emperor to survive, his private person must remain an enigma, a mystery.

Braxton stood at the entrance to the compound's main building. The emperor dismounted. Braxton bowed, stepped aside and kept his head lowered as the Emperor of Japan walked past him and into the building.

Both the emperor and Braxton observed diplomatic

etiquette and stood silently after entering the room chosen for the impromptu meeting.

The Japanese prime minister was accompanied by his minister of trade. Braxton directed Ramsey and Seiko to remain in the room.

The emperor turned to his imperial chancellor and asked him to stay. Braxton then instructed Major Barrett to join them. Tit for tat, the British and Japanese had maneuvered for equal representation.

The emperor declined an offered chair.

"Prince Braxton, words cannot express our gratitude for saving our son's life. Your actions have spared our country great sorrow and possible upheaval. Again, I thank you. You bring honor to your family and your country." He paused and then continued, "You are a man of honor who can be trusted." The emperor paused again, offering a slight nod. The Japanese delegation uniformly and simultaneously twitched, stunned at the emperor feigning a bow. This act had never been seen during the thousand years emperors had ruled Japan.

The emperor continued. "Prince Hirobumi will unveil the purpose of our visit." The emperor took a seat, situated a small distance from the conference table.

Braxton bowed, and said, "Thank you, Your Imperial Majesty. You honor my house and my country with your visit to this consular sovereign ground."

Braxton then invited the prime minister to sit, motioning to a chair alongside the table. Braxton sat opposite him. The prime minister signaled his minister of trade, who placed documents in front of the prime minister and Braxton.

"Prince Braxton, it is with great honor that we present to you the same document you submitted a year ago. His imperial majesty has directed us to accept the proposal as written by your government. With your permission, we will sign the documents now."

The prince royal maintained his emotion-free countenance. He rose from his seat, faced the emperor, and bowed.

"Thank you, Imperial Majesty." He bowed to the prime minister, and said, "Thank you, Prince Hirobumi."

Together, the courtier and Major Barrett managed the documents. Nothing was said as the men signed and affixed their seals. The rustling of papers and shuffling of instruments were the only sounds in the room.

As the papers were placed in separate porfolios, servants entered the room carrying trays laden with Champagne and crystal glasses. Baccarat flutes filled three-quarters full, were presented to the assembled men.

Braxton raised his glass and said, "Your Imperial Majesty, Prime Minister, Lords, and gentlemen, a toast. A salute to a growing friendship, mutually beneficial trade and eternal trust between our nations!"

———

News of the preferred trade agreement spread throughout Tokyo and the rest of the country. Braxton's staff executed the trade arrangements with Japanese merchants and manufacturers. All were eager to partake in a trade treaty sanctioned by the emperor and his government.

The prince felt the burden of diplomacy lifted from his shoulders and was now comfortable spending time obtaining a more personal knowledge of Japan and its people. He required two months to solidify his own trading interests with Japan.

He had promised the emperor's children he would spend more time with them, regaling them with stories and teaching them about horse racing. He felt close to the family, at times wondering what it would be like to have children of his own, children with Valentina.

One day, sitting in the imperial garden, he turned to the emperor and empress and said, "Above all I have experienced in your country, one special thing comes to mind."

A sparkle in the empress's eyes and a gentle smile caught the emperor's and Braxton's attention.

"What stirs your thoughts, my empress?" the emperor queried. "I believe I know of what the English prince speaks."

"And how would you know that my empress?"

"I am a mother and a wife. I can see it written on his face and in the ways he has changed." She paused a moment, fanning herself, and from behind the fan continued, "A more confident and peaceful carriage, for one."

Braxton raised his eyebrows and offered a questioning gaze.

The emperor took the empress's hands in his and turned toward Braxton, "My prince, my wife is very perceptive, and I never take issue with her in matters such as this. Prepare yourself to be unmasked," The emperor said, smiling and chuckling.

The empress lowered her fan. She had turned a light shade of red, then tucked her chin and gazed downward. "I think you have someone special in your life and you are planning on starting a family."

Braxton smiled and said to the imperial couple, "You have graciously allowed me to witness the love you share between one another and your children. Your family embodies what is good in the world. I hope one day I will be so fortunate as to have such a family."

———

Braxton purchased the British compound from its Japanese owner.

He was now the landlord. The embassy placard remained on display. Officially, the land was no longer a consulate or sovereign property. As a courtesy, the Japanese government did not force the issue.

The entrepreneur prince began the process of determining who in his entourage would remain in Japan. He hired local Japanese to augment his staff. His goal was to create a predominately Japanese team. They were provided a moderate salary. They were also offered additional payments based on net profits.

The books of the new Anglo/Japanese offices were available for inspection by those participating in the profit sharing. All swore a sacred oath to keep information regarding the Anglo/Japanese business activities confidential. Honor to one's employer was considered a sacred trust in Japan.

The trade agreement with Japan also had a provision for establishing a bank in Tokyo and branches in other cities. Count Aramis, Braxton's cousin and a principal in the Chiacontella banks, arrived in Japan four weeks after the trade document had been signed.

As Aramis had no experience in the Far East, Seiko spent a great deal of time familiarizing Aramis and his staff with Japanese culture, customs, and business. Seiko would remain in Japan advising the new bank and remain deeply involved with the conglomerate.

———

Months of planning for the next leg of the journey had begun during the previous winter. While Braxton was in

Japan, he had placed his personal train in service hauling cargo and oil throughout Russia and Europe.

The rail tonnage had increased to the point where substantial profits from the Russian Conglomerate had to be invested in upgrading existing track and bridges. Thousands of miles of track and hundreds of bridges were constructed or improved. More cargo trains were procured to meet the Russian Conglomerate's requirements.

Anticipating departing Japan, Braxton arranged to have his personal train carry English-manufactured machinery from Calais to Calcutta. His personal cars had been refurbished after experiencing two brutal Siberian winters.

Prince Braxton and his entourage would be met by his train and Its renovated cars in India.

14

—————

FRAGRANT HARBOR

Dearest Valentina,

Finally, we are departing Japan. We set sail in a fortnight. By the time you receive this letter, we will have arrived in Hong Kong.

Singapore follows a month or two after that. It is my plan to arrive in India prior to winter taking hold.

The prime minister has arranged for two warships to transport my men and supplies along the coast of China. I remain Royal Envoy. The British Governor, Sir George Brown, is expecting my arrival.

As to Singapore, I have written the governor a letter outlining what I shall require. I am not so sure what we will find in Singapore. The hell-bent transformation from a small fishing village to a major trade center in less than fifty years intrigues me. It sounds like a fertile trading field of sorts for someone like me. Opportunities must surely abound.

I have heard nothing from you since my last letter. Of course, thousands of miles and an ocean separates us. Do you still love me?

Braxton's correspondence went on to profess his love for Valentina. He imagined their letters might pass in the mail and that a hoped-for message from her might reach him before departing for Hong Kong.

———

Cascading, turquoise-infused ocean waves foamed against the wind. The brilliant sun's rays refracted off the verdant rolling sea, as the steel hull split the turbulent waters, bound for Hong Kong's Victoria Harbor.

The harbor's entrance was framed by towering emerald-green mountains. Billowing clouds allowed a shimmering rainbow to reveal itself, fluttering between plumes of white clouds dancing over, under and all about an azure sky.

"My God, this is beautiful," Braxton remarked to Major Barrett.

The two men stood on the warship's bow plowing ahead into four foot swells.

Braxton, attempting an Irish brogue, said, "Look! T'is a bit of Ireland."

"Yes, Your Royal Highness," the major responded, pointing and saying "I believed that is the peak we have heard about, Victoria Peak. It is supposed to be the highest point on the island, over 1,800 feet high."

"They say the roads are so steep even the rickshaws cannot make the climb. It is accessible only on horseback or horse-drawn wagons and carriages. It sounds like something we shall have to attempt!" Braxton insisted.

The wind and sea spray covered the men as they held onto the ship's railing. They stood mesmerized by the rich panorama of mountains and harbor. Steam and sail-powered ships of every nation passed by from every direction. It looked as if hundreds more lay at anchor.

"Sir," a voice shouted, struggling to be heard above the

sea and wind. "The captain said to tell you signals received from shore indicate the governor and his wife, Contessa Roma, will meet you at the wharf."

Turning to acknowledge the messenger, Braxton responded in a loud voice, "Thank you, Ensign."

Entering the harbor, cannon fire from the Fan Lau Fort's battlements spewed forth smoke. Soon, the thunder of the cannon's report reached the warship, the first of eighteen that would sound to announce the arrival of His Majesty's Imperial Royal Envoy.

Braxton saluted the British warships standing at anchor. The officers and crew lined the decks, dressed in whites and standing at parade rest. One French frigate and a Dutch ship honored the prince's arrival with all men on deck, the ships festooned for the occasion. From the bow up to the mainmast and back down to the stern, a celebration of brightly-colored signal flags, unit citations, courtesy flags, pennants, ensigns and rank flags repeatedly snapped in the sharp winds.

An hour later, Braxton's ship had moored, and the gangplank lowered to the dock.

Uniformed men manned the side. Prince Braxton faced the stern of the warship and saluted the British flag. The high-pitched boatswain's whistle pierced the air as the Royal Envoy walked down the gangway festooned in the red, white, and blue British bunting.

A military band played Hail Britannia. British expatriates crowded the pier waving miniature union jack flags, cheering the first member of the royal family to have visited the colony.

Governor Sir George Brown, Contessa Diamantina Roma, and the Colonial Administrator, Sir William Henry Marsh, stood at the bottom of the gangplank. Surrendering to the capricious wind, the contessa folded her parasol. The gentlemen struggled to keep their hats on their heads.

"Your Royal Highness, welcome to Hong Kong," the governor said. Pleasantries were exchanged. The governor, the contessa, Sir

Marsh, and Braxton boarded an elegant four-horse open landau.

Prince Braxton waved to onlookers, many throwing flowers, cheering, and bowing as the carriage rolled past. The wind subsided as the party retreated from the harbor.

"Sir, we hope you will honor us by allowing my husband and me to host you at our home, Government House." Contessa Roma said.

Braxton smiled and tipped his hat, recalling he had heard mention of the contessa's beauty and that it lay in her expressions, rather than her features. She was, indeed, charming.

"It would be my pleasure, Contessa Roma."

The streets were narrow and humming with Chinese peasants, laborers, and merchants buzzing about as bumblebees harvest pollen in a fast-colorful garden. Like in Japan, all their movements appeared intentional and eerily frenzied.

The carriage driver did not try to force his way through the throng. Unlike the Japanese, he melded with the flow.

From the elevated carriage, Braxton marveled at the sea of rattan hats shaped like shallow, inverted saucers with pointed tops. Some Chinese men wore decorative bandanas wrapped about their heads. Simple reed sandals protected their feet. Uniformity was evident in their loose-fitting, earth-toned tunics and trousers. Geta, sandals fashioned of an elevated wooden base, produced a peculiar sound on hard surfaces. The click-clop of wooden soles traveling over the stone streets caught Braxton's interest.

Braxton noted that, like Japan, rarely could he make eye contact with the peasants or coolies.

The banter amongst the people hummed along, accented with seemingly random, crisp, high-pitched voices. Most bowed respecfully as the carriage passed, not lifting their conical hat-clad heads until the vehicle had moved on.

Japan's streets were cleaner and more orderly. The Nippon were more western in their dress and mannerisms. Hong Kong appeared less developed, somewhat parochial. This city had much more in common with the rural Japanese villages than Yokohama or Tokyo.

Braxton pinched his chin, looking out upon the city and thought to himself, does a seemingly less well-ordered culture offer less in the way of trading opportunities? It bothers me that the dichotomy of the Japanese and Chinese cultures does not favor the Chinese. The Japanese covet China. How will this play out? What does this mean to the British should these cultures clash?

The contemplative envoy's thoughts were interrupted when Sir Brown said, "Your Royal Highness, your needs for housing your military escort and your administrative personnel have all been addressed. There is room at Government House to quarter two additional men. We have secured a modest home to house the civilians. The military contingent has been supplied quarters with the colonial garrison." "Splendid," Braxton answered. Through his smile he thought, I cannot possibly function as envoy and run my own affairs in someone else's home. I asked for my own quarters. It was clear in my instructions. I will not refuse and offend them now, but I will need to make other arrangements. For now, I shall accommodate them until I learn all I need to know.

"George and I are hosting a reception and dinner in

your honor tomorrow evening at Government House. We hope that meets with your approval and allows you time to rest after your voyage," the contessa beamed.

"Yes, of course. That sounds like a capital idea. Thank you so much, Contessa, Governor."

The carriage commenced its climb up Government Hill toward the governor's official residence.

Sir Marsh offered, "If you have time in your schedule tomorrow, we would like to provide you an opportunity to visit the real Hong Kong." The contessa moved with a start and covered her mouth with her lace handkerchief. She blushed, but found the strength to interject, "Sir Marsh, I doubt you can show his Royal Highness anything he has not already seen. After all, he has experienced Venezia and Carnivale."

Braxton's mind raced back several years to Vienna and Carnivale. In the waning morning hours of Carnivale, incognito and dressed as the ancient Greco-Roman god Mars, he had compromised women and men alike, or so they had presumed. The scandal had rocked Europe and had served his purposes, foiling many of his enemies.

The contessa's reference to Carnivale was careless. Not only was she presumptuous, but indelicate. Could his proximity to the infamous events at Carnivale prove dangerous? Her clumsy attempt to get close to him was an inadvertent warning shot across the bow. Her tendency to gossip could be harmful to him and made it quite clear he would have to remove himself from under her roof as soon as possible.

Braxton coughed into his clenched fists and said, "Contessa, I understand your family is originally from Venice."

"Yes, that is true, Your Royal Highness."

The prince steadied his voice, and with a down-turned mouth, said, "My mother's family, the Chiacontella are Italian."

Contessa Roma elaborated, "Not only is your ducal family Italian, but one of the oldest noble houses." The contessa had addressed her remarks to all three men riding in the carriage. She appeared to fancy herself an authority on the Chiacontella, and continued, "They are said to be one of the richest banking families in Europe, perhaps the world." The contessa paused, and continued, "Though, very little is known for certain. They are so very private and do not flaunt their wealth."

The hair stood up on the back of Braxton's neck. The Venetian countess speaking of his family in such familiar terms rankled the Chiacontella in him. The audacity to suggest she was intimately acquainted with their affairs was vulgar. How dare she speak with such familiarity to him, her husband's senior, and the Imperial Royal Envoy?

Prince Braxton leaned forward, facing the contessa opposite him, and said, "As am I, Contessa, very private." He sat back in his seat and glared at her, revealing cold eyes atop a steely mouth.

The four sat in silence as the horses labored up the hill toward Government House.

That evening, at a casual dinner hosted by Sir George and the Contessa Roma, Braxton was determined to keep the conversation far away from his personal and business interests. He was, to them, His Majesty's Royal Envoy and nothing more.

"What is it, Your Royal Highness, that we can do to accommodate your visit while in Hong Kong?" Governor Brown asked.

"As you know, Sir George, I am here on my father, the king's, business. I also have interests of my own, but they needn't concern you." Braxton looked over at the contessa and then to the governor. "I understand, Sir," The governor said, visibly embarrassed, scowling at his wife.

The Contessa Roma's cheeks flushed.

Braxton focused on the governor and Sir William and said "I will be examining all government offices. You will, of course, open your administrative files for review by my clerical team. It goes without saying, I will be inspecting all military installations and fortifications. You will assemble a full military review. The latter should be scheduled as soon as possible."

No one spoke. The click of silver flatware against the China dinnerware was the only sound.

Braxton spoke to Sir William Marsh, "I look forward to our day together tomorrow. Perhaps we could explore Hong Kong unannounced. The day would be so much more productive if I am not recognized. I have used this ploy many times. It has often proven to suit my purposes." Braxton placed his flatware on his plate, still addressing Sir Marsh, "I shall be dressed in a summer suit and hat. It would be best that we have no more than two Chinese men attend us. I would prefer they be fluent in English and familiar with the business district. If we go on horseback, we could take a look at the peak. What say you?" Braxton sat back in his chair.

Sir William smiled broadly, replying, "Perfect, my Lord. That is indeed the best way to see Hong Kong, or the Fragrant Harbor, to which it is often referred." The administrator raised his glass.

―――――――

The following morning, Braxton, Marsh, and two English-speaking Chinese retainers set off from Government House on horseback.

"Other than the Victoria Peak, what else would you like to see, Sir?"

"I hope to visit several different hongs."

Marsh sat up straight in his saddle, and stared at the prince, before asking, "You know about the trading houses? The Jardine's, Dent & Co, and Russell & Co.?"

"I know a little bit. I would like to learn more."

"Excellent, I shall make introductions. Discreet, of course. But not today. But let us ride by the hongs. Perhaps you might want to mingle with the traders. That should do the ticket." Marsh said, displaying a self-satisfied grin.

"That will do just fine." In a subdued tone, the prince continued, "No one is to know who I am. No more 'your royal highness.' Today, I am John Braxton."

Very well, Your Royal...excuse me, John." Braxton grinned and offered his hand.

Sir William, bewildered and amused, snorted a short laugh and shook his head.

The first half of the day was spent in the expatriate trading quarter of Hong Kong. Braxton and Marsh were dressed in white cotton trousers, shirts, and summer jackets. They wore wide- brimmed straw hats to protect themselves from the sun. The royal's command of Spanish, Italian, German, and French facilitated his conversing with foreign traders. Braxton experienced a surge of adrenalin as he discussed trade and economics with like-minded strangers. He remembered every face and every name.

"It is well past noon, and I am famished," Sir William said, as they rode alongside a street vendor. "Let us sample the cuisine!"

Marsh dismounted, as did Braxton. The two retainers tended to the four horses as Sir William introduced the prince to the local fare.

"John" ordered two more servings of jiaozi, sesame balls, and tea eggs. "Let us give these to the retainers. We can tend to the horses while they consume their food.

Then we shall discuss a favor I should like to ask of you, William."

Marsh, once again amused with the English prince, said, "Whatever you say, John."

The retainers huddled over their bowls, eating, chattering and gesturing with their chopsticks while Braxton and Marsh held the horses a short distance away.

"There are two more things I would like to accomplish today. The first is to familiarize myself with Victoria Peak. The second is to call upon an opium den."

Marsh's head drew back, his eyes blinking rapidly.

15

THE DEN AND BEYOND

Braxton's eyes, lit with a mischievous glow, squinted in the sun. Marsh stammered, "John, you are full of surprises."

"Oh, there are more surprises to come, of that you can be certain."

Marsh cocked his head quizzically as the prince said, "Remember, all of this is confidential. You know I can have you shot, or would you prefer hanging?" Braxton raised his fist above his head to charade a hangman's noose about his neck.

Sir William, not knowing where to look, his mouth ajar, said nothing.

The prince placed his hands upon his hips and laughed.

Sir William stared, then broke into his own shaky laugh.

"My Lord, you truly shocked me," Sir William said, slapping the prince on the back.

Braxton grinned a broad smile and nodded, whispering, "Call me John."

———

The trek up Peak Road was steeper than Braxton had anticipated.

He marveled at how the different forms of conveyance, all horse- powered, went up and down the steep winding gravel incline.

Chinese servants and vendors walked the hill. Very few rode on horseback, or sat aboard the horse-drawn wagons laden with goods, tools, and food.

Large homes dotted the hillside. Most were painted white and were roofed in colorful tiles. Broad verandas attested to the profits being made from the burgeoning trade. Elegant women carrying parasols seated in elegant carriages paraded up and down the Peak Road. This was the Hill District. Only British expatriates and government officials were allowed to live in certain areas of the Hill District on the peak. Mansions littered the incline.

The party continued their climb.

"This is absolutely beautiful," Prince Braxton said, looking out over the city and the crowded Victoria Harbor. "I had no idea there was so much development. What is that over there?" he asked, pointing across the harbor.

Sir William stood up in his stirrups, shielding his eyes from the sun.

"That is Tsim Sha Tsui. And to the right is Kowloon Bay." "There is so much to see in Hong Kong. Opportunities bound."

They continued their trek, navigating their way in and out of carts, people, and carriages coming and going in both directions. "I would appreciate it if you would make inquiries as to the availability of a house for me. I will have need of one for a couple of months," Braxton said.

"It will be my pleasure, John."

Suddenly, screams cascaded down from the road above. The sound of neighing horses followed as a chorus of panicked, high- pitched Chinese voices erupted. The four men's horses reared up on their hind legs. One of the retainers was tossed off his animal.

Crashing sounds were soon followed by wooden barrels careening down the hill, some bouncing off the side of the road to the left, plummeting down the steep embankment.

"Get off the road!" Braxton shouted. The three remaining riders yanked their reins to the right and drove their mounts into the steep underbrush opposite the precipice. The fallen man crawled up after them, narrowly avoiding being trampled by his own horse.

More casks ricocheted and bounced down the hill. The ones not launched off the cliff's edge to their demise ripped open, spewing out flour, rice, and red wine. Five shrieking and gesticulating coolies scurried down from the upper road, inspecting what was left of the shattered drums.

The chaos soon passed. The multitude of carriages and carts resumed their journeys as if nothing had happened.

"That too is part of Hong Kong," Sir William sighed.

———

Later that afternoon, the prince and Marsh returned to the city and proceeded to an opium den, one popular with foreigners.

"May I ask, what is your interest in opium?" Marsh inquired. "Mostly economic. I understand a great deal of money can be made. It is one of my many interests including, silk, tea, jade, and pottery. Maybe more."

Marsh continued, "The opium trade, as you may know, started over a hundred years ago. In fact, the British are the ones who brought it to China, and many other parts of the world, including North America and Europe."

"Yes, I know. It was initially grown by the East India Company and exported. I understand the opium trade was supported by our government in an effort to offset the tea trade imbalance with China." Braxton paused and placed his hands in his pockets. He said, "Do you know that ten percent of the Crown's revenue comes from duties placed on tea imports?"

"Ten percent? My God, that is an astonishing number."

"It is a big concern to the government. If something should happen to our tea imports, the government...let's just say it would be catastrophic."

Marsh marveled, "So that is one of the reasons you are here? To ascertain how best to protect the British economy?"

The prince laughed quietly, then said, "I wish that was entirely true. I am here on behalf of my father's government and my own interests. Now, let's take a look inside. I want to know more about this opium. If I am to consider trading in it, I would like to become familiar with it."

Sir Marsh put out his hand to stop the prince for a moment. He lowered his voice, "John, have you ever seen or been to a den? Ah Sing's in London, perhaps?"

"How could I? Everyone knows me in London and in the cities I frequent on the continent. I know little of the real world. I have learned much since initially leaving England almost six years ago.

"I beg of you, John. Opium can be addictive and has destroyed many men, their families, and their fortunes. Are you sure you want to partake?"

Braxton inhaled through clenched teeth while gazing down at the oriental carpet on which they stood. He rubbed the back of his neck. "My Aunt Ekaterina lived in physical pain and mental anguish of one sort or another all her life. She would often drink from a mysterious bottle she kept close to her person. One day, she neglected to put the bottle in her bag. The grand duchess dozed off during one of our conversations. Curiosity drove me to inspect the bottle. It was laudanum. I was ten years old. I assumed if it was good enough for her, I should give it a try. I took a tiny gulp. Nothing happened, or so I thought.

"Ekaterina appeared to be nodding off and was soon breathing heavily. It was rather obvious that our conversation was over, and I decided to return to my rooms. I began to feel somewhat confused as I navigated my way back to my quarters in the palace. The furniture and paintings along the promenade became a bit fuzzy and seemed to move about. That amused me more than concerned me. By the time I reached my rooms, I felt rather relaxed, even giddy.

Then my mood picked up. I was uncritically happy. As I have always been overly serious and self-directed, this was quite new to me. The rest of the day turned out to be one of the more pleasant days of my life. It was the opium in the laudanum that brought me out of myself. I would like to revisit that day."

———

Later that evening, Braxton sat propped up against Sir William Marsh in a rickshaw. His confused gaze and dry mouth attested to his having experienced the poppy extract.

"Where are we?" Braxton asked.

"On our way back to Government House, John."

"John, who is John? Is my brother here? God."

"No, Your Highness," Sir William replied. "I beg your pardon." "Why are we going there?" Braxton mumbled. "I don't like that place, or that woman."

"They're hosting a dinner party in your honor this evening."

Braxton did not respond. He rested his head on the back of the seat and dozed.

Upon arrival at their lodgings, Sir William assisted the prince into the house through the back entrance, up the service stairs and into his rooms. The Chinese staff they encountered respecfully looked the other way as the two men passed.

The Englishman placed Braxton in the care of his valet, and said," I shall make the necessary excuses. He should be fine in the morning."

Apologies were made and the planned formal dinner was rescheduled due to the guest of honor having contracted "food poisoning," so everyone was told.

———

A week passed. Prince Braxton moved into a large house on Victoria Peak. He assembled his staff and set about his business, free from the watchful eyes of the Contessa Roma.

Braxton's time in Hong Kong was spent inspecting the governor's and Sir Williams' administrative operations. He met with the East India Company and the three largest hongs: the trading firms Jardine's, Dent & Co., and Russell & Co.

The prince spent time and energy on developing relationships with foreign dignitaries and business leaders. Unlike Japan, Britain ruled Hong Kong. As Royal Envoy, he spoke for the king and prime minister. His royal and diplomatic status opened many political and commercial doors. Braxton spent the bulk of his efforts on developing his conglomerate's interests through third parties, as he had done in Japan.

It had been three years since the prime minister and the king had asked Prince Braxton to serve as Royal Envoy and Viceroy. At that time, the prince had developed sprawling economic interests in Europe and Russia. At that time, he had not been to Japan and had no interest in trading with that island nation. He had expressed his desire not to sacrifice his outside interests. He'd reasoned with the prime minister that his succession to the throne was unlikely. His two older brothers were likely to produce heirs, further removing him from the succession.

The entrepreneurial prince saw no reason to live a life based on the improbable. After initially refusing the government's request, the prime minister acquiesced to Braxton's presumption he would never become king. The young entrepreneur forged an understanding with the king and the prime minister that he could pursue his interests as long as they remained at arm's length.

Protecting his independence, Braxton refused compensation and shouldered the cost of the expedition. The military men and the costs of transportation were shouldered by the government.

Burgeoning trade and abundant opportunities kept him in Hong Kong for four months. When he departed Hong Kong for Singapore, he had duplicated his Japanese business and trading interests, albeit not on so grand a scale.

———

Major Barrett, his troops, Braxton, and his cadre of clerks boarded two British warships for Singapore. In less than three months' time, winter storms would visit the China Sea.

The HMS Invincible and HMS Devastation departed Hong Kong early in the morning. The tide had crested, and the harbor waters were placid as glass. Braxton stood on the bow and inhaled the salty sea air. The prince observed merchant ships, both sail and steam, lining the docks. Soon the docks would spring to life, but not quite yet. The rising sun lit up the surface of the harbor's waters and showered the emerald green mountains enveloping Hong Kong in a golden light. Braxton saluted the Victoria Peak. "Good bye."

The young prince was glad to be at sea, away from commerce and politics. No one could reach him here. He remained on deck until the ship had entered open waters. The massive vessel beneath his feet felt as though it was propelled from behind by a gentle rolling sea. As if it was gliding atop the turquoise sea. All tension escaped his body and a smile crossed his face as he observed eight dolphin swimming alongside the front of the ship. He was certain they were welcoming him to their world.

16

THE LION CITY

The prince entered one of the warship officer's staterooms. The ship's captain had given his quarters over to the royal. The fleet admiral had offered his lavish quarters, but Braxton had declined the offer. He had reasoned the naval officer, nearing retirement, and having served the empire well, need not be inconvenienced. The prince also realized not displacing the gentleman would reflect well on him and his family.

"Second best is still good," Braxton said to his valet. "Yes, Your Royal Highness."

"All seems in good order. Leave things where they are. Come back after you are settled in your quarters. I am dining with the admiral this evening."

"Yes, Sir. Thank you, Sir," the valet replied. He bowed and exited the cabin.

The accommodations included a bed against the bulkhead under one of the two large portholes. Four leather upholstered chairs surrounded a low mahogany table. A large desk faced the other porthole. The wall opposite the portholes was paneled in teak. A montage of etchings depicting historical naval battles covered most of the teak paneling. The remaining steel bulkheads remained uncovered. A smaller space adjoined the cabin. It was lined with cabinets, built in drawers and what appeared to be a large wardrobe. In the center of the room stood an expansive wood and glass chart table.

Braxton searched through one of his bags and withdrew a simple silver frame. It held a picture of Valentina, her lustrous, black hair cascading down her back. She wore a simple cotton dress and was half seated on a swing, pushing back with her legs, her hands grasping the ropes. Her sparkling eyes danced from within the black and white daguerreotype. Braxton yearned to kiss the full, laughing lips, smiling at him.

The love-struck prince placed the frame on the desk beside a brass lamp. He removed several pieces of linen writing paper from a drawer. The stationary was gold embossed with "HMS Irascible" and a small line drawing of the massive battleship underneath. He helped himself to a pen in the writing set anchored to the top of the mahogany desk.

Dearest Val,

I hope this note finds you well. As I mentioned in my previous correspondence, your letters finally started to arrive in batches when I reached Hong Kong. I suppose the four thousand miles that separate us must have had something to do with that!

We are en route to Singapore. It shall undoubtedly prove to be another marvelous experience. I wish you were here to share it with me.

Hong Kong was not what I had expected. In my previous correspondence, I mentioned the differences between Nippon and Sino cultures.

I don't think the Chinese are yet prepared for westernization. The Chinese are not positioned to face the challenges they will inevitably encounter. It is imperative they protect their economy and borders from the overtly ambitious Japanese.

My business interests are more and more tied to both nations' wellbeing. It is a bit unsettling what could be undone should the Japanese stir things up in their efforts to expand their empire. The British government, I hope, will take heed of my warnings. Hong Kong and China are vulnerable to any conflict, be it trade or military. To have you here with me, by my side, in transit to the British Colony of Singapore would be the perfect balm for my troublesome concerns.

I so love and miss you.

I've heard Singapore is beautiful and thriving. Like Hong Kong, at the turn of the century it was but a fishing village. Today, it is a bustling international trading center.

I do not anticipate much to occupy me during my stay, other than waving the Union Jack. Yet I thought the same thing about Hong Kong, only to be wrong. But I am gratified my sojourn turned out to be worthwhile.

There may be an opportunity to invest in rubber and shipping in Singapore. We shall see.

My timing appears to be fortuitous. Government instability, labor unrest, and an economic downturn have led to depressed prices throughout Singapore and Indochina. Most shipping lines are losing money and many plantations are bankrupt.

I still have vast sums to invest. Frankly, the more I study the situation, the more I look forward to availing myself of any opportunity. Yes, shipping, because it is a significant cost for trade. Yes, rubber, as it is evolving into an essential commodity used in manufacturing. Tin is another interesting commodity. There are vast mining reserves in Burma. Of course, the French colonies have tin mines and seem to be doing quite well. You may be aware that it is increasingly utilized in coating steel. Tin cans, I suppose, are one of its more prominent uses. Pewter is made from it. Did you know it is used in soft solders? It serves as a kind of adhesive for metal. I find that intriguing, particularly as I am currently aboard a vessel made of steel held together by bolts, screws, and solder. There are also many household uses of which I had never cared to notice. I am taking note now!

Do I drive you crazy going on and on about my interests? I am sorry if I do, but without you, that is all I have. I am sorry to learn your father, the czar, is not well. Though, from your letters, it sounds as though your cousin Maxim and you are thriving in your capacities as co-regents. The burden you share with Maxim is tremendous. Be sure to husband your health. I fear I have neglected my own.

It pains and frustrates me to have realized, and now admit, this journey is wearing on me and I am quite exhausted. There never seems to be a moment of rest. The government's demands and the burdens I place on myself are adversely impacting my health. I will have to share with you an incident in which I sought respite while in Hong Kong. One which turned out to be quite embarrassing. I narrowly escaped scandal. It is funny now, but not when it occurred...I shall share more later.

In my last letter to the prime minister, I asked that my time in India be kept to a minimum. I need to see you. I have to see you. I fear you may give up on me. That would be a loss I could not bear.

You know I love you. I genuinely want to spend my life with you. We have been separated for so long. Please write and tell me you love me as I do you.

All my love, Brax

———

Prince Braxton and Admiral Sir Jackson Hunt sat in the officer's stateroom aboard the flag warship. The admiral was dressed in his dress-mess uniform and the prince in white tie.

Four port holes ran along one wall. The cabin's oak panels glowed in the lamplight. Furnishings upholstered in leather rested on a polished wood floor. Fine dinnerware and sterling flatware set the table. A gently rolling sea framed the mood.

"I must admit, Admiral, I am always amazed at the very civilized life aboard naval vessels." Braxton took a deep pull on his cigar. He raised the cut crystal tumbler, observing the candlelight refracting through the amber-colored Scotch. "Dinner was excellent."

"Thank you, Your Royal Highness. But as you can imagine, most of us at sea live quite simply. When I was a junior officer there were three of us stacked one atop the other, six to a cabin. We each had a small cabinet for our uniforms and personal affects. There was one writing desk and two chairs between us."

"I think that would be incentive enough to make every effort for promotion to the senior ranks as quickly as possible," Braxton laughed.

"Indeed, it is, Sir."

"On another subject, Admiral, I understand things are not going well in Singapore. I have heard the economy is racked by falling rubber prices and that the severity of the crash has unhinged the government."

The admiral sat for a moment in silence then cleared his throat.

"It is not my place to be involved in or comment on politics sir. I am a naval officer. My expertise is confined to those policies that involve the navy. I wish I could offer more, Your Royal Highness."

"I understand, Sir Jackson, but I won't accept your being totally unfamiliar with the crisis. As royal envoy, I have a responsibility to assess the situation. It is important that I avail myself of all assets, including naval assets such as you, Admiral. Would you deny your king and country your humble opinion?" Braxton held his gaze on the flag officer.

A shallow smile crossed the admiral's face. "I have heard you are a clever man and wise beyond your years."

An orderly entered the cabin, removed the dishes and poured each of the men another Scotch. He relit the admiral's cigar. Braxton declined a light.

"Will there be anything else, Sir?" the orderly asked. "No, that will be all for tonight."

"Thank you, Sir." He saluted and withdrew.

Admiral Hunt sat back in his chair and said, "In my opinion, the Singapore economy is indeed a crisis. There are many opposing in play here. The French have their interests, as do the British. Then there is the indigenous population and the Chinese to the north. One must understand it is the West and East pitted against one another and amongst themselves. This conflict will not be settled in our life time. Certainly not mine. Maybe not even yours."

Braxton was dumbstruck by this insighful, yet brutal revelation.

He had received an answer, however he was not confident he completely comprehended what he had heard. Intuitively, he knew the situation was highly nuanced. "I have always been somewhat unsure of understanding the 'Irish' question, but this is even more rife with variables and much more difficult to fathom."

The navy man explained the situation in Singapore in more depth.

Braxton nodded as his words validated what Braxton had shared in his letter to Valentina.

Braxton said, "Not so long ago I ran into a similar but much larger political and economic crisis in Russia. I was fortunate enough to get involved in mining, lumber, oil drilling, and railways. I spent years working day and night to help lift them out of that morass. It proved mutually beneficial. The country is now on a sound economic footing. Trade between Hong Kong, Japan, and Russia is thriving.

Perhaps I can leverage some of what I learned in Russia to help the people and the government in Singapore."

The admiral grunted, and said, "Why else would the prime minister put my fleet at your disposal?"

Braxton smiled and lifted his glass."

———

Their arrival in Singapore coincided with a still plummeting economy. Coupled with the government's instability, this worked to Braxton's advantage. Labor strife had all but brought trade to a halt, the strife a consequence of the struggling economy and politics.

Overextended rubber planters had sold off significant portions of their plantations. Braxton calculated that with current rubber prices and distress sales abounding, he could recoup his planned investments in two or three years. He subsequently made a substantial investment with two prominent English planters. He limited his involvement to scrutinizing the balance sheets and participating in decisions regarding long-term finances.

———

Braxton sat in the governor of Singapore's office. "I appreciate your hosting me, Sir Cecil," Braxton said. Cecil Clementi Smith, a tall, angular, and impeccably dressed career civil servant, held out a rosewood box filled with cheroots.

"Thank you," Braxton said, and helped himself to one of the slender rolled cigars.

"It is my pleasure, Your Royal Highness." Sir Cecil paused and sat back in his leather desk chair. "You have come at a rather challenging time. Let me take a moment to apprise you of the current situation."

"Please do."

"As you know, I have spent most of my career living and studying the Chinese cultures. It has been an enlightening and worthwhile experience. Nevertheless, I find the situation here in the Singapore Straits, frankly, dire. Corruption is rampant. We are dealing with secret societies and an exploding population. These secret societies intimidate and abuse the working class and trade in the prostitution of women and young boys. Disease plagues the lower classes and has severely impacted trade and commerce. No doubt you are familiar with the decline of the rubber trade?"

"Yes, Governor. I am aware of the calamity."

"During your stay in Singapore, I welcome your input and counsel regarding these matters."

"I appreciate your confidence in me, Sir Cecil, but I do not believe I have the background in such matters. How might I be of service?"

The governor pulled out a thick file filled with papers and newspaper clippings.

"I have been following your activities since you were a young man. I had the good fortune to be at the Ascot Races when your horses cornered the Queen Anne Cup. I believe you were not yet fifteen at that time. Amazing. Frankly, I've been fascinated by you ever since. This folder will attest to my interest. My nephew, Lord Ramsey, has kept me abreast and often sends me clippings."

Braxton coughed, having heard Sir Cecil mention Lord Ramsey's name. My God, what might this man know?

Ramsey is close to my family, and one of my most trusted associates.

The admiral continued, "I imagine it is my way of staying in touch with what is going on back home. And in this instance, throughout the world." He tapped the thick folder with one hand and smiled at the prince.

Braxton looked at the folder and back at the governor, and said, "Governor, you have me at a disadvantage."

"How so?"

"I certainly do not have such a comprehensive dossier on you." "There is not much to tell. I am a humble civil servant and scholar of all things Chinese."

Braxton pursed his lips and grinned.

Sir Cecil picked up the file and placed it in a drawer. "It is my understanding you provided a great service to the Russian co-regents, Prince Maxim and the Grand Duchess Valentina. Your contributions were, on the surface, primarily commercial. More importantly, you were instrumental in helping quell civil unrest in difficult times. Your compassion for the Russian people is well documented. We would like to avail ourselves of that expertise."

"Thank you. I am, of course, at your service."

"Begging your pardon, Your Royal Highness, you are the royal envoy. I am at your service."

17

———

KNOTS LEFT UNTIED

Two weeks after his arrival in Singapore, the prince received a letter:

Dearest Braxton,

I trust this letter finds you well. Hopefully, it has reached you before your departure for India. I would so hate for it to take weeks, or even a month, to reach you.

I miss you and want to see you. I would come to India and strap myself, body and soul, to your side if I could. However, Father is very ill. Maxim and I both are overwhelmed with that, and the unsettled undercurrents associated with a transition of power.

If father would abdicate, my cousin Maxim could solidify his position and things would be simpler. In the past, I would not have dared write that in a letter, but Father's secret police are now loyal to Maxim and me, or so we believe. The attempt on Maxim's life still lingers in my thoughts. If they were not to remain loyal to us, I do not think we would survive my father's death and what could easily be a violent succession. I pray for Maxim daily.

If I could resign the co-regency, I would. When that day comes, a smooth succession demands I be here to support Maxim's assumption of the Russian throne.

Marriage. We speak of it so often in our letters. I have reached out to Maxim. He is in favor of you and me marrying, but he suggested I speak to my father. Father is of a favorable bent to our union.

Father is leaning toward giving his blessing on the marriage of Maxim and your sister Carmen, but he has little faith in your Parliament agreeing to the match. Father believes the union between Maxim and Carmen would be good for Russia; however, he does not think you and I can announce our engagement or marry before they are wed. You can imagine how that took the wind out of my sails after believing he was supportive of our marriage, then adding the caveat delaying our plans. Once again, with him, there is always a nasty twist.

When I asked him why, why we could not proceed, that wily and all too familiar cagy stare descended upon his face; that look that telegraphs he has an agenda from which he cannot be dissuaded. In short, he said once Maxim and Carmen wed, he will support our marriage. Until then, I think it is best we keep our plans to ourselves.

As for patience, I have none. I feel horrid asking you to wait. You will return home soon, perhaps by then we will be able to wed. That being said, we cannot sit idly by. It is imperative we stay true to our desires.

I am afraid it is time for you to get involved. It pains me to ask, but do you think you could petition your parents and your government to act on Carmen and Maxim's marriage?

Please be direct. Our future together depends on it. I love you, Braxton.

Val

Braxton chaffed with the knowledge the czar and England held Valentina's and his future in their hands. He did as Valentina asked and wrote his parents and the prime minister.

Your Royal Majesties and Prime Minister,

As you are in regular receipts of my reports, I will refrain from addressing anything but a personal matter concerning my sister, Princess Carmen.

Please excuse the somewhat severe tone in this letter. The time has come for plain speaking. This letter rises from deep within my heart as a son, a brother, and a senior member of the royal family. If I were to express my opinion as the royal envoy, I would still be of the same mind.

The government has sat for some time on the matter of Carmen's betrothal to Prince Maxim. While I am not privy to the details, it is painfully obvious both Carmen and Maxim are ill-served.

No doubt, some feel their marriage might shift the balance of power in Europe. Perhaps that is exactly what needs to happen. The Germans, Austrians and Italians are forging a stronger bond. Why not match them? Form an alliance with Russia! Certainly, Austria and Germany would think twice about waging war against the British, French, and Russian Empires.

It is time for the government to approve the marriage. Such a union would help secure peace for the British Empire.

Most importantly, Carmen and Maxim are in love. I beseech you to make every effort to offer a nod of approval. Without implied consent, the czar will not publicly consider the match.

Sincerely,
Braxton, Prince of Wales

———

Braxton's cousin and banking manager, Count Aramis, arrived in Singapore from Tokyo. The prince had summoned him to assist in a takeover of a floundering American shipping line, Pacific Transport.

The prince, Count Aramis and Mr. Robert Carlton, the president of Pacific Transport, met in his office.

Prince Braxton opened the meeting with, "Mr. Carlton, thank you for hosting us today. We appreciate your hospitality and look forward to the possibility of working with you."

"You're very welcome, Your Royal Highness. We, too, are hopeful this might lead to a mutually beneficial working arrangement."

Braxton said, "I hope you understand that in my capacity as royal envoy, my involvement must remain at arm's length. For that reason, Count Aramis will serve as my personal liaison. Please note, these discussions are in no manner linked directly or indirectly to their majesties or his majesty's government." He paused and waited for the shipping line's president to fully comprehend what he had said.

Mr. Carlton thought, and then responded with a knowing smile, "I understand."

Braxton nodded and continued, "Thank you, Sir. I would also appreciate total confidentiality."

"Yes, Your Royal Highness."

Braxton rose from his chair and walked over to the floor-to-ceiling window. Folding his arms, he looked out upon the docks and harbor.

Count Aramis said, "Mr. Carlton, it is not our desire to dwell on the challenges that are facing all businesses associated with the rubber industry. The falling markets are negatively impacting everyone, particularly your shipping line, Pacific Transport. These are difficult times. We are here to find a solution to the challenges so many are facing."

The men sat silence for a moment.

"Yes, Count," Mr. Carlton said, his face now drawn, his clasped hands resting on the boardroom conference table. He looked back and forth between Aramis and Braxton. "I must admit, I was a little surprised to receive your request for a meeting. It is not often one meets with men of your stature. Normally, we deal with intermediaries. This is most unusual."

Braxton did not respond to Carlton's comments.

Aramis remained silent, his hands resting atop a dark brown leather porfolio.

Carlton inhaled and asked, "What do you propose? Why exactly are you here?" In a more hopeful tone, he asked, "Are you interested in hiring ships to transport your goods?"

Braxton turned from the window and faced the two men, his hands in his pockets. "Please indulge me, Mr. Carlton, as I would like to provide you with a little background on my interests. Perhaps you are aware of my holdings in Russia. I am heavily invested in lumber, mining and oil drilling. My conglomerate owns and controls the railways from Vladivostok to Western Russia."

"I heard you have purchased interests in several rubber plantations. Why? The market has crashed." Both the prince and the count were perplexed with why Carlton had deflected the conversation.

Braxton returned his gaze to looking out the window, as if not facing the other two men would somehow remove him in his capacity of royal envoy from being perceived as participating directly in the conversation. He remarked, "Yes, the rubber market has crashed because of corruption and greed. The French, Indo-Chinese, and parochial interests are shortsighted and have cut off their noses to spite their faces. Your shipping line's insolvency is proof enough the market has collapsed from within, as the international demand for rubber and tin cannot be satiated due to labor strife and ineffective governance. It saddens me to say this surreal travesty is self-inflicted."

Prince Braxton paused for a moment and then looked directly at the American. "The need for rubber is exploding in Europe, America, and Japan. Japan has its eyes on China and Eastern Russia. They will soon be accelerating their military build-up. The Americans have grown too rich to sit idly by as Germany, late into the game, seeks to acquire colonies. The French and Austrians are caught in the middle. They will have to arm as well.

"Oil, rubber, and steel are the raw materials needed for war and trade. Need I say more?"

Mr. Carlton cocked his head and said, "Frankly, I had no idea of the magnitude of your firm's involvement. I had heard rumors you were involved with the Russian Consortium. Is that why you are so interested in transpacific shipping?"

Braxton turned back toward the window. He withdrew a cigar from his jacket pocket, cut and lit it.

Aramis waited until the prince finished lighting his cigar to respond, "We have been interested in oceanic shipping for years. But we did not know where to look. Also, we were reticent to involve ourselves in an industry where we had no expertise. As you might imagine, our European and Russian projects require all our energy."

Mr. Carlton sat back in his chair and asked. "I am not sure what you are saying. Again, are you interested in contracting my company to transport your goods?"

Braxton and Aramis said nothing.

Mr. Carlton moved uncomfortably in his chair. His lips flattened as he asked, "Gentlemen?"

"We have something else in mind," Aramis replied. "You think you are in a position to pressure me to sell!"

"That is correct, in part," Braxton said, still facing the window. He let the cigar's ash fall to the carpet.

Carlton sat up straighter and gripped his chair's arms. "I did not comply with your request to meet today to sell my company!"

Count Aramis ignored the statement and interjected, "His royal highness has developed trading interests in Japan, Hong Kong, and now Singapore. We sell and transport oil to all three geographic regions. We are paying entirely too much to ship the oil. Also, we have coal, and copper interests in China. Our Japanese and Chinese textile export profits are marginalized by the cost of shipping throughout the Far East, North America and Europe."

Mr. Carlton's face had lost its color.

Aramis continued. "We are finding it difficult to meet Europe's and North America's demands for porcelain. Also, the highly-prized yellow fabric nankeen, and likewise tea, silk and opium. Why? Two reasons. The availability of reliable ocean transport and the irregular costs associated with said transport."

Carlton leaned forward, both arms on the table and exclaimed, "Then why are my ships sitting at anchor, empty? Why have you not hired them?"

"That is a good question, Mr. Carlton," Braxton said. Turning from the window, he pulled one of the chairs out from the conference table, placed it next to the window and sat down.

Count Aramis went on to explain, "We are willing to make a cash infusion of £250,000 into your company. We will also provide the funds for the purchase of two ships and will finance the building of three additional vessels to be built in Liverpool. For all this we ask for fifty-one percent ownership and a proportional participation in your company's profits. This arrangement would require you to continue to run the company. We also require preferred shipping rates."

Braxton added, "This arrangement prevents the shipping line from defaulting on its debts and restores your personal wealth. Again, we require you remain at the helm."

The president of Pacific Transport rose out of his chair and paced the wall along the windows overlooking the harbor. He stopped and starred out. Turning back, he asked, "Anything else?"

"Yes," Braxton said. "Years ago, I founded and continue to underwrite an academy situated on one of my family's estates. It is called the Aurelio Palace Academy. It was created to educate the children of the estate's staff. It grew and now attracts young men and women from throughout the British Isles. Their education is focused on commerce, law and government service."

Carlton appeared distracted as he returned to his chair.

Braxton continued, "We are hiring many of the graduates and placing them throughout our commercial organizations. We will require you allow us to place recent graduates within your company here and in your offices in San Francisco."

"Why do you two feel I would even consider this offer?" Braxton folded his hands in his lap and said in a cold voice,

"Because your ships sit idle. You have not paid your crews in months. Half your ships will be in receivership in less than a month. That is why."

Carlton shot to his feet and demanded, "How are you so familiar with my business affairs?"

"I purchased your debt," Braxton snapped back. "Christ! Why?"

"Because if I had not, you would have lost your company weeks ago. What little work you have in shipping I contracted through a third party I own. It is my shipping contracts and owning your debt that keeps your fleet afloat."

"Why would you do that? Why did you not you come to me directly, weeks ago?"

"Because you still had some cash on hand. Now you do not. Also, as I own your debt, I in fact, own your company. I am not here to ruin you. I am here to garner your attention." He paused. "I believe I have it."

Mr. Carlton swallowed and asked, "Once again, is there anything else?"

Aramis looked at Braxton. Braxton shook his head slightly and motioned with one hand toward the American.

"That is all, Sir," Aramis said.

Mr. Carlton rose from his seat. Braxton and Aramis also stood.

"I will take it under advisement and get back to you within the week."

Mr. Carlton did not make an effort to show the prince and the count out of the office.

Four days later, Pacific Transport's board of directors accepted the prince's offer.

18

AL HIND

Braxton soon tired of the the volatility associated with trade and commerce in Singapore. He felt he was leaving the management of the shipping line and of the plantations in capable hands. Both enterprises were run by people having vested interests in their success.

The prince departed soon thereafter for Al Hind. On the voyage to Calcutta, Braxton wrote Lord Ramsey in Tokyo.

Dear Ramsey,

It relieves me to say I am on the final leg of my journey. Three years have passed since I've seen my family or set foot in England. I must admit that this adventure has proven far more difficult than I had anticipated. Yet I have learned a great deal and have succeeded in meeting my father's and the government's expectations, but at a great cost to my health.

I appreciate the work you; Aramis and Seiko have done to consolidate my business interests in Japan and Hong Kong. India is my last remaining destination. My intentions are to experience as much of that great land as I can manage. You may be aware of the many chal-

lenges facing the viceroy and the British government in those vast and varied princely states. This is the first time I have approached an assignment with trepidation. I shall attempt to familiarize you with what lies ahead.

Calcutta, a great and troubled city, promises to be my first trial.

The capital of our Indian empire is not well situated geographically to rule the large sub-continent. It would be as if London were located on the furthest northwest corner of Ireland, and in a country thirteen times larger than the United Kingdom. This isolation is made all the worse by poor roads and little rail service.

Calcutta is two cities within one. The divide is between that of "White Town", which is composed primarily of our countrymen, and "Black Town", populated by non-whites.

The city is excessively overcrowded and equally vibrant and experiencing rapid growth and expansion. Infrastructure improvements and private building projects are woefully inadequate, striving impossibly to overtake and keep pace with the demands of its populace.

It is so very difficult to define the races or nationalities of this melting-pot of a nation. Perhaps the most efficient way to describe the populace is that of the Indians being comprised of four principal ethnic groups - white, yellow, black, and brown - they have proven to be the most well-suited for British rule, as many strive to assimilate our customs. They are westernizing and becoming at times more English than the English. However, underneath all this, seethes anarchy; a hotbed of Indian nationalism.

An additional variable, that of the archaic caste system. I cannot fathom what useful purpose it serves. It relegates a large cross- section of its people to poverty and a desultory existence.

All the aforementioned is only part of what I have been charged with delving into and reporting back to my father's government. Alas, that does not speak to the remainder of the vast continent. Frankly, I do not know how I will go about sorting out the challenges confronting this vast country. This may be the most difficult assignment I have ever undertaken. For the first time, I must reach deep within to regain the confidence, desire, and energy required. I am fatigued.

For that reason, I am stepping away from the day-to-day operations of my business interests. It will fall to you, Aramis, and Seiko, to take up that mantle. In the meantime, please gather the others together and submit a recommended proposal to include not just the Far East business, but those in Russia, Europe and England.

I am mentally and physically exhausted, Ramsey. Perhaps I can find time to regain my strength before commencing my tour of the subcontinent.

Rest assured, I have every confidence that you, Aramis, Seiko and the management staff will rise to the occasion, surpassing my expectations.

Warmly, Brax

————

King Richard and Queen Mercedes sat in the Crimson Drawing Room overlooking the park at Windsor Castle. The heavily gilded white walls framed red damask wall coverings situated behind paintings of previous kings and queens.

"Richard, I am concerned about Braxton."

"I know, my love. You have been worried about him since before the fire, decades ago in the Aurelio Palace. And your concerns are often-times warranted," Richard said squeezing her hand.

Mercedes continued, "His letters the past six months have lost their luster. They do not reflect the same upbeat, bon vivant Braxton. I have previously kept my own counsel, so as not to alarm you."

"I understand. I have sensed something different as well. He has continued to perform his tasks admirably as royal envoy. The prime minister sings his praises to the cabinet. The minister of foreign affairs and the colonial secretary have both made mention as to his reports being invaluable. I suppose that is why I have not brought my concerns to the government. Perhaps I should have, as it is quite unfair to our son."

The queen placed her tea on the table, sat up straight, folding her hands in her lap and said, "I have taken things into my own hands."

His interest piqued, Richard looked over at her and sighed, "Mercedes. He is not a boy. He is a man about the government's business. We are not to interfere."

"I have reached out to Cosimo. He agrees. Braxton has been absent far too long and no one in the family has laid eyes on him in years, other than Lord Ramsey and Count Aramis. He too has expressed concern as to our son's exhaustive pace."

"And?"

"I've asked Cosimo to join our son in Calcutta."

"Calcutta? That is halfway around the world. Is Braxton aware of this?"

"I know exactly where it is, Richard. And no, Braxton has not been told."

"When does your brother plan to depart for India?"

"He sailed from Brindisi last week and will board a train for Calcutta once he arrives in Constantinople. He should reach Calcutta in a fortnight."

"How is that possible? No contiguous rail service exists between Constantinople and Calcutta?" Richard asked, challenging his wife's statement.

"Ferry service connects passengers. He will find his way. I am not concerned."

"I wish you would have discussed this with me earlier."

"I posted my letter to Cosimo detailing my worries. In the letter I mentioned he might use bank business as an excuse. He wrote back stating there was no requirement for excuses, and that by the time I had received his letter, he would have departed Chiacontella." She paused, adjusting her shawl, and continued, "I was taken quite aback with Cosimo's having immediately picked up and set out for Calcutta. But as he had had mentioned Aramis also having remarked in letters as to Braxton's harried pace, it further confirmed my concerns for Braxton's health."

Richard turned his attention to the expansive park outside the window. "I have always known your brother to be a good man. This simply confirms it."

"He loves you, me, and our family," Mercedes sighed. Richard's heart skipped a beat. Yes, he loved Cosimo as well,

deeply. He had since they had been young men, desperately in love with one another; before he had met Cosimo's twin sister, his wife, Mercedes.

———

Upon his arrival in Calcutta, the Indian population embraced the legendary prince.

As Braxton made the necessary preparations for his tour of India, he wrote in a memorandum to Major Barrett:

It is imperative we take note of the topography and the weather we will likely encounter during our tour of India. The land is decidedly arid in many parts. Food and water will be in limited supply and should the train suffer mechanical problems, little access to parts and labor will be available.

As this pertains to the train, I am directing the two engines be overhauled. Also, that the undercarriages of all the cars following their journey from northern Europe be refurbished.

In addition, please ensure provisions are adequate to sustain our party for up to 90 days should we encounter difficulties along the way. Provisions must include adequate coal, water, food, and ammunition.

Calcutta's slower pace was welcomed by Braxton. Over a four- week period he regained his health and felt energized. He grew restless and resumed his diplomatic duties.

A week later, Major Barrett addressed the prince, "Your Royal Highness, the crew has completed your requested overhaul of the engines and cars. The train is fully provisioned per your directions."

The two men were seated at a worktable on a large stone terrace on the second floor at Government House. They wore the traditional white knee length shorts and opened collar short-sleeve shirts. The men were kept comfortable in the sweltering heat by a punkah; the large swinging fan made of heavy ornate fabric was attached to the ceiling. To keep the fan in motion, a punkah wallah pulled on a rope strung through pulleys attached to the punkah.

"That is welcome news, Major. I would like to confirm my instructions have been followed to the letter."

"Yes, Sir, they have."

"Have all my orders for preparation of the train and basic food stuffs been carried out? Two additional coal cars and two tanker cars carrying water? Basic food stuffs sufficient to last three months, feed for the horses and the usual tools and replacement parts for anything that might go amiss with the train?"

"Yes, Your Royal Highness." "And ammunition?"

"Yes, Sir. We followed your orders detailing that it be distributed among the various carriages, troop carriers, civilian personnel cars, and your private carriages."

"Excellent. We will depart on the second of January. Hopefully, the milder winter climate will make the trip less arduous."

"Yes, Sir. Is there anything else?"

"Finalize arrangements with the viceregal offices. Inquire as to whether the viceroy has need of any additional accommodations."

———

The hot weather had not yet arrived when the train pulled out of Calcutta. Warm fly-infested air whirled about and had covered the once gleaming emerald train in yellow dust. It reminded Braxton of England and the heavy mid-spring pollen he had come to dread. The prince stood on the rear plaform of his personal car. He observed how the black coal smoke spewing from the steam engine's stack trailed the train, converging with the track disappearing into the distance.

"Your Royal Highness?"

Braxton turned around to see his valet. "What is it?"

"The viceroy has extended an invitation for you to join him in his car."

"Inform the marchioness, with my compliments, I will join him shortly."

The servant nodded, backed into the car and closed the door.

The prince turned back around and gripped one of the struts supporting the metal roof overhang. The Fifth

Marchioness of Lansdowne. A capable man. He proved himself as Governor-General of Canada. Now he has been charged by my father's government to serve as the king's representative, as viceroy, taking on a herculean task ruling India. How can anyone succeed in resolving this multifaceted and culturally convoluted flummox of a nation.

———

That evening, the royal envoy and the viceroy conversed over cigars and brandy as the train rumbled along the undulating pitch- black countryside. Kerosene lanterns had been dimmed. Both men had shed their jackets and cravats. The viceroy had followed Braxton's lead and rolled up his sleeves as the yellow dust had blotched their sweat drenched, once-white shirts.

The prince drew primitive designs in the yellow powder layering the wood table, thinking, this dust is relentless.

"Henry, Prince Braxton addressed the viceroy, Henry Petty Fitzmaurice, What do you see as this country's future? And the British Empire's place in it?"

"That is indeed the question I ask myself every day, Your Royal Highness. One word would sum it up. Tumultuous. As you know, my Lord, the people of India are ruled by their own indigenous leaders, these leaders serving under the paramountcy of the crown. We see ourselves as their benefactors."

"Yes, so I have heard; over and over, though I am not convinced they take the same view of our presence in their country. I would have difficulty viewing it as a paramountcy if I were in their place."

"Your point is well taken, Prince. When I first arrived

in India, I was of the same mind. India is complicated. For many of its people the status quo functions adequately and continues to be effective as a tool to bring them into the nineteenth century. On the other hand, we are hated by millions of their people. But I have come to believe that in the long run all the peoples of this country will prosper from our tutelage."

Braxton mulled over what the marquess had said. "And the riots, rebellions, abject poverty? The corruption and horrific treatment visited on the masses by their own leaders, the maharajas? The feudal caste system suffocates the masses. What can be done?"

"Education. But time is not on our side," the viceroy said. "The unrest is moving forward at an accelerating rate. The more we educate all ranks of society, the more knowledge and freedom they seek. The struggle is not unlike growing pains. The pain is invisible, but it is agonizing. We have been relentless in establishing a pathway for them to follow, one step at a time. God knows they need and want such a course."

The white handkerchief Braxton used to wipe the sweat off his brow came away covered in black coal dust and yellow powder. "How long will this grime be with us?"

Lansdowne chuckled and said, "The coal dust, for the duration.

The yellow will change to a rusty brown soon enough."

"Back to your point, it is my guess it is the ruling class, the upper castes, that are the chief impediment," Braxton said.

"That is my estimation as well. Those who have power do not care to relinquish it and are fighting vigorously to hold on. Then there is the longstanding undercurrent of religious strife between sects, the Hindu, Buddhists, Islam and Sikhs, to name a few. Importantly, much of the religious conflict was of our making, by attempting to unify India under one rule."

"An endless quagmire whose depths escape comprehension," Braxton moaned.

———

Their journey took them to all corners of the continent. When there were no train tracks to take them into remote areas, they traveled by horseback or on elephants. The entourage was transported by camels in the deserts of Kaziranga.

Braxton wrote several letters to Valentina during his journey.

Dearest Valentina,

This land is so vast and varied, mountains soar into the heavens and valleys then fall to depths almost out of sight. Expansive, garden-like plains disappear into the distance. Yet scorched, arid lands are not infrequent. Cities are filled to bursting with the wretched poor by the hundreds of thousands. High above the squalor sit sumptuous palaces of mythic proportions. People lay starving while sacred cows wander the streets, untouchable.

I am fortunate to have had the forethought to bring carloads of grain. But in all honesty, the grain was purposed to feed us and the animals if we could not purchase needed supplies en route. I have found a better use for it. We often extend our stops to portion out grain and food stuffs to the poor. It breaks my heart. I would not and could not describe the deprivation. Deprivation alongside untold wealth. I have petitioned God many times why he would allow this. These are not heathens, but a people at the mercy of things beyond their control.

If there was ever a time in my life when I wanted to be king, it would be now, so I could do whatever I could to assist this mass of starvation and ignorance. But alas, not even the most powerful nation in the world has the resources to mitigate these crimes visited upon a wretched humanity.

I have written my father and the government on this matter but am at a loss to proffer a remedy. My reports have been clear and concise, leaving nothing to their imagination. It will be up to them as to how they move forward. But again, the solution escapes me. This is a land of many different cultures, languages, and religions. It is not one country; it is a rich kaleidoscope of peoples conjoined yet mixing no better than that of oil and water.

I may have discovered my Achilles heel, having seen firsthand man's inhumanity to man visited upon millions. It has crushed my spirit.

I am weakened by my journey. My return home cannot come too soon.

As always with all my love, Brax

Braxton was so disheartened by the reality of his tour through the poverty he found in India he took no steps to advance his own economic interests. He spent his days strategizing ways to organize and finance an attack on hunger, and medical efforts to ease the pain and suffering he had witnessed.

The prince realized he would merely be able to make a dent in the poverty he had witnessed. He appealed to the Indian princes he had visited to assist in underwriting these activities. The sums were large, but not by the standards enjoyed by the wealthy maharajas.

Humoring Prince Braxton's demands was a small price to pay to the British sahibs, hoping they would be left to their own devices.

Braxton returned in the blistering summer's heat to Calcutta. Cosimo, Duke de Chiacontella, had arrived months earlier, having spent his time establishing a branch of the Chiacontella Bank in the teeming city.

After first laying eyes on his nephew when entering the prince's rooms at Government House, the duke shuddered. The ghostlike young man did not rise and embrace his uncle in his customary fashion, but looked up from his chair, his eyes having lost their color, his face gaunt.

Dr. Roundtree, standing next to Braxton nodded and said, "Your Grace. The young, clean-shaven, dark-haired physician wore white linen trousers and an open collar cotton shirt with a stethoscope draped around his neck.

"Uncle," Braxton murmured.

Wide eyed, Cosimo asked, "Braxton, my boy, what has happened?"

Braxton swallowed, and lips slightly parted, looked up toward Roundtree and offered a slight nod.

The doctor pursed his lips and exhaled. "His royal highness has, in my opinion contracted Idiopathic Adenitis."

Cosimo cocked his head and said, "Idio what? I have never heard of such a thing. Are you sure? You are rather young, are you not, doctor? Please, Uncle, listen to him," Braxton said in a guttural whisper, his eyes closed, and his head leaned back against the high- back leather chair.

"Go on," Cosimo said, his gaze directed at the doctor.

"The prince is suffering from an illness that has affected many young people. It is typically found in those between the ages and 15 and 25. It is rarely seen in adults approaching 30. Nevertheless, I have no doubt he has contracted Idiopathic Adenitis. It is a disease that causes extreme fatigue, fever, sore throat, headache and body aches."

Cosimo clasped his hands behind his back. "And the prognosis?

How did he acquire this illness and why have I not heard of it before today?"

Braxton's head tilted to one side; his eyes closed, his chest rhythmically taking in shallow breaths.

Dr. Roundtree moved away from his patient towards the other side of the room, motioning the duke to follow him.

In a whisper, the doctor continued, "While in Berlin last year, I attended a lecture by Dr. Nil Filatov, a Russian physician. Intrigued by this malaise that for centuries had confounded physicians, Filatov shared his research, giving the illness a name and offered his findings on a viable treatment. It is not exactly an illness that often affects the upper classes."

Cosimo gave a quizzical look and remarked, "But he is a royal prince, a prince of the blood?"

"The lower classes live in closer proximity to one another. They share drinking vessels, eating instruments and all those items utilized in hygiene and nutrition. Your grace may not have heard of the illness as your family must certainly have limited your contact with those not in your circle."

"I suppose you are correct. And the prognosis?"

"Time. A lot of time and a great deal of rest. Fluids, nutrition, rest and time."

"How much time?" "Months."

Cosimo placed his hands on his hips, whispering intensely, "Months!"

Roundtree rubbed his chin and looking directly at the duke, confirmed what he had said.

"Yes, months."

A cough sounded from across the room. Both men jerked their attention towards Braxton.

———

The duke had often wondered if Braxton would ever stop striving to acquire more wealth long enough to conjoin his existing business interests. He was relieved to learn that Braxton had not, in fact, expanded his business enterprises during the previous five months.

Taken aback by how physically run down and depressed his nephew had become, he made arrangements to remove the prince from the capital, Calcutta, to the viceroy's cooler, mountain retreat.

His nephew's health issues weighed heavily on Cosimo, yet he did not communicate to his sister, Queen Mercedes, his very real concern for Braxton's full recovery. It was at the retreat that Cosimo sequestered Braxton from all professional and political activities.

They remained isolated at the lodge and its gardens for a month.

During the initial ten days, Braxton was not allowed to speak with anyone, correspond, or read any newspapers. He spent the first three days resting in bed. The following five days he took walks avoiding sunlight. Day nine and ten he ventured outside only in the early morning and at dusk.

Cosimo then provided Braxton spiritual notes and chants to ponder.

During this time, they engaged in conversation and played games of chess, backgammon and took short walks. This practice lasted three weeks. On the thirty-first day of his confinement, Braxton had a visitor.

The prince sat meditating in the lotus position on an

intricately patterned oriental wool carpet. His uncut, sun-streaked hair was tied at the back of his head. He wore loose-fitting, white cotton trousers and a high-collared jacket.

"Braxton?" a familiar female voice inquired.

He opened his eyes, not changing his position, and beheld Valentina. She stood dressed in a light blouse and a comfortable full- length cotton skirt, the hem partially covering cloth slippers. Her dark hair fell to her shoulders. Her bottom lip pressed into her upper lip as her chin quivered slightly.

Braxton's blank countenance changed as his mouth formed a gentle smile and his eyes came to life. He unfolded his legs and brought himself to a standing position.

They approached one another, then paused at arm's length, their eyes moistening. Valentina opened her arms and Braxton moved forward. Wrapping their arms around one another, their heads rested on each other's shoulders. Their bodies pressed against each other; they stood silently for several minutes. Braxton then drew back and took one of her hands in his, drawing her to a nearby ornately carved, wood-framed couch covered in colorful silk cushions.

They sat holding hands, staring into one another's eyes. Valentina reached up and placed her hands around his face, drawing him to her, kissing his lips gently. He sighed quietly.

Valentina murmured, "It is good to see you, my love." The prince smiled and nodded. "I have missed you so." "And I you."

Braxton rested his head back, closed his eyes and asked, "When did you arrive?"

"Several days ago. Your uncle and I agreed it was best

we give you more time to rest before interrupting your recovery."

"I see." He paused, and said, "Perhaps that was best." His head remained laid back with his eyes closed. "How long will you be able to remain?"

"As long as you will have me."

He lifted his head and looked into her aquamarine eyes and asked, "Forever?"

"Darling Brax. We are forever."

———

Valentina and Cosimo limited their time with Braxton, encouraging conversation for only short periods of time. Into the sixth week of his convalescence, spiritual discussions filled their times together. No mention was made of business, politics or the outside world.

One day, while walking in the viceregal lodge's garden, Braxton and Valentina found a place to rest under a large banyan tree. Its thick canopy shielded them from the sun.

"Valentina, how did you hear of my illness?"

"I knew nothing of your illness until I arrived at the lodge. Of course, I suspected that something was amiss when Major Barrett informed me you both were here, you and Cosimo. It sounded so unlike you to separate yourself from your duties for what he said had been weeks."

"But you never wrote telling me of your plan to join me." "No, I did not. One day I spoke with Maxim and told him I suspected you were not well and perhaps needed me. It was a premonition I then chose to act upon. In short, I was unnerved and departed St. Petersburg the following day. For months, your letters had given me pause. It was as if an increasingly hollowing man was writing those letters."

"I am so grateful you made the arduous journey."

"It warms my heart to hear you say so. I was concerned you may not have felt that way, my having arrived uninvited and unannounced."

Braxton turned his head and gently smiled at Valentina. "Please, do not ever feel I would not want you at my side under any circumstances."

Braxton leaned over and kissed her.

"Val, I have made a very important decision." The prince sat as erect as his tired body would allow.

"What is that?" Valentina said looking into his eyes. "I am going to divorce my mistresses."

Valentina sat up and with a quizzical look on her face and said, "My word, that sounds ominous. What exactly do you mean?"

"When we were alone on the tundra in that beautiful sleigh, that glorious night ..."

"Ah yes, that glorious and tragic night. The last time we spoke." He continued, "You mentioned mistresses, yours and mine." She laughed softly, remembering how she had alluded to

Braxton's obsession with his growing business empire. "That was a bit metaphorical, but nonetheless true."

"I love you Valentina, with all my heart. I have no use of mistresses.

I shall shed them, divorce them."

Valentina placed her hands in her lap and gave him a sidelong look.

"My dear," he continued, "Before I arrived in Calcutta, I had begun making arrangements to relinquish the day-to-day control of my business concerns. As you can see by my current circumstances, it proved to be fortuitous that I had done so."

"Yes, I would agree, Brax. But do go on."

"I shall return to England and resign my position as

royal envoy." "Will your government accept your resignation?"

"That remains to be seen. Nevertheless, I will press my point hard."

"What then?"

"If you will have me, it is my dream we will be married."

Valentina closed her eyes and leaned her head back, breathing deeply. She opened her eyes, then spoke quietly to Braxton, "If I will have you? You silly fool." She wrapped her arms around him and initiated their first passionate kiss and embrace since her arrival in India.

———

"Uncle," Braxton said, forty-five days into their stay at the lodge, "I am feeling better and need something to occupy me."

"You have Valentina and me, nephew."

"Yes, and for that I am very grateful. Without your taking charge of my health, I may have perished. Having Valentina here has also lifted my spirits. I believe I owe the two of you my life and well-being. But." Braxton stood and paced. "Would you please make arrangements to have the correspondence that has surely piled up brought to me? By that, I mean business and personal letters and packets."

"Braxton, I cannot do that. What I mean is, you have no business correspondence."

The prince stopped mid-step, facing his uncle he placed his hands on his hips and glared at Cosimo.

Cosimo continued, "It has all been handled by Valentina and me.

All matters have been addressed. What we could not resolve was forwarded to either Seiko or Ramsey, per your instructions prior to your embarking on your tour of India."

"I see," Braxton said pressing his lips together in consternation.

Cosimo placed a cigar he had been smoking in an ashtray, rose out of his seat and made his way across the room.

"And my personal correspondence, Uncle?"

"I have it here," the duke said, reaching in and withdrawing a twelve inch-thick packet from an adjacent armoire. Your personal correspondence remains unopened."

Rubbing the back of his neck, Braxton inquired, "No one, not even my family's letters, have been opened or answered? It has been almost two months. They shall have been frantic!"

Cosimo handed the packet to the prince and said, "I wrote your parents, your brothers and your sisters. In my correspondence I explained that under doctor's orders you were not to correspond or in any way be in contact with the outside world until you had regained your strength. I informed them it was nervous exhaustion. I saw no need to share the details with them."

"How did they react to the news, Uncle?"

"They all insisted they come to India to gather you up and return you to England."

Braxton's alarm morphed into a chuckle, "That would be truly astounding, the emperor and empress of India, along with their grown children in tow, journeying to India to rescue their sickly, fully- grown son."

"Precisely," Cosimo interrupted. "That is why I informed them the trip would be wasted and entirely unnecessary, as they would not be permitted to see you, much less transport you back to England at that time. They acquiesced and made me promise I would send you back to England as soon as you could travel."

Braxton thought for a moment then, pursing his lips, said, "Dear uncle, I am surprised they gave in so easily. Particularly John. He would certainly have insisted on coming."

Cosimo, still standing, stretched his neck side to side and murmured, "Well, I took the liberty to inform them Valentina was here."

Braxton's mouth fell open. "Uncle!"

Cosimo smiled, turned, and walked over to his chair. He picked up his smoldering cigar from the ashtray, took a seat and puffed away.

———

Another two months passed before Braxton could contemplate his imminent departure from India. A week earlier, Braxton had returned to Calcutta and Government House. He sat in the logia contemplating the panorama of the vast gardens giving way to a thriving Calcutta, the Ganges River and mountains in the distance. In a strange and exotic way, this is a beautiful country. It has revealed to me so much of human nature and opened the doors wide into my own soul. The prince closed his eyes and rested his head on the back of the chair.

He drifted back into the memories of his journeys through Europe, Russia, Japan, China, Singapore and finally India, dwelling on the peoples he had met, with whom he had interacted, and those he had seen from afar. Absorbing those images and overcome by the accompanying emotions, he sprang up and out of his chair, reaching for the nearby balustrade to steady himself. Those people, those millions of souls making their way through a very hard and unkind world. Why am I here? Why was I chosen to see all this? I feel powerless. No one can alleviate all the injustices that overwhelm their lives.

The prince wiped light perspiration from his brow and took a seat atop the balustrade overlooking the gardens. An unexpected cool breeze whipped in, cooling his body and soothing his raw emotions.

I want to return to England, to make a life with Valentina. But some strange pull insists I remain in this land and help the Indian people find the solutions to their problems.

As his departure date approached and the prince again ensconced himself in his business affairs. Instead of digging into his newly- discovered spirituality, he returned to his old way of thinking. The people of this great nation have the potential to return to their ancient glory. It is their past greatness that will serve as a foundation for supporting the creation of a prosperous future. The Indian people must take charge of their lives. They must not emulate the British.

They must pursue their own greatness. My travels have taught me this.

———

Braxton, Valentina, and Cosimo boarded his train in Calcutta and departed for Calais. Calcutta's stifling heat, red dust and humidity accompanied the train but a few days. They wound their way through hills and mountains, snaking along precariously perched passes and onto broad open plains, hurtling north west toward Delhi.

Temperatures along the northern route were slightly tempered by the seasonal monsoons. Heavy rains thundered on the railway carriages' metal roofs, stifling conversation for hours. Winds beat against the train, violently rocking the rail cars. The passengers remained seated for their own safety.

The windows were kept tightly closed against the torrential monsoonal rains. Blanketed by a thick humidity, most everyone wore loose fitting cotton garments and fanned themselves.

Braxton and Valentina sat alone in his private car at the rear of the train, side by side in overstuffed chairs, each reading a book. They looked up occasionally and smiled at one another.

Perspiration plastered Braxton's light cotton, short-sleeve shirt against his back, chest and arms, outlining his athletic frame. He occasionally wiped his brow.

Valentina, abandoning propriety, wore a short-sleeved, ankle- length white cotton nightdress, also laden with moisture as it it lay against her skin. Little was left to the imagination.

A blast of wind rocked the car. A startled Valentina grabbed Braxton's hand. The prince placed his book in his lap and took hold of her hand with both of his and leaned over. Through the saturated cotton nightgown, he kissed her breast. He looked up into her aquamarine eyes and murmured, "Everything will be fine."

Valentina let her breath out slowly. She placed her hands around her prince's head and drew his lips toward hers.

Their passion was matched by the roaring of the wind and rain.

Braxton took hold of her nightgown and drew it up and over her head, tossing it to the side.

The rain intensified and the car drew darker. Valentina unbuttoned her lover's shirt. She used both hands to unbutton his waistband and fly. She slid Braxton's shirt off his shoulders and caressed it down his sweaty back. Her hands continued around his body and up onto his chest. She pulled his head down to her heaving breast. His shorts soon joined his shirt at his feet.

They wound their arms about each other, joining the rocking motion of the train with their own writhing.

After a time, the raging cacophony around the train ceased. The sun peeked out from behind the clouds and shone brilliantly through the rain-scrubbed glass.

Later, Braxton and Valentina stood naked in the open doorway at the rear of the car. Holding hands, they stared out at the empty plain and soaring ominous black clouds disappearing into the distance. The only sound was that of the clickity-clack of the wheels traversing the track.

They returned leisurely to their lovemaking.

———

Hours later, the now verdant rolling countryside rushing by, they returned to the rear plaform, fully dressed. She wore a light blue off the shoulder, open-back loose-fitting cotton gown; he was in tan linen trousers and a white singlet. Each held a glass of sherry.

Valentina intertwined her fingers in the hair on the back of Braxton's head and forced his face toward hers, saying, "I want to do that again before this trip comes to an end."

His mouth falling open, and his head tilting slightly to the side, Braxton replied, "Mademoiselle." Then with a slight smile and a provocative tone, continued, "Mademoiselle, I am yours to command."

Once again, they tossed their glasses to the wind and embraced.

———

A week later, having recently crossed the Bosporus, the train was churning its way through the Balkan Mountains. Crisp cool air rippled through the half-opened windows. Valentina sat in her day dress, sipping her Russian tea and looking out the window.

Trees in the upper elevations had begun to turn to crimson red, sparkling gold and riotous orange. She sat back, sighed, and reached for a breakfast pastry.

Braxton intercepted her hand in his, and said, "As you know, my dear, tomorrow we arrive in Vienna." He paused and pleaded playfully,

"I believe I have honored your request enough?"

Valentina sat up and looked down her nose, replying, "I would blush if I could, however I have no shame when it comes to you, my darling."

Looking down at her hand in his, he said pensively, "I dread tomorrow. These months together have been the happiest in my life.

The thought of you returning to St. Petersburg, and I to London, tears at my heart."

She placed her cup on the table and raised his chin with her free hand. They looked into each other's eyes as she whispered, "I, too, dread our looming separation. What I fear most is we may not see one another again for a very long time. Perhaps even not again, never to marry."

Braxton's eyes widened and in a frightened tone he said, "Whatever can you mean?" He took short breaths insisting, "We will be married! We have agreed!"

She placed a hand on Braxton's knee to steady herself while rising from the divan. Valentina walked the few steps to the door closed against the rear plaform. She turned, wiping a tear with a finger, and faced Braxton. "We have been living in a fantasy these last several months. A dream, a dream from which I have dreaded waking up." She walked back to the dazed prince staring at her, his mouth slightly ajar.

The grand duchess took both his hands in hers. "Braxton." She waited a moment. He had not changed his look nor acknowledged his hands in hers.

"You know I am right." She sat back and placed her hands in her lap.

In a sober voice she began again, "Who are we to pledge to marry? Neither you nor I can make that decision. The truth is, your father, the king, and my father, the czar, will dictate our fate."

The veins on the side of Braxton's neck flared as his stare hardened. His body shuddered. He thought, I cannot allow this to happen. I have lost her once and cannot bear to lose her again.

The prince released her hand and stood. He paced the length of the car, then increased his pace and pounded his right fist into his left palm. "You should not even think such things, much less say them." The prince's face reddened. He turned around and insisted, "We must persevere and not relent! We must be in control!" He clasped his head in his hands and sunk to the floor on his knees, crying out, "How can you be doing this to me again? Just like in Siberia. I could have died, and you deserted me! You will not deceive me again!"

Valentina rose, her hands folded at her chest, imploring, "You are frightening me, Braxton. You are acting irrationally. Why do you speak to me this way? I never deserted you. There was nothing I could do! I remained with you for weeks. I was ordered back to Moscow by my father." Valentina realized she was holding her fists clenched to her side. She breathed deeply and released them.

Valentina continued in a softer tone, "Braxton, please understand, I do want to marry you. I am not leaving you. I love you. I am in love with you and hated leaving you in Siberia. I had no choice!" Now weeping, she took a step toward him.

Standing, he violently shook his pointed finger at her and shouted, "How can I believe you when you are giving up on us without trying?"

Valentina stopped her progress mid-step, still twenty feet from him, her face afire. "Giving Up? I have done no such thing." Placing her hands over her heart, she continued, "I was revealing my fears, because I thought I could trust them in your care!"

In a sarcastic retort the prince replied, "That is a far cry from what I heard you say."

Standing at the far end of the railroad car he grabbed hold of a mahogany cigar humidor and cried out to Valentina in desperation, "This is what you have done to my heart!"

He hurled the humidor into a large mirror. Glass fragments exploded all about the end of the car. Braxton ignored the debris, his hard-soled shoes crunching the shards as he continued to pace in a tight circle.

Valentina, shocked at his behavior, was once again reminded of her father, the czar, and his uncontrolled rages. She attempted to calm Braxton as she had often assuaged her father, with a sympathetic gaze.

The prince saw her look and interpreted it through his anger and pain. He shouted, his eyes red with rage, "You are looking at me as if I were a child! Stop it! I insist!"

Braxton ran two fingers inside his collar wiping the sweat from his neck.

A fearful chill ran through Valentina's body. She sank down into a chair, her knuckles white as she clasped the chair's arms.

Braxton walked past her, threw open the door and charged outside onto the rear plaform. He wrapped his arms around himself, attempting to control his abrupt and overwhelming anger.

The rocking carriage and the echoing sound of the wheels rolling across the rails haunted the car's interior. The engine's whistle sounded in the distance.

Valentina rose and crossed to the writing table. She penned a note, then folded the paper in half and placed it under Braxton's cup and saucer.

She quietly stepped over the treacherous pieces of glass and exited the car at the opposite end.

Thirty minutes later, Braxton stepped back into the car, his head held down, recalcitrant and embarrassed. "Valentina, I am so sorry. Please forgive me. I lost my head. Perhaps it is my illness. I never wanted to frighten you or upset… " He looked around. "Valentina?" The forlorn prince spied the note removed the it from underneath the saucer.

Braxton,

I have not witnessed such anger in a man since that which I was forced to endure from my father, starting when I was only a child. What I saw in your behavior today is something I had promised myself never to suffer again.

My heart is broken. I promised myself years ago I would never again live with what I witnessed today.

I am retiring to my compartment for the remainder of the journey. Please do not make any attempt to see or speak to me. I do not wish to see you. I shall detrain in Vienna.

Valentina

Braxton stared down at the note clasped between his

hands. He folded the note and tore it into tiny pieces. He placed the remnants in one hand and covered them with the other. He walked out onto the plaform and cast them to the wind.

Braxton shoved his hands into his pockets and said, "Aramis would have understood."

19

HOME

An unseasonably frigid early autumn rain pelted Braxton's train as it pulled into the Aspang Train Station in Vienna the following morning. A heavy fog blanketed the rail yard. Dark clouds ensured there would be little sunlight to brighten the dreary day. The driving rain and hissing steam muted the clatter of iron clanking against iron as the cars rolled to a stop.

Braxton stood on his private car's rear plaform wearing the clothes he had worn the previous evening, bareheaded, coat-less, unshaven. Leaning over the rail, he stared through the mist toward the front of the train. Rain beat down on his head and face, soaking his clothing.

Steam, mixing with fog and rain, framed the dim morning light, slightly obscuring a lone figure disembarking the train. Porters followed carrying trunks and multiple pieces of luggage.

Braxton's body trembled. He leaned forward and grasped the plaform railing, his brain whirling. He turned his chin back and forth shoulder to shoulder, the pace quickly accelerating as he watched what must be Valentina vanishing from his life. He held his head in his hands and mumbled, "No, no, no, no."

The train whistle pierced the air as the iron wheels began their labored turn on the track. Surreal reality emerged with the slamming of each hitch connecting the cars to one another echoing in the foggy mist, steam escaping. Sounds of clanking hitches growing closer until the last car, Braxton's car, lurched forward.

Braxton's eyes filled with tears. He looked upward gripping the car's rear plaform rail, letting loose a full-throated sound, not unlike that of a wild animal in the throes of a terrifying death. "VALENTINA!"

The prince's valet rushed out onto the plaform shouting, "Sir! Your Royal Highness!" He threw a blanket around the collapsing prince, dragging him into the car and placed his crumbling frame on a divan.

"Please, Sir, remain here. I will get another blanket."

Prince Braxton rolled to one side, collapsing face down onto the cushions. His hands and forearms covered his head while the pillows muffled his sobs.

The train continued its journey across Europe.

————

A telegram was brought aboard the train in Munich and delivered to Braxton.

Dear Brother STOP Wilhelm and I are in Paris for several days STOP Please do take a day or two with us STOP It has been years STOP I insist STOP Diedre Braxton replied via telegram.

Dearest Diedre STOP Thank you for your kind invitation STOP My schedule demands I continue on STOP My regards to you both STOP Much love STOP Braxton

Arriving two days later in Calais, he boarded the royal yacht dispatched by his father and sailed for Dover.

A letter from the prime minister awaited him aboard His Majesty's Yacht Elfin:

Welcome home, Your Royal Highness.

England awaits your arrival on its shores, arms opened wide. Sir, please forgive me for being unable to fulfill your request for a private return. Parliament would not hear of it. If the public were deprived of a chance to welcome their favorite son home, there would surely be a public outcry.

Your Royal Highness is a national treasure, a hero who must be on display for the people to admire and embrace. Saving the life of our new ally and trading partner, the Japanese Emperor's heir, is reason enough to celebrate. This, coupled with the tremendous goodwill you have endeared in Southeast Asia and the Indian sub-continent is quite astounding and demands celebratory recognition. The Crown and this government have never been held in such high esteem. For these successes, the empire owes you, the Prince Royal, our gratitude.

The correspondence went on to outline the events that would follow when he disembarked in Dover. Braxton's popularity had to be exploited. He would be received with great fanfare accompanied by enormous crowds. Bands would play and flowers and confetti would certainly shower him as he rode through the streets toward Buckingham Palace.

Having finished the letter, Braxton crumpled it in his hands. I had hoped for an obsequious response, not a defiant disregard for my wishes. His chest tightened thinking back to that cold gray Vienna morning. I am not a returning hero. I am of no good to anyone. I have failed at the most important thing in life. I am a fool, lost, damned and forsaken by my love.

Braxton gazed into a mirror hung on the wall of the

comfortably appointed yacht's stateroom. The glass reflected a downturned mouth, the whites of his eyes covered in streaks of red, a gray pallor and a face consumed by grief.

————

Arriving at Buckingham Palace, Braxton's parents received him in the White Salon. He bowed to them both. The prince shook his father's hand and turned to his mother and wrapped his arms around her.

"Mamma, I am home."

As his mother's arms tightened around him, Braxton let out a sigh and felt the overwhelming anxiety drain from his body.

In a tender voice she replied, "My darling son, I have missed you so. Today, my heart is full."

————

Later that evening, the members of the royal family sat chatting informally amongst themselves.

"It is so good to see you, dear brother," Prince John said. His wife, Louisa, smiled in agreement.

Prince Braxton had folded his hands in his lap, struggling to keep his reeling emotions under control. His face was oddly expressionless as he responded, "Thank you, John. It is good to be back. I have missed every one of you. Distance and years certainly cause one to appreciate one's family."

"You appear subdued. Is there something troubling you, dear brother? Braxton's oldest brother Dominic queried.

Braxton tilted his head and gripped the arms of his chair.

Struggling to focus on Dominic, he replied in a clipped tone, "Why do you ask?"

Queen Mercedes offered, "Perhaps you are exhausted from your journeys. You have been traveling for weeks." She then looked from Braxton, to Dominic, and then directly at the king.

King Richard squinched his eyebrows and pressed his lips together, not sure why his wife had directed everyone's attention to him. Fumbling, stalling in search of words that might diffuse the unexpected tension in the air, he said, "Ahem. I am disappointed Diedre and Wilhelm were unable to come over from Paris to join us. I must say, it is unfortunate and rather odd." He pulled on his beard and shifted his weight. "Their having decided not to come over and what not."

Braxton's mind drifted off, vaguely fixating on an ephemeral.

Valentina. He hardly noticed the footman announcing his sister-in- law.

Dominic's wife, the Austrian grand duchess Princess Mathilde, entered the room carrying the infant Princess Rose. A nurse followed with the toddling Prince Adolphus in hand.

"Good evening, everyone one! Look who I have brought to meet their uncle!"

Deep in his thoughts reliving the fierce last moments he had shared with Valentina, Braxton managed to gawk at the entourage entering the room. He swallowed hard, attempting to give them his attention.

"Has the cat got your tongue?" John teased. "Have you not seen children before?"

The prince did not respond, fearing he would break

down, thinking, those beautiful children, like those Valentina and I might have had one day.

"Really son, what has come over you?" the king inquired.

The prince gave his head a quick shake and sprang to his feet. In a rattled voice he said, "So sorry, do forgive me. My thoughts had drifted elsewhere."

Stretching his mouth into what he hoped was a smile, he walked over to Prince Adolphus, knelt and took the curious young prince's little hand. "Nice to meet you Adolphus. I am your Uncle Braxton." In an artificially jolly voice, struggling to maintain control of his emotions, he continued in a shaky, high-pitched voice, "When we get to know one another better I shall be your favorite uncle!"

The sensitive Adolphus threw himself into Braxton's arms. Uncle Braxton teared as he wrapped his arms about the child and stood. Adolphus pushed back a little. Raising his cherubic face, he peered into his uncle's eyes.

Braxton released a barely inaudible sniffle, wiping away the tears that threatened to burst forth.

"Hello nephew."

Adolphus reached up and, using his small, fleshy palm, patted his uncle's face twice. Then he burrowed into Braxton's arms and settled his head on his uncle's chest.

"I think you two have become fast friends," Mathilde said. Adolphus's uncle kissed his nephew's forehead and whispered,

"Yes, that is exactly what I could use right now. A friend."

———

Later that day, after his family left the room, Prince Braxton's personal secretary entered carrying a shallow sterling silver tray holding a thick envelope.

"Your Royal Highness, his excellency, the Russian ambassador, Baron George de Staal previously delivered this letter for you to his majesty. The king directed his private secretary to have it sent on to you via courier. It arrived while you were out this morning."

Braxton removed the letter from the tray, recognizing the unbroken seal. It was that of Prince Maxim.

"Odd. Why would the ambassador have this? And send it to me via my father? Quite out of the ordinary. Perhaps Maxim had no idea where on earth I was."

"Sir, it appears to have come via diplomatic pouch. I suspect it is either of a diplomatic or private nature, perhaps both."

Prince Braxton grunted. "Interesting. It appears not to have been opened, the seal remains intact." He shifted in his chair, reached for the lamp and adjusted the light. "Thank you. You may go."

Alone in the dimly-lit Renaissance House library, Braxton closed his eyes, placed the package in his lap and leaned his head against the back of the chair. What could this possibly be? Why would Maxim send something to me through diplomatic channels?

Attempting to quiet his mind, he leaned back in his chair, eyes still shut. She would not, she could not.

He sat back up and said out loud, "Ridiculous. She would never say anything to him. Impossible, she could not have arrived in St. Petersburg earlier than I arrived here. Maxim could not have known about our disagreement. This cannot be about that!"

Tearing open the packet, he found two envelopes

inside. One addressed to him with Maxim's seal. The other, the czar's seal, addressed to the king.

This is all so irregular. I shall have to return the czar's letter to my father.

He set the letter for his father on the table next to his chair and looked down at Maxim's missive. What could this be? Braxton felt a shakiness in his limbs. Fear of more disappointment. He inhaled. Just get on with it!

Breaking the seal and removing the letter, Braxton smiled, warmed by the familiar sight of his friend Maxim's handwriting.

Greetings Braxton!

I pray this letter reaches you in a timely manner, having no idea on which continent or subcontinent it will find you, India, Asia, Europe?

You are most likely wondering why I have exerted great care to ensure both these letters arrived intact. Perhaps it is because it required a great deal of effort and cajoling on my part to get the old man to come to his senses and listen to reason.

He was initially stunned and then amused to find that Valentina had left for India. The czar did not seem to mind her not asking his permission to leave the court. The old codger was actually amused and ascertained she must be very fond of you. Quite an understatement. In any event, he probed and probed until I had no choice but to confirm his suspicions.

He holds you in high esteem. As you know, he has heaped praises on you many times in recognition of your part in replenishing the trea-sury. He still relishes having a part in bringing the Chiacontella bankers to their knees, figurative and literally.

The aging monarch is no fool and quite cognizant of you having helped provide Russia with an economic future. He has asked for you many times. His disjointed memory frustrates him. And yet, he was very aware you left Russia without your having asked his permission. It is not as if you are one of his subjects; nonetheless, he misses you.

He once ordered me to send a company of soldiers after you and bring you back. As fortune would have it, he soon forgot he had. That happens with more frequency.

In short, the czar has agreed to your marriage to Valentina. You both have my blessings and I wish you the very best! I trust you will share this news with her should she be with you when you receive the letter. I had no idea which of three continents the two of you were on, as Valentina wrote weeks before of your plans to depart Calcutta for Europe within a fortnight.

The letter to your father contains a very generous marriage contract. There is but one caveat. You and Valentina must forfeit any rights that your children or their descendants may have to the Russian throne. Other than that, you get Valentina and a king-sized dowry. Once again, I could not be happier for you both.

On a selfish note, please feel free to name any of your children after me. M-A-X-I-M-U-S. After all, had I not cajoled you into putting your life on hold and saving Russia, you would not today be the richest man in Europe! It is the least you can do, dear friend...of course, I jest.

Fondest regards, Maxim

Braxton placed the letter on top of the one addressed to his father. Rising out of his chair, he proceeded to a nearby table. He picked up a decanter, poured a full measure of Scotch and walked through one of the French doors onto the terrace. Waning sunlight mixed with a light snow covering the terrace blinded him for a moment. The Scotch heated his body and the letter warmed his heart.

Oblivious to the damp snow and chilly temperature, he left foot prints in the skiff of snow blanketing the terrace. Sipping the Scotch and then staring at the glass, he took note of gently falling snowflakes disappearing into his amber beverage.

A signed marriage contract. If and when my father signs the contract, she is mine. Even if she does not want me. So very tragic for her yet provides hope for me that she might reconsider. He sighed.

Well, I shall certainly not force her into a marriage she does not desire. I will not, however, interfere with the negotiations. Perhaps there is some hope for us. Time. All we need is time.

———

Braxton was informed his attendance would be required at the prime minister's weekly audience with the king. The prince petitioned his presence be postponed until the following week. His petition was promptly denied. He was commanded to attend the king.

The day of the audience, Braxton first rode horseback to visit Dominic and Mathilde at Kensington Palace, knowing full well there was a strong threat of rain.

Arriving at the palace, he dismounted and looked up at the sky, noticing the roiling, darkening clouds. Leaves blew across the cobblestones as he handed the reins off to a palace groomsman. Surrendering his coat and hat to a footman, he entered Mathilde's drawing room.

With sparkling eyes, Mathilde exclaimed, "Why Braxton, so glad to see you! Though it is quite a surprise. Did you not have enough of us the other evening?"

Grinning broadly, he replied, "Hello Mathilde!" Absentmindedly, he forgot the customary greeting of a kiss on her cheeks and made his way directly to Adolphus, playing with a small wooden horse on the carpet near the fireplace. While continuing to dote on his nephew, Braxton said to Mathilde, "Shall I misrepresent the truth and tell you I was riding by and sought shelter from the threatening storm?"

"I suppose you could, but you know I would ascertain that not to be the truth," she replied with good humor.

"Then I shall admit that it is but a half-truth. I came directly and uninvited. Oh, and I did find shelter from the storm."

At this point he lay full length on his side next to the little prince.

"Hello, Adolphus. We meet again. You do not mind do you, that I sought you out?"

Adolphus picked up his toy horse and handed it to Braxton.

His uncle's face lit up. "Oh my, you are indeed generous sharing your toys with me. Tell me, does he have a name?"

Adolphus still learning to talk, struggled out "Valorious." Braxton's jaw dropped. "Did you say Valorious?"

The toddler nodded and said, "Fast horsey. Your horsey."

"Indeed, it is!" Braxton said turning, smiling up at Mathilde sitting in a chair next to them. His cheeks went lightly pink with pleasure. "That is so kind my dear. How thoughtful of you to bring me into your lives even though I have been so far away."

"My dear Braxton, you have been in my life since we first met in Vienna. Your brother, nephew, niece, and I love you very much."

Braxton's face softened, feeling an effusion of warmth and happiness. "And I return that love for you and your lovely family."

The contented uncle set about playing with Adolphus narrating to his willing listener and playmate the story of Valorious, the "Unbeatables" and their Queen Anne Stakes victory of years past.

An hour of play and chatter passed before nanny

arrived and whisked Adolphus away for a nap. "Goodbye, nephew, I shall return again soon and we shall resume our play!"

"Bye-bye," Adolphus said walking hand in hand with Nanny, turning and waving.

"Bye-bye," Braxton said, waving back as they exited the salon.

Rising off the floor and finding a seat in a chair next to Mathilde, he said, "I love that boy. What a treat it has been to spend a few precious minutes with him. I hope you do not mind my visit. Perhaps you will humor me and allow me to return."

The princess wriggled her eyebrows and snorted a laugh, saying, "Of course you may return at any time!"

"You are so kind." He paused, swallowed, and looked down at the carpet as he continued. "You have no idea how much this means to me."

In a warm voice she responded, "Braxton, we are your family and we will always be."

He forced a broad smile and with a twinkle in his eyes, jumped up saying, "I must go. Expected at Buckingham Palace. I tried, I even petitioned to get out of the meeting, but alas, I am off to meet up with the king and prime minister. God only knows why they commanded I attend them there."

———

He left the warmth and protection of Kensington Palace.

Embracing the downpour, he cantered back to Buckingham Palace, churning the sodden turf and splattering mud over the two miles across Hyde and Green Parks. His visit with Adolphus and the invigorating ride to Buckingham Palace had lifted his spirits.

Entering the palace, he anticipated appearing in his soggy state would suffice to excuse him from the audience, allowing him to return to Renaissance House and retire to a warm bath.

Drenched, he boldly presented himself to the king, queen and prime minister.

"Your Majesties, Prime Minister. Forgive me, I was assaulted by a squall and am forced to show you insufferable disrespect in acquitting myself in such a dreadful manner. Surely you will give me leave and allow me to return another day?"

The prime minister chuckled, commenting, "Your carriage, it sprang a leak?"

"Up to your old tricks, eh Braxton? Thought you might have outgrown that by now," his father stated in a stern voice.

His mother, not generally included in these weekly audiences, sat up straighter and placed her hands firmly in her lap. "Braxton, remove yourself at this instant. You will return forthwith properly attired."

The prince let a look of surprise jump across his face. No one had spoken to him in this manner since he was a child.

Still amused by his shenanigans and attempt to be dismissed from the audience, Braxton was yet frustrated with his failure to have his own way. "My apologies Mamma, Father, Prime Minister." He bowed and backed out of the room. As the footmen were closing the doors behind him, he heard laughter coming from the audience room. He was relieved to know they were amused, albeit his plan had not been successful. Unfortunately, he would have to change and return.

An hour later he was back, properly attired, his hair combed but damp. He was offered tea. His mother had ordered warm soup for him to consume while they met. Again, this was not acceptable protocol, but Braxton always seemed to be able to claim the exception.

"Your Majesty," Braxton asked his father, "Would you allow everyone to sit around the table close to the fire? It would be so much more comfortable, and I could finish my soup without decorating my waistcoat with it." Again, he was indulged. Soon all were seated at the table sipping their tea and nibbling on biscuits, grateful for the fire's warmth while watching Braxton devour his soup. Wind and an icy rain continued to pelt the palace windows.

As Braxton had carefully detailed his journeys in weekly reports over the years he was absent from England, the four were current on relevant aspects of his adventures. Conversation flowed smoothly.

The queen interrupted the chatter to ask, "What are your plans for the future, son?

"Mamma?"

"Yes, what is it you are planning on doing now that you have returned?"

"If she will have me, I will marry Valentina."

The king, queen and prime minister exchanged confused looks. "If she will have you, Your Highness? I do not understand. Both the grand duchess and you have been..." The prime minister stopped mid-sentence.

Braxton expected his mother or the prime minister to have something to say.

The king surprised him, interjecting, "Your mother and I have no objection. Your sister Carmen has been politicking on your behalf. We have reason to believe the czar will agree if Parliament endorses the match. As you know, the czar was initially against the marriage due to Russia's tenuous succession issues. Little did we know the matter ultimately rested on your sister providing Maxim an heir.

Your sister Carmen, having given birth to twin boys, has softened his position. The succession appears to be secure."

Braxton placed his soup spoon beside his bowl and fished the czar's letter from his coat pocket, handing it to his father.

Taking note of the seal, the king exclaimed, "It is from the czar!" The queen and prime minister sat up and leaned in the direction of the king opening the envelope and removing the stationary. He began reading the letter, his lips moving, his jaw dropping the deeper he dove into the correspondence.

"Richard, please. What does it say?" pleaded the queen.

Braxton interjected in a sardonic manner, "It is a marriage contract, Mamma."

Incredulous, the prime minister asked, "Really?"

The king extended the letter toward the prime minister. Mercedes reached over and snatched the letter, sat back, and commenced reading.

His majesty looked at Braxton, commenting, "It would appear that it is done. I see nothing objectionable contained therein. All that remains is for Parliament and I to ratify it."

The queen handed the contract to the prime minister. The three sat silently waiting for him to read its contents.

The prime minister's face flushed as he fidgeted uncharacteristically. He began, "I must share with you; Parliament is not very excited about the union. Having Princess Carmen in St.

Petersburg is a powerful statement. It balanced the marriage of Princess Diedre to the Kaiser. The French, Austrians, and Spanish are concerned that another match between the Imperial families would be ill-advised from a diplomatic and alliance perspective."

Braxton interjected, "What is it you and the cabinet want from my family? There must be some Machiavellian scheme lingering here somewhere." His voice hardened as he continued, "What is it Prime Minister? My marriage to Valentina is inconsequential, as neither of us will assume either throne. This is ridiculous."

The king interrupted, attempting to quell the tension. "Prime Minister, may I suggest we get on with our meeting? This marriage contract has nothing to do with our gathering here today. Neither her majesty nor I, nor you or my government, were aware of its existence until now. However, I must say, and do pardon me for saying this, but I think your reaction to the letter is unkind and unnecessary."

The prime minister rubbed the back of his neck and adjusted his seat position.

"Prime Minister?" Braxton queried, mentally ordering himself to stay calm.

The prime minister placed his hands squarely in his lap, sat up straight and said, "Your Royal Highness, the government would like to invite you to resume your role as royal envoy and represent their majesties in Canada and the United States."

Braxton remained visibly agitated by the prime minister's earlier comments. He exploded, "Why me? Have I not done enough? There are others. Dominic is the heir! As the future king, surely he has more gravitas than I."

The king and queen exchanged looks, the king placing one of his hands atop hers.

The prime minister replied, "No one has achieved the gravitas and renown accorded Your Royal Highness."

"That really is not the point. I have other plans."

"And what are those, son?" The queen asked repeating the question she had asked earlier.

Braxton thought for a moment, folded his arms and turned to his father, "Pappa, I ask your permission to discuss the details of this demand here and now, in Mamma's presence."

The king turned to Mercedes.

Mercedes nodded saying, "It is fine with me Richard. This is indeed a very important family matter. Braxton is being asked to represent the crown on your behalf. It is yet another request intruding on his private life. Once again, it requires him to put his personal life on hold." She paused, then with a curious look said, "However, as I recall, no member of the royal family has been to the Commonwealth or America."

"Prime Minister?" the king asked, directing his attention to the embarrassed politician.

The prime minster swallowed and answered, "I have no objection to Her Majesty's presence."

Braxton stood tall and assumed a commanding stature.

Addressing the prime minister, he said, "These are my terms." He looked at his attentive yet somber parents and returned his gaze to the prime minister.

I will perform the duties of royal envoy to Canada and the Americas. In return, my marriage to Grand Duchess Valentina will be ratified by Parliament before my departure. The marriage announcement will not be made until I return. And Parliament will also make the constitutional changes necessary to allow me, if elected, to sit as a member of Parliament, not in the House of Lords, but in the House of Commons."

The king raised his eyebrows, the queen quickly drew her head back and the prime minister tightened his jaw while tapping the fingers of one hand on his pant leg.

"That is a tall order," the king said.

The queen interjected, "I do not agree."

The prince finished with, "Those are my conditions."

The three of them could see the prime minister's mind reeling.

However, he had not objected yet. Finally, he spoke. "The prince has long been seen by the world as an out-lier. He is an entrepreneur and a worldly man who has lived beyond the court and certainly outside the boundaries of our vast empire for all his adult life. The people expect him to challenge the order of things. Am I not correct?"

The king and queen nodded.

"Prince Braxton has a unique way of inspiring admiration and hope in others. That is why the government wishes to employ his talents abroad. It is the cabinet's opinion we might be able to keep Canada close and maintain the respect and cooperation of the United States through his persona and reputation." He looked directly at the prince and said, "You are of the modern world. The empire must join the modern world to survive. I feel you are the person to lead us there." Silence filled the room.

Braxton said somberly, "You see trumpets, fanfare, and flags waving. I see burdensome travel, long days, and a life I cannot call my own. Nonetheless, I am willing to do this to achieve my heart's desires. To have Valentina as my bride and to further serve the people of the British Empire."

The queen motioned the prince to her. She took his hand. Looking up to him she said, "You do not have to do this."

Braxton returned his mother's gentle smile with one of his own and mouthed, "Thank you, Mamma."

Braxton withdrew his hand, returned to his seat, and said, "I have studied this and have not identified any conflict in the constitution that would prohibit my standing for Parliament. I possess no hereditary title and have no standing in the House of Lords."

Rain and wind continued to beat against the 14-foot-tall windows lining one wall of the audience chamber. Thunder cracked and lightning followed, lighting up the room.

The king rose from his chair and paced the length of the room. On his third turn round, the queen, wrapping a brilliantly colored wool shawl about her shoulders, joined him. They proceeded to the far end of the room speaking quietly. The prime minister and Braxton sat in silence waiting for them to finish their private conversation.

Several minutes passed before their majesties rejoined them at the table. The queen rang for the footman and ordered a light dinner and port.

The king asked, "What is it, Braxton, that causes you to consider abandoning your commercial interests and standing for Parliament?" Braxton thought it best to stand as he spoke.

"When I was traveling, I came across many cultures and peoples, most of them quite unlike the English; in fact, startlingly different than we are. As would obviously be the case, most of the populations I encountered are ruled by Englishmen, either directly or indirectly. I was astonished to note the disparity in the lives led by these persons of diverse cultures versus the lives lived by the English. It is remarkable and alarming to see how our government has insisted on creating small replicas of England, even in the starkest environments that bear no comparison to our island, either physically or culturally. The English abroad shelter themselves and virtually hide from those they rule.

"I am not condemning or judging my countrymen, I am stating facts. Our honorable countrymen certainly do their best to rule wisely. But quite frankly, the results are less than spectacular. I spent months and tens of thousands of pounds sterling trying to help abate some of the sufferings by which many of our colonized people live and die. The task is monumental and perhaps out of reach."

Braxton continued speaking as three footmen entered the room carrying three plated dinner trays and placing them on the table.

"When I created the Aurelio Palace Academy long before my first journey, it was a somewhat vain and perhaps self-serving attempt to provide a quality education for the less fortunate. But the situation in India is entirely beyond my ability to comprehend, much less ameliorate."

Braxton then turned to the queen.

"Mamma, Uncle Cosimo arrived in Calcutta at a critical time. I am so grateful you had the foresight to send him. He saved my life. I was emotionally and physically at my end. Without his care and encouragement, I do not know if I would be alive, much less in good health. With Cosimo's and Valentina's nurturing, not only have I regained my health, but I have acquired an improved perspective. You may be aware the businesses I have built are strong and have provided substantial assets and income, far more than I would ever need for myself or our family.

"This good fortune must be put to work and used wisely. I intend to continue to grow this wealth and use it for the good of those who can most benefit from it. To balance my life for the future, I have delegated many of my former responsibilities to capable people I trust."

Braxton moved behind his parents and placed his hands on their shoulders.

"What I cannot delegate is assuming a forward-looking role in helping our country maintain and expand its effectiveness as an empire. This means having the courage to do what is right for all our people in all our dominions. This duty is not limited to ruling them, but to empowering them to lead prosperous and healthy lives. Our country needs to be directed in this way to maintain its economic and humanitarian leadership. The power of the British empire is slowly being eroded by many of our colonies learning from us, then seeking their own autonomy. On my journeys I observed first-hand we are losing ground, economically and politically. There are cracks in Britannia's imperial 'foundation.' I do not want to see my father, brother, and nephew preside over a crumbling empire. I can wield true influence in the House of Commons. I have no hereditary title and am fifth in line to the throne. The likelihood of my being involved in the succession is beyond remote. However, I am loyal to our family and would never renounce my or my heirs' rights to the succession."

The prince placed both hands in his pants pockets. He took a moment to think and then continued. "I can, however, see the logic as to why you are asking me to continue my role as royal envoy. However, I will not perform in this capacity forever."

Braxton poured everyone a glass of port and sat down.

The prime minister rose and strode to the fireplace. He stoked the coals and added two more logs.

Braxton sat fiddling with the stem of his crystal glass. The king and queen held each other's hands and watched the prime minister toy with the fire.

Turning to the king, the prime minister asked, "May I offer my thoughts on this matter, Your Majesty?"

The king nodded affirmatively.

"My dear prince, it goes without saying you have more than caught me, and I suppose their Majesties, off guard. It pains me greatly to hear of the suffering you have observed in your travels. However, it does my heart good to learn you have been able to analyze what you have seen and formulate a plan to address it.

Respecfully, and I beg your forgiveness for being so frank, I think even with all your travels and experiences and uncommon intelligence, you are somewhat naive. I was naive when I was your age."

Braxton cleared his throat and said, "I beg your pardon, Minister." The king sat up. The queen's lips parted then closed.

"Please my lord, no offense is intended. All young men, even the most gifted, experience a moment of ideological foment in their lives. Naïveté is one of God's gift to the young, empowering them to do impossible things. I do not take exception to what you have described as our strengths and weaknesses in governing the Empire. But I believe it goes without saying the British have proven to be magnanimous and compassionate while ruling over primitive peoples. On this point we shall have to differ, Your Royal Highness."

Braxton sat back in his chair, folding his arms and looking toward the window, transfixed by the lightning storm and dismissing the prime minister's rationalizations about the effectiveness of British colonial rule.

The prime minister, oblivious to Braxton's displeasure, continued, "Even as revenues are increasing substantially, we are, in fact, seeing signs of international economic competition and political unrest in our dominions. Addressing this dilemma will be difficult. We need all able bodied men of character and wisdom to help guide our nation. I have faith in the British people. I have confidence they will rise to the task of supporting the needs of our empire. Prince Braxton, you embody what the empire needs to advance into the future. It is the empire's good fortune to have your contributions continue in any manner in which you wish to offer them. With the king's consent, I will petition Parliament for all you ask."

Braxton realized he was unlikely to convince the prime minister of his own point of view. In a somber voice, accepting the futility of trying to sway the prime minister otherwise, he answered, "Thank you, Prime Minister."

The king assumed a fatherly tone, saying, "Braxton, through the years your mother and I have continually marveled at what you set out to accomplish and how you have consistently exceeded our expectations."

The king took a moment to sip his port and continued, "But once again you are pushing the boundaries. You are requiring us to consider advocating actions that defy tradition and could undermine the nation you so altruistically seek to strengthen. As far as your renouncing your succession, remember, that is not an option."

His majesty slammed his hand on the table, shocking the queen, prime minister and Braxton. "I refuse to discuss it." The king sat back, folding his hands in his lap, and pronounced, "The empire should be so fortunate as to have Braxton as its king and emperor."

Braxton's eyes widened; he swallowed.

The prime minister looked down at his lap and mumbled, "Here, here."

Mercedes bit her lower lip, her eyes moistening.

Richard continued, "We all agree that the possibility is quite unlikely." The king pointed his finger at Braxton and said, "You know I could make this topic moot should I award you a hereditary title. As it happens, I had intended on creating you a hereditary peer, a Duke. You seem to have blocked that with this new scheme of yours to sit in the House of Commons! As it would interfere with your plans, I will not extend the offer at this time. But remember, when you marry, it is customary for royal male progeny to be created dukes. Your mother and I want what is best for you and the nation."

Mercedes looked directly at the king who caught her eyes as she made a slight nod.

The king began again, "Braxton, Prime Minister, Her Majesty and I will support the marriage and permission to stand for Parliament. Prince Braxton will of course have to agree to serve as royal envoy to North America in the interim."

Braxton allowed a small smile to cross his face. The queen sighed gently. The prime minister sat back in his chair and the king reached for his port.

"Thank you, Father, Mamma, Prime Minister. Your trust and confidence honor me. I will serve Britain faithfully in any capacity for which I am tasked."

The prime minister waited for the signal the audience was over. Once given leave by the king, he rose, bowed, and departed.

Richard, Mercedes and Braxton retired together to the sofa next to the fire. They sat closely, speaking quietly and lovingly.

————

Prince Braxton had assumed the lease on Renaissance House when his parents ascended the throne and moved into Buckingham Palace.

It was now time to update his father and the government on his activities prior to departing for the Americas. As was his habit when making his reports, he addressed them both.

Your Majesty and My Lord Prime Minister,

In preparations for my departure to Canada, I thought it best to bring you up to date on my personal business activities.

Lord Ramsey will remain behind to manage my affairs. Please note, I have removed myself from day-to-day operations and am now "Counselor to the Board of Directors." Let there be no doubt, I will remain firmly in control of my business interests. Having awarded Lord Ramsey with the chairmanship allows for an arms-length management and discretion in ownership. It is my hope this arrangement will lessen the chance for potential scandal or embarrassment to the crown of government regardless of any unforeseen circumstances.

Your Majesty, you have on at least one occasion, voiced your concern regarding the expenses associated with funding the Aurelio Academy. It has been my good fortune to be able to endow the academy sufficiently to cover its expenses on into the next century. As for under-writing the academy for the long-term, the board has agreed to solicit and accept contributions from its graduates as they move on to income-producing endeavors.

The racing and breeding stables under Josh's leadership continue to prosper and remain a leading breeding and training facility in England and Europe. I am grateful and pleased to say the facility is one of my more profitable enterprises. It is my intention to continue to use this income to fund the Academy.

Regarding Parliament approving my request to marry Valentina and run for the House of Commons, it appears we may be encountering opposition. I am not at liberty to divulge my sources, but be forewarned, our arrangement is in jeopardy.

Respectfully yours, Braxton, Prince of Wales

———

Several days prior to writing the king and prime minister, Lord Ramsey arrived unexpectedly at the Aurelio Palace.

While the prince was in the Ducal Library at Aurelio

Palace, the major domo entered and said, "Viscount Ramsey has requested an audience, Your Royal Highness.

"Lord Ramsey? Here?" Braxton said looking up from his desk in the ducal library. A fire crackled behind him; gas sconces illuminated the painting he had commissioned depicting his parents in coronation robes. Braxton had convinced his parents to indulge his request they sit for it, by offering to donate funds for the building of a children's hospital in their names.

"Please, show him in!"

Two footmen opened the massive 20-foot-tall double doors leading from the rotunda into the library.

"Viscount Ramsey," one of the footmen announced.

Braxton rose from his chair and moved over to the colonnade spanning the center of the soaring Romanesque chamber. He then strode down the center of the columned corridor.

"Ramsey, so good to see you! What a wonderful surprise. I trust all is well?"

Ramsey bowed to the prince. They embraced and proceeded back toward the fire.

"Please, sit," the prince said, motioning to a chair by the fire. "Give me a moment to stoke the fire."

Ramsey did a double take, saying, "I do say, Braxton."

The prince chuckled, acknowledging Ramsey's disbelief at his tending the fire himself. "I rarely allow servants to manage the fire. It would only be a distraction and I enjoy minding it as it helps clear my head." Braxton tossed two logs on the fire. He strode the short distance to a table holding a decanter and poured part of the cut crystal's contents into two snifters. "Cognac, my friend?" he asked, handing one off to Ramsey.

"Thank you, Braxton."

"You are very welcome," the prince replied, taking a seat in a nearby chair.

Flames fed by the aged, split oak logs spewed upward no less than five feet. A toasty warmth stretched out into the enormous room.

"Pray tell, what brings you unannounced? It must be important, or you would have sent word of your pending arrival."

"May I speak confidentially?" Ramsey asked, moving slightly forward in his chair.

"Why, of course. We are alone."

"Very well, how shall I begin?" Ramsey set his glass down, turning toward the crackling fire rubbing his hands together. "Carlo Ratini cabled me and asked that he and I meet in Paris immediately. I was in St. Petersburg at the time."

"That was indeed fortunate, finding yourself conveniently in St. Petersburg. Had you been in Siberia, the trip to Paris would have been arduous and quite time consuming."

"Yes. The entire time he has been part of the Intelligence Operation, Ratini has never asked to meet on such short notice. As you know, I had asked him to place several of his best men around London to keep an eye out for anything that might adversely affect your time in England."

"Yes, Ramsey. I remember. At the time I thought it unnecessary, but it appears I must have been wrong, otherwise, why would you be sitting here now?"

Ramsey sat back and sipped his cognac.

"Ratini and I met at a restaurant, La Tour d'Argent, on the Quai de la Tournelle. It has a fabulous view of Paris."

"The cuisine is not bad either. I know it well. But why would you choose such a conspicuous place to meet?"

Braxton asked, his full attention suddenly directed at Ramsey. He began again, "I must admit, the restaurant's candlelight provides some semblance of discretion. The small quartet conceals most conversation. Still, though, it is certainly not private."

"I had little choice. Ratini insisted. I too, thought it rather peculiar and was concerned Ratini had had a lapse in judgment. It was impossible to contact him and change the venue."

"I would have been disappointed had you not had reservations regarding the choice of venue," Braxton remarked, sitting back in his chair.

"We were well into our second course, having not discussed anything of import, when the owner, Frédéric Delair, presented himself at the table. Introductions were made." Lord Ramsey paused, shifting his weight in the chair and in an incredulous tone said, "And Ratini invited him to join us!"

"Join you! My word, that was a bit pas socialement acceptable." "Wait, my lord. The story unfolds in a rather spectacular manner.

As it has been a few years since you have been in Paris, Delair has acquired quite a reputation."

"Yes, I believe he has made his restaurant the 'cause celebre' vis- avis 'pressed duck.'"

"Well done, sir! I beg your pardon, not the duck, but your familiarity with his claim to fame."

Both men chuckled.

"I understand it is quite a process, rather gruesome, but I am not familiar with the details," The prince admitted.

"I will acquaint you with the details momentarily, my Lord. Delair offered to present the renowned entrée and we, of course, accepted. He first joined us at the table. He is a rather rotund man. I believe he enjoys his own cooking.

We were fortunate to have a large table a bit removed from the other guests.

"Shortly, what appeared to be an undercooked duck was presented table-side. Delair, rose from his chair and commenced carving on the foul. It was most certainly undercooked, as the meat was redder than pink. He removed the breasts and placed them to the side. The remaining meat was skillfully carved from the carcass and placed in a drum, a cylindrical wood drum of sorts, resting just above a copper pan, the pan perhaps two inches in depth. A screw- like top was turned squeezing blood and marrow from the meat and bones contained therein. Quite a sight to behold, not at all appetizing. I believe Ratini rather enjoyed it. I did not."

Braxton laughed. "This is quite the entertainment. Go on with your story, please."

"The juices in the pan were combined with butter and brandy. The blood sauce was then poured over the breasts, the meat sliced into strips and served."

"And?"

"Yes, it was delicious, rich tasting, just a bit gamey."
"Fascinating. What do you call this piece de resistance?"

"Canard à la Presse."

"I see," the prince said. Braxton then smiled slightly and shook his head, asking, "But how does this relate to your meeting with Ratini?"

"It was a cover for Delair to have time to relate some extraordinary information. During the table-side theatrics, he spoke quietly, rendering a tale that eclipsed even his presentation of the pressed duck. And that is what brings me here.

'Once we had heard all that Delair had to recount, at my request Ratini rushed me to the station, not a moment too soon for the last train's whistle sounded as I climbed aboard. I reached Calais midmorning, purchased a ticket on a packet boat, crossed the channel and here I am, voilà!" Ramsey said, gesturing with outreached hands.

Braxton offered a bemused smile, then in a monotone inquired, "Is Ratini aware of our association?"

"He has never indicated so. Remember, he has only seen you in the Mars disguise. But any reasonable man might make assumptions, knowing our close business association."

Braxton harumphed and said, "I was afraid of that. One can never be too careful." He refilled each of their glasses. "Please continue.

What did Monsieur Delair disclose?"

"He first told a story and then tied it forward to today. A possible scandal threatens you personally. It comes from a very dangerous French woman, currently living in England; a woman who apparently possesses a deep hatred for you."

The prince shot out of his seat. "Me? Why me?"

Lord Ramsey placed his glass on the table, steepled his hands at chest level, looked into the fire, then directly at Braxton and said with a slow and deliberate cadence, "It appears she associates you with the Mars campaign."

Braxton's face blanched. He reached back and steadied himself on the chair. Staring across the room, he inhaled three times then sank down into the chair.

Gathering himself, Braxton said, "This Delair, what do you know of him?"

"I posed that same question to Ratini on the way to the station. As you recall, he was one of the men who delivered the Mars letters in Venice. He has been in our employ all this time."

Braxton sighed. Pressing the palms of his hands to his eyes, he said, "We are indeed fortunate to have been made aware of the situation. Well done on Ratini's part. Regardless of what Delair has uncovered, without their diligence we would not be in the position to have been forewarned." He motioned with his hand as he said, "Continue with the story."

Lord Ramsey, with a deliberate quiet exhale said, "One couple figures prominently in the story. Perhaps you remember them, the Comte et Comtesse de Bérengar?"

The prince crossed his chest with one arm and stroked his chin with the other hand.

"They sound quite familiar. I believe she is English by birth, and he from an impoverished noble French Swiss family. It was her money that kept them afloat. He gambles a lot and is known for having attempted blackmail on several occasions. He was also known to have been rooting about my uncle's bank in Paris, making inquiries. Offering money for information. His actions were at the very least, disconcerting." Braxton gave a light snort and said, "I recall his activities helped plant the seeds for the very creation of the Mars project. Quite the cad. I thought him dead, or so I had been led to believe."

Ramsey continued, "The morning following Carnivale, the day they both received the Mars letters, was the end of the Comte and Comtesse de Bérengar."

Braxton sat up straight. "What do you mean?"

"It appears that upon receiving the Mars letter, the Comtesse, in a separate boudoir from her husband, began shrieking. She dismissed her maid, secured her peignoir de jour and made straight for her husband's rooms, her letter in hand. All of this was told to Delair by the comtesse's maid.

"You may find this quite interesting. It had been Delair, then in your employ and rather than Signore Ratini, who had been the one to deliver the two letters to the comtesse and the comte the morning following Carnivale. Delair had, that morning, been seen by the maid, recognizing him to be one of her past love interests. The following day she sought him out, revealing what she had seen take place in the Bérengar palazzo.

"As you know, my Lord, ladies' maids are privy to many of their ladies' secrets. That is why we can trust the personal details she related to Delair."

"Ramsey, could you move this story along? It is rather dragging on."

"I beg your pardon. I am getting to the crux." Ramsey began again. "The comtesse stopped just short of her husband's bed chamber. Peeking inside, she spied him quite undone, even hysterical. The comtesse could not contain herself and laughed hysterically. It was obvious to her that Mars had also compromised her husband."

The prince interrupted, "Compromised? In what way?"

Ramsey shifted uncomfortably, momentarily giving thought to his own passionate love affair with Braxton's brother, Prince John, years earlier. An affair Prince Braxton had ascertained and accepted long ago.

The prince thought, Ramsey really has no idea I was Mars and what transpired that bacchanal night at Carnivale, or of my relationship with Aramis.

Ramsey continued, "I can only guess it was of a carnal nature." "I see. Please continue."

"While she had always suspected her husband's proclivity for men, as told to Delair by the maid, the comtesse's suspicions were now confirmed by the Mars letters. She went on to verbally assault her husband, using the well-worn English term 'bugger' and all other manner of vulgar pejoratives. She was loud, crass, violent, and obviously enjoying every moment. It appears her husband had scorned her in the past when she first confronted him with news of what she thought must be his 'mistresses.' She came to suspect otherwise and had grown to hate him, as she felt he had squandered their marriage and their fortune, her fortune, with his gambling.

However, it was not the gambling that did him in financially; but the upkeep of very expensive young men, many young men."

Braxton remembered placing the comte on Mars' list of those to be punished because he was suspected of attempting to blackmail a manager at the Paris Chiacontella bank for information on Braxton's enterprises. The comtesse was on the list for having encouraged gossip regarding his brother John. Braxton wondered for a moment if somehow the comte and his brother were connected.

Ramsey said, "It appears the comte snatched the comtesse's letter, crumpled it with his own and threw them into the fire. She proceeded to pound on his back as he stirred the letters into the burning coals, calling him more vile names and promising to ruin his reputation. "Suddenly the comte whipped around with a gold- covered poker in his hand. He commenced beating his wife with it. The maid recounted how he must have struck her 10, 15, maybe even 20 times. It appeared unnecessary to go to all that effort, as the comtesse was probably dead on the second or third stroke. He had cracked open her skull on the first strike."

Ramsey was now leaning forward, highly animated, he accented the narrative, moving his hand about, emphasizing one action and then another.

Prince Braxton sat, his eyes having grown dull and his facial muscled slackened. He uttered, "My God."

"The comte's richly embroidered silk dressing gown

was covered in blood. Now raving, he ran to the roof brandishing the blood- covered poker as if it were a scepter, the devil's scepter. His evil, cackling laugh echoed from the stairway throughout the palazzo.

"Reaching the roof, he ran directly to the edge, spread his arms wide, and jumped. His flight from the palazzo's heights did not go unnoticed. His chest and head splattered on the quai below, his lower body hanging out over the canal, the carcass then flipping violently into the water."

"Good God!" Braxton sputtered. "I cannot imagine. The poor girl.

I pray this is the end of it. But what does all this have to do with today? It has been years."

"It has everything to do with Mars." "How so?"

"It appears the daughter, Hélène, witnessed the entire episode."

"How awful," Braxton remarked. "No child should have to witness such horrible events between her parents."

Ramsey sat back in his chair, waiting for the tension in the room to abate. He then continued, "Yes. It also appears Hélène hated her mother and worshiped her father. Further investigation has led us to believe she was left irreparably scarred by this event and became quite mad. She was unequivocally convinced Mars was the cause of her father's demise."

Braxton's stomach turned, realizing the part he, as Mars, had played in this tragedy. The ends certainly had not justified the means. Cosimo, is this really what you had wanted me to learn when you gave me Machiavelli's book in Capri so many years ago?

"There is more, is there not?" Braxton whispered.

"As she was not of age at the time, she was sent to live with her mother's family in Mayfair."

"And?"

Ramsey rubbed his hands together and took a deep breath. "That is where it should have ended. However, it appears that is where it began.

"Since then, Hélène has come of age and into a large fortune.

Though her mother's fortune had been lost, what remained of it was invested in a South African diamond mining firm, Debeers. She is quite mad, but she is also beautiful, intelligent, resourceful, and driven."

"Are you quite certain, Ramsey?" A look of incredulity ran across Braxton's face.

"Yes, my Lord. She has adopted her family's title and is forging through society surreptitiously disparaging your family's name."

"But why?"

"Delair believes she speculates you are or were involved in the Mars campaign. She hints at something about your brother, John. As I said, she is rather intelligent, and her deductive reasoning appears to be working in her favor. It would not surprise me if she had heard much during her parents' squabbles. Again, she is quite intelligent."

The men sat silently for several minutes.

The prince rubbed the back of his neck and bristled, "Then she is a real threat. In an odd way, her behaviour is her parent's legacy."

"It would appear so, Sir."

"Have you and Carlo Ratini any thoughts on how to rid my family of this problem?"

"Signore Ratini has a rather heavy-handed solution. I cannot say that I have thought of an alternative."

"What does he suggest?"

"He recommends taking steps requiring discretion. Regardless of the measures that must be taken, they will not in any way implicate the crown or the government."

"Is he suggesting violence of any kind?" "Of that, I am not certain, my Lord."

Firmly, and with conviction, the prince replied, "I shall not countenance any such thing. This girl must be protected from herself and my family protected from her. Nothing untoward. Have I made myself clear?"

"Very clear, Your Royal Highness."

"There are other options. Rest, a holiday, perhaps the continent or India. She needs to be sent far away. If necessary, there are doctors and hospitals that can help her."

"Yes, my Prince."

Braxton murmured, "I cannot be directly involved."

Ramsey stood and walked about the room. "Of course." He paused and turned, facing the prince. "Most importantly, please remember, Hélène is not in her right mind. Hostesses have had to eject her from their homes for her alcohol and perhaps laudanum- induced tirades. But no one speaks of it. Those in the ruling class feel their positions are threatened by this very wealthy, very irrational aristocrat."

Braxton and Ramsey sat contemplating for a few moments. The prince leaned forward, and in a quiet voice said, "I have an idea."

———

King Richard, Prince Braxton, and the prime minister were seated in the Audience Room following the monarch's and minister's weekly meeting.

"Father, the prime minister and I have sketched out a tour of sorts. A trip to show the crown as modernizing, allowing members of the royal family to become productive members of society. A tour of the British Isles."

Wrinkling his brow, and in a tenuous tone, the king asked, "That is interesting. Where did this idea originate?"

The prince averted his gaze and looked downward. The prime minister stared blankly at the king. "Braxton?"

Braxton sat, tight-lipped.

His majesty continued, "Your uncharacteristic silence answers my question. This is about you, is it not?"

The king and minister waited for Braxton to respond.

The king continued, "You and your desire to run for Parliament and marry the grand duchess?"

The prince nodded and said, Valentina." his hands clasped in his lap.

"Tell me exactly what you intend to accomplish," his father said.

Braxton answered, "The tour will certainly have a positive impact on parliament's support and improve the Crown's standing."

"How, exactly?" interrupted the king.

"Modernizing the Crown. Showing the royals to be more engaged in the lives the commoners live. When addressing the people, during the tour, I will introduce the idea that minor royals, such as myself, should be allowed to do something with our lives as opposed to sitting idly by, squandering our time here on earth. In effect, becoming engaged, working for the people side-by-side. I will be asking the people to petition and support members of Parliament to vote to permit junior royals, such as myself to be released from the confines of our gilded cages. Again, becoming productive members of society." He paused and then admitted, "Of course, I will touch on my hope that I might be able to marry the woman I love. It will be an appeal to the hearts of the common man."

The king sat back, his chin resting on his hands. "I

think it is a capital idea. You should take your brother John with you. It will make you appear less self-serving.

"And son, I would like to see special attention given to Ireland and Scotland. I have deep concerns regarding the Irish unrest and other anti-monarchist sentiments in the north."

———

Prince Braxton soon set off on a tour of Wales, Scotland, and Ireland. He lost no time ignoring the royal custom of never expressing a political opinion. He blatantly encouraged constituencies to support the two votes soon to come before Parliament that would affect him directly. Braxton appealed to the people's emotions, playing on his celebrity and popularity as "The People's Prince."

"I am asking you, the people, for my freedom to live my life as I like, such as you are permitted to live yours. And to marry the woman I love."

When newspapers and the occasional heckler made remarks about this break with protocol, he addressed the concerns in his speeches saying, "It is my life and my family's lives. It is not at all political, but quite personal!"

Initially, during his travels throughout the British Isles, it had been very difficult for the prince to move beyond the wooden speaking plaforms that had been erected to allow the crowds to see a member of the royal family. In his inimitable style, Braxton soon remedied that situation. One day, while addressing the crowd from atop a plaform, he said, "I have no idea why I am standing so far from all of you. Can you hear me? Do you want to hear me? I feel a bit like I am on display."

"Well, aren't you, my Lord? Like a fine horse or bull!" shouted someone from the crowd.

Laughter broke out.

Braxton joined in the fun, grinning wide, ear to ear. "I am afraid you have a point, Sir!" He paused for a moment. The crowd quieted down.

"Do stay put for a moment, I shall be right down."

The prince hopped down the stairs leading off the side of the plaform. The streets were soggy from the morning rain. He sloshed through and was reminded of his time in the forests, mines, and oil fields of Russia. The familiarity of slugging through the muck and being among the villagers relaxed and invigorated him. The crowd drew back, taken by surprise by this young royal apparently quite comfortable tramping through the mud. Many attempted a clumsy bow or curtsey. "For goodness' sake, please do not bother with all that. It seems a bit odd, does it not? How shall we ever have a go at talking? I want to hear from you. Actually, I am quite tired of hearing from me," he chuckled.

"Have you a tavern that will let the likes of me in?"

Minutes later he was ushered into a local pub. The place was soon packed to the rafters, the word passing quickly through the village that the prince was drinking with the common blokes. The prince entertained his listeners with the adventures he had experienced in Germany, Vienna and Russia. The stories of Japan and India mesmerized many. The women wanted to know as much as they could about Grand Duchess Valentina. He was made to promise he would return with her in tow one day.

He regaled the ever-increasing crowds with stories of his and Valentina's mutual work on the Russian plains and in Siberia. The prince shared with the people her efforts to improve the living environment of the people. He provided a glimpse of the woman who had uncovered and rid her country of "the wicked nobles" who had attempted to assassinate her cousin, Grand Duke Prince Maxim. There was little doubt in anyone's mind this woman was strong and would make a suitable wife for "their" Braxton.

When Braxton's three-week campaign came to an end, he returned to London to find his efforts had been effective. The prime minister and the leader of the House of Lords lent their support to Braxton's cause. The Commons and the Lords voted in favor of allowing junior royals to run for seats in the House of Commons. The second vote, confirming the marriage contract between Braxton and the Grand Duchess Valentina, easily passed the Commons and the House of Lords.

It was agreed that while the prince was in North America, the betrothal would be announced. The marriage would take place in London shortly after his return.

Valentina had yet to answer Braxton's letters.

———

"I suppose you and Valentina are quite pleased with Parliament approving the marriage," Queen Mercedes speculated.

"I cannot confirm that either way, Mamma." Braxton said twisting his napkin in his lap while at tea with Mercedes a few days after his return to London.

"Surely, you jest."

"I wish I were. But truthfully, we have not communicated since she disembarked in Vienna. I had been quite the cad. She would have nothing of it. Valentina left me."

"Was it that temper of yours? "How did you know?"

She rose out of her chair and sat next to him on the divan. The queen placed her hand on top of his. "I have witnessed impatience and a solemnity since your return.

Your heretofore flowing enthusiastic conversations have been absent. You spend less time with the family. You have shown no interest in things that bring you pleasure. You are short tempered and, quite honestly, a bit difficult to be around. A mother usually senses these things. You are remorseful and your heart appears to have darkened. And unless asked, you never speak of Valentina."

"Mamma, what caused you to believe it was my temper?"

"You and I are a lot alike. The bond we have had since the day you were born is all I needed to speculate what was the source of your discontent."

Braxton breathed a heavy sigh. "Thank you, Mamma. You are correct. Still suffering a bit from my illness, my temper got the better of me. Valentina's father's temper had, on more than one occasion, threatened her life. She would not stand for it."

"She is a wise woman. I would have done the same." Braxton placed his head in his hands. "What am I to do?" Mercedes inhaled and placed one hand on the prince's back.

"There is not a great deal one can do in these situations. It will take time and prayers. Continue to correspond, even if she does not reply. In those letters do not allow yourself to be self-deprecating, but share your feelings, all your feelings. Include her in what you are doing, invite her into your inner thoughts and your daily life. That is all one can do. Above all, show yourself to be strong and resolute.

And still in love with her."

20

1890 - CANADA & THE EIFFEL TOWER

Braxton was not overly excited about the Canadian visit. He could only shiver when he thought of the cold of Siberia and what he might experience in Canada. To help eliminate that possibility, he delayed his trip three months. He would not leave England until the middle of May, sailing directly to Quebec.

On the night before his departure, he retrieved a special envelope and card from the false bottom of a valise he kept in his possession at all times.

The prince remained depressed about the state of his relationship with Valentina. The clear, crisp spring evening wafting into his rooms at the Aurelio Palace was replaced in his mind by a cold, haunting feeling of gloom. He wrapped his arms about himself, plagued by the thoughts of what his actions as Mars, God of War. He thought of how he might have inadvertently played a part in the death of Hélène's parents, the comte and comtesse. This poor girl, so severely wounded by the violent deaths of her parents. How proud and arrogant of me to assume the only repercussions from my Machiavellian "Mars" scheme would be those which I ordained.

What on earth can I possible do to ease the misery of this unfortunate young woman?

In an effort to shake off the imagined cold, he rose from his writing table, put on his frock coat and closed the windows. He sat down to write.

My dear young comtesse,

I write to you on Mars stationary only to validate the authenticity of this letter. It is not meant to frighten you, but to assuage you. I pen this letter, haunted by what are the unintended consequences of my actions.

When I initiated the Mars scheme to silence those who were wreaking havoc on my business interests, I never imagined my actions would harm the innocent. These consequences tear at my heart and soul. Should there be a miracle, charm, or incantation that could remove this from our past, I would give anything to have it invoked.

But alas, that is not possible. Though I am not deserving of your forgiveness, I beg it of you.

As to your life, please do not continue the path of spiteful revenge you have chosen. It will neither bring your parents back, nor will it remove the dreadful memory or pain of having lost them. There is no perfect remedy. It is the long, slow dulling of the painful agony accompanying the passing of time that will beget some respite. Your current path will not bring about beneficial gain for anyone. The course you currently chart can only harden your heart and poison your soul. As to beneficial gain, should there be one, that schadenfreude shall be visited only upon gossips and newspapers.

They shall surely profit, their actions being at the expense of others, the innocent and troubled, leaving them miserable in their wake.

You are young, intelligent, beautiful, strong-willed, and blessed with station and wealth. Please use those gifts to live a worthwhile and meaningful life. It is not too late for you, but oh so late for those who came before you.

Sadly,
Mars, a foolish, cruel, repentant soul

———

Braxton was breakfasting late the next morning when Ramsey arrived unannounced.

"I beg your pardon, my Lord. The matter is rather urgent."

"Well, first things first," Braxton said, handing him an inconspicuous package containing the Mars letter to Hélène.

"Please have Signore Ratini surreptitiously deliver this to the Comtesse Bérengar."

"In Paris, my Lord?"

Braxton jerked back his head, asking, "Why Paris? I understood her to be in London."

"She was my Lord, until the Duchess of Marlborough had her escorted from the ball the duchess was hosting last evening."

"Tell me more, Ramsey."

"The fracas is in all the papers. I am surprised you have not seen it, my Lord."

"No, I have not read the morning papers. I have been otherwise engaged."

Pointing to the Times atop Braxton's breakfast table, "There, my Lord," Ramsey said.

The prince picked up the paper. "Where?" "Several pages in."

The prince turned the pages until he found the article to which Ramsey referred.

"Please sit, while I read this."

Ramsey accepted the invitation, helping himself to tea and a biscuit. Minutes later the prince placed the paper on the table. "My God, it says she was literally cast out. Her carriage driving off with her shrieking, "You shall see! You shall see! I will fly! I will fly from the highest heights!"

Viscount Ramsey muttered, "What on earth could she mean? Did you read the part where the footmen had to bring her down from the top of the house as she was determined to fly? It says she wore a peculiar cape draped across her shoulders and attached to her ankles and wrists. She was set to jump, launch herself off."

Ramsey sipped his tea, watching as Braxton read the full article. He then continued, "And did you read where she had announced to everyone at the ball, 'Go quickly to the garden. I shall only be a moment. Watch from above, for I shall surely fly!'"

Braxton began reading the article aloud. "A stampede of sorts erupted. A rush of ladies in gowns, tiaras, fluttering fans, brilliantly uniformed officers, gentlemen and excited voices exited the ballroom onto the terrace and into the torch lit gardens. Everyone looked up at the mansard roof, only to be cheated of the spectacle by the duchess and footmen thwarting her deadly intention."

The prince looked up from the paper and said, "She has definitely been driven mad."

Ramsey interjected, "She is now on her way to Paris. She apparently never returned home but instructed her coachman to take her directly to Dover."

The article went on to tell of the comte and comtesse's deaths following their receipt of the Mars letters.

"Do you still wish Ratini to deliver this letter?"

"Yes, please. Hopefully, she will read it before something dreadful occurs. Instruct Ratini to keep a close eye on her. I do not want that letter to fall into the wrong hands."

"Yes, my Lord."

Prince Braxton departed England later that day.

As Royal Envoy, he traveled to Canada on the soon to be decommissioned Royal Yacht Elfin, a ship that had served Braxton well many years ago when he purchased his first railroad. He hired private rail cars for his overland travels, traveling across the continent from Quebec to Ottawa, Winnipeg, Edmonton, and Victoria. He marveled at the size and beauty of the country.

Prince Braxton spent a great deal of time with the Governor General and his wife, the Princess Louise.

Not long before his arrival, the princess had suffered a leg injury.

She had been thrown from a sleigh when a snow bank had given way. The sleigh had been pushed off its course and separating it from a team of two horses, sending it careening down a hillside. She was not entirely ambulatory when the prince, a friend of her family, arrived in Quebec.

Connected by their similar sleigh accidents, Braxton and Princess Louise found mutual comfort in each other's company. The princess proved to be a good listener and deeply sympathetic. Braxton shared the details of his relationship with Valentina and his concerns about their future.

One morning, several days following his arrival in Canada, Princess Louise was seated in the morning room enjoying her breakfast. She wore a summer wool day dress boasting a brilliant cornucopia of hand painted flowers covering the bodice and sleeves. As her husband was away on business, only she and Braxton were at breakfast. She felt comfortable enough to leave her luxurious, brunette hair down on her shoulders.

Prince Braxton entered the room, and exclaimed, "You look lovely, Louise."

"Thank you Brax. Do make yourself comfortable."

Removing his coat and placing it on the back of a chair next to him, he replied, "I believe I will. Did you sleep well, my dear?"

"Yes, indeed. My leg does not pain me as it once did. Today is the first day I shall not have to prop it up. I suspect I will tire early on and surrender to propping it up as the day moves on." She attempted a smile.

"Ah, perhaps not. You appear to be mending well."

A footman entered carry a silver tray piled high with correspondence. A thick envelope was positioned at the bottom of the stack.

"Thank you," the princess said. The footman bowed and left the room. "Let me see, what do we have here?" She sorted the letters into several small piles. "So glad your letters are finally arriving, though I do not see anything that might be from the grand duchess. Pity." She handed several envelopes to Braxton.

The prince glanced at the letters he had received and placed them to the side.

"My goodness, look at this," she said, holding up the thicker envelope. "It is from my sister Fredericka. I believe she is spending half the summer in Paris and the other half in the south of France." The princess paused for just a moment, then continued prattling, "I know why the envelope is about to split at the seams." She laughed and continued, "The darling is always sending me newspaper clippings and articles of note. She feels sorry for me being so far away from 'civilization' as she would have it. Frankly, I do not miss 'civilization' a wit." She proceeded to open the large envelope.

Braxton looked on, his mind consumed with thoughts

of Valentina, hearing little of what Princess Louise said. He did not eschew her upbeat company, but it was Valentina's companionship he yearned for.

Louise, holding Fredricka's letter in one hand, pushed the stack of articles toward Braxton. Still focusing on the letter, she said, "Here Braxton, search for the one about the Comtesse de Bérengar. You know, the young lady who leapt off the Eiffel Tower. I believe she was the one who fancied herself a flying squirrel or some such animal."

Had Louise not been focused on her sister's letter she would have seen her breakfast partner's face assume a gray, ghostlike pallor.

Clasping his napkin to his mouth, he sprang out of his chair, ran through the opened French doors onto the terrace and forcefully vomited on a bed of flowers.

The princess looked up to find the prince had vanished. Shortly after, a footman entered the breakfast room.

"Your Highness, His Royal Highness sends his regrets as he will not be able to continue breakfasting this morning."

She placed the letter she was reading on the table, and wondered aloud, "Heavens! Whatever could have happened?" She gathered up some of the items on the table. "Well, here, I cannot imagine what could have transpired for him to have vanished. Take these," she said, flustered, handing the stack of articles to the footman. "Perhaps His Royal Highness will have time to enjoy them when he has dealt with whatever has taken him from me."

The footman, having gathered up the articles, was taking his leave when Princess Louise said, handing him Braxton's letters, "Take these as well, mind you."

———

An hour or so later in his rooms, the prince had changed his shirt and cravat and was reviewing the articles the princess had sent him. Warily, he searched for the article she had brought to his attention prior to becoming ill in the garden.

The article read:

The investigation of the young Comtesse Hélène Bérengar's recent demise on the Eiffel Tower's embankment and the River Seine has been completed. The official cause of death: suicide.

The investigation chronicled a story originating at Marlborough House, the London home of the Duke and Duchess of Marlborough: Witnesses confirm the comtesse had behaved in a less than appropriate manner while a guest of...

Nothing of import was illuminated until the part where the young girl arrived in Paris early the following evening. She had made her way to the Eiffel Tower, recently constructed on the unfortunately named Mars plaza, alongside the River Seine. As the construction of the tower has not been completed, it was not yet open to the public. The investigative report went on to say she had bribed her way past a guard and climbed the 906 feet to the observation deck. A watchman had taken note of the intruder and caught up with her as she stood astride iron beams, her arms outstretched, cloaked in a most unusual garment. The light wind lifted what was certainly a cape into a form closely resembling that of a large bat.

When the guard attempted to dissuade her from jumping, she exclaimed she would soar out over the river, make a gradual descent over the Seine and deposit herself on the opposite bank. The man stated she said something to the affect she would take flight, not unlike the nocturnal flying squirrels or perhaps a bird.

She then thrust herself forward and out into the pitch-black night. The billowing clothing failed to slow her hurtling descent. Her body slammed against the angled iron lattice work, ricocheting off the tower. The comtesse then crashed onto the stone embankment, the rapid angled decent of her fall forcefully propelled her into the Seine. The body was recovered the following morning.

Braxton's worst fears had been realized. An innocent young woman was dead, the result of a ruse of his creation meant to protect his own selfish interests.

He rang for a servant. When a footman arrived, he gave him five pounds sterling and asked him to purchase a large bottle of laudanum and bring it back to him, along with a bottle of Cognac.

The footman returned with the medicine and a bottle of Domaine du Mazureau Vieux. Braxton asked not to be disturbed. He spent the following three days alone in his rooms, accompanied by the opiate and alcohol.

On the fourth day, Prince Braxton emerged clean shaven and freshly dressed, ending his journey of angst and remorse. He neither offered an apology nor an explanation for his three-day retreat.

Ramsey's letter, one of the three Louise had handed him, explained Ratini had delivered the Mars letter to the comtesse when he had caught up with her on the Mars plaza beneath the Eiffel Tower. She had accepted it, scowling, and said not a word. She merely placed it in a pocket within the folds of her clothing and proceeded in the direction of the tower.

Ratini had remained on the plaza and was present when she met her end, crashing onto the plaza and rolling into the River Seine. As fortune would have it, the packet had either fallen from her as she dropped to the ground or was disgorged from her clothing when she hit the stone plaza. Ratini was able to unobtrusively retrieve the unopened letter from Mars. He subsequently made arrangements to return it to Lord Ramsey.

———

Prince Braxton had expected more economic vitality in Canada than he observed. The populace was intermittently spread out, not unlike that which he had seen in parts of Eastern Russia. The country was littered with thousands of clear lakes, forests rolling on for an eternity, undulating plains and mountains to rival the Alps. No doubt, mineral deposits and, perhaps even oil, lay undiscovered.

Braxton had occasion to see the ambitious railway construction underwritten by the Canadian Pacific Railway. He was poised to invest in the project until he found the company unwilling to make the changes necessary for increasing safety for the Chinese labor. His protestations to the Canadian government fell on deaf ears.

Braxton departed Canada for America from Vancouver.

21
———

AMERICA & JOE

Accompanied by only his valet and secretary, Prince Braxton traveled on to San Francisco via packet steamer. He found San Francisco's rough and tumble world exciting and invigorating. The economy was booming. Longing to experience all the city had to offer without the patina of royalty, he did not immediately inform the British consul of his arrival. Instead, the prince resided in modest accommodations until he was unmasked three weeks after his arrival. The British consulate quickly insisted he move to the Palace Hotel.

He continued to lay plans for expanding his business interests in America. As Braxton was familiar with forestry and logging, he promptly sought out other investment opportunities.

Two months into his stay and with his secretary in tow, Braxton made his way to the Pacific Transport Shipping line, his shipping line, the one he had purchased in Singapore almost a year prior.

"Good day. I am here to see Mr. Carlton, the Managing Director," Braxton said to the clerk staffing the large mahogany desk in the shipping lines towering oak lobby.

"I beg your pardon, Sir, but do you have an appointment? Without one, I do not believe he will see you–without an appointment I mean. Are you by any chance from England?"

"Yes, why do you ask?"

"Well, Sir, your accent sounds English, you know what I mean, Sir?"

"Perhaps an accident of birth," the prince returned, congratulating himself inwardly as to the dryness of his wit.

"May I have your name, Sir?"

"His Royal Highness, Prince Braxton of Wales. Son of the King of England."

The clerk rose from his chair, took a step or two back and stammered, "Sorry, Sir. I didn't recognize you, Sir. I'll be just a moment. I will announce you now, Sir."

Moments later, following the clerk up the main stairs, Braxton was met by the flushed Robert Carlton.

"Your Royal Highness, I beg your pardon, I had no idea you were in America, much less San Francisco." Braxton stuck out his hand. The two continued up the stairs and to the director's office.

"It is a pleasure to see you, Sir. As you know from my monthly reports, the firm has been doing quite well since you bought into the company, infusing it with cash, retiring our debt and fueling expansion."

"Yes Mr. Carlton, I am well pleased with the manner in which our partnership has come together. Particularly in the manner you have enthusiastically carried out my directions," Braxton said, hoping to assuage any regrets that might be lingering following the aggressive bargaining that had placed the company under his control. He continued,

"It pleases me greatly to have been part of a relationship that has returned the shipping line and you to prosperity."

Nodding his head, the middle-aged, well-dressed man blushed again. "Yes, it is a pleasure to see you as well, Your Highness. I may have resented your takeover a bit at the time, but ego aside, I have learned much and have prospered. My deepest thanks."

"It is my pleasure, Sir. Your diligence has improved both our circumstances. The tonnage we currently transport exceeds even my expectations. My offices in Vladivostok, Tokyo, Hong Kong, Shanghai, and Calcutta sing Pacific Transport Shipping Lines' praises and refuse to consider shipping with anyone else."

His face beaming, his chest puffed out and his hands inserted in his waistcoat's pockets, Carlton asked, "How may we be of service, Sir?"

"While I am in San Francisco, which may be for some months, I require an office for myself and one for my secretary. Naturally, I would like to have introductions to some of the business leaders in the community. My interests lie in forestry, mining, shipping, and oil. Perhaps you could manage introductions to individuals having like-minded commercial interests."

"It would be my pleasure."

"Oh, and yes, Mr. Carlton," the prince said, as he removed an envelope from an inside coat pocket, "please find enclosed instructions for ordering four additional freight steamers. I have obtained lumber shipping contracts while in Canada. That is the good and the bad news, as I believe I may have placed the firm in a tight spot, perhaps exceeding its capacity. I will of course, leave it to you to seamlessly bring things together."

Stammering, Mr. Carlton replied, "Yes, yes, Sir, I will,

of course." "And Mr. Carlton, you will find another order for twelve shallow-

bottomed steam barges. While in San Francisco I have begun negotiating contracts with farmers and growers between here and Sacramento. Details for both scenarios are enclosed. If you should have any questions, please reach out to my secretary. Best of luck, Mr. Carlton."

Having nothing to say, the director nodded, which served him well as his jaw had dropped giving every appearance it had locked in place.

———

Braxton decided to put aside his English clothing and adopt a more American style. America was such a different country than he was used to. He felt compelled to try to integrate into American ways. He had never seen or felt denim and could not understand the stiffness of the fabric.

"You'll like 'em once ya wear 'em for a while," the general store manager insisted. "The wearin' and washin'll soften 'em up." He handed a short stack of pants to Braxton. "These canvas trousers'll soften up sooner, but they won't last like the blue jeans, even with the saddle pant in the seat."

"And this flannel shirt. It will soften up as well?" Braxton asked. "Yep, but wear these underneath the Levi's and flannel," he said,

tossing him two pair of red long johns. "They"ll keep ya warm in the cold and cool in the heat."

Braxton held up the one-piece underwear, marveling at the color, long sleeves, and trap-door bottom. "Is this what I think it is?"

"Yessireee!" The manager laughed.

"What is this? This shirt with the cotton panel and buttons? Only in red?"

"Heh, heh, that'll come in handy. That is a bib shirt. There ain't much time for washin' or cleanin' up 'round these parts. That bib does just what it says it'll do: keep ya tidy. Big demand for red," the manager smiled, enjoying the proper Englishman's reactions.

"And footwear. Boots. Do you carry them?"

"The finest made these days, Sir," he said, pulling out several large boxes from underneath a work table. "Lucchese slant-heel boots.

Take a look at these. Last ya forever. Try 'em on so you can figure out your size. Sizes is differn't in boots."

Now a well-dressed cowboy, the Englishman felt a bit self- conscious the first day he ventured out. His skin chaffed in the stiff materials. He had purchased enough clothing to rotate them out so he hired a washerwoman to wash and rewash until he found them comfortable enough to wear. The boots altered his gait, making it slower and less assertive. He thought, I look the part and I'm even beginning to feel it.

A couple of bandanas, a Stetson hat, leather gloves and a sheep- skin coat rounded out his new clothes. He would soon grow to prefer the attire. When I return to England, shooting on the moors will be so much more comfortable in these American clothes. What a sight that will be!

The prince then hired a man to teach him how to shoot an American Winchester rapid-fire rifle and master the Colt single- action and double-action revolvers. He found learning how to ride a western saddle practical and utilitarian, wondering why the Europeans had not adopted it for their own use.

After a day or two passed, Braxton noticed his secretary gawking at his western attire and remarked, "I find the

Americans so practical. Even their comfort is sensible, as is their western saddle. So easy to sit. And all the things one can do while riding. A splendid invention."

Braxton never felt obligated to indulge in another western pastime, that of chewing tobacco. Watching men place the dried leaves between their jaw and cheek and chew vigorously, only to spit the juice out wherever and whenever they liked, disgusted his British sensibilities. He found the spittoons strategically placed in many drinking establishments more decorative that utilitarian, as he had seen many aim for the device, but few ever hit it successfully.

———

The American transcontinental railroad had opened new markets for goods arriving from Russia, China, and Singapore. This particularly piqued Braxton's interest, having struggled so hard to establish rail lines across Russia to carry lumber, mine ore, and oil. Surely there were opportunities for the Russian Consortium to export to America. The Americans had their own oil and mountains of lumber. Perhaps his mines produced ore needed in America. Certainly, the orient's tea, opium, tin, rubber, and fabrics had a place in this growing nation. He expanded his shipping to accommodate the demand he would create as he discovered new markets during his planned journey across the United States.

Braxton purchased several large parcels of land in the outlying areas around San Francisco. Developing large plots of land for manufacturing had been one of the early ways in which he had begun to build wealth. Many years ago he had purchased interest in an English railroad, then options on property along the route where he planned on laying track. He had prospered from leasing land to manu-facturers and building homes for the workers. The prince hired contractors to develop the land along the same lines he had done when he purchased his first railroad and developed land between London and the Aurelio Palace.

By the time he was set to depart San Francisco, the prince had been successful in all his business goals. His activities during his eight-month stay expanded Pacific Transport's shipping from the Far East into his West Coast business center, his gateway into the North American continent.

Braxton had always been curious about the American mining and cattle businesses. His experiences in Russia had well prepared him for mine inspections and respective financial analysis. He was cautious not to be sucked in by the romanticized folklore of the American West. The only way he felt he could make an informed decision regarding investing in anything would be to visit the mines first hand. He decided to experience the American stagecoach system and, with his valet and secretary, embarked on the long, arduous journey over the Rocky Mountains and down into the boomtown of Denver, Colorado.

———

Braxton began making plans for the exploration of mining opportunities in Colorado. He would leave his valet and secretary in Denver to take care of daily business.

Weeks earlier, he had sent for several of his more seasoned Russian mining engineers to join him. The prince and his engineers would be led into the mountains on horseback by a party of prospecters familiar with the western mining territory. The party leader, Joe Richards, had purchased options on one of the mines they were going to inspect. He was looking for investors. Braxton hoped this expeditionary venture would help him evaluate, as had been done in Russia, the various mining opportunities.

———

Other than the lodge in India, the prince had never been this far away from civilization and his own hectic life. The journey was slow, hot, dusty, and remote. Braxton embraced every aspect of it. He learned to sleep on the ground under the stars. He experienced freezing, cold, rainy nights and hellishly hot days. And he became fast friends with the lead prospector.

Muscular and lean, Joe Richards was Braxton's age. He was an inch or two shorter in height but inches broader in the shoulders. His looks were what Braxton thought of as the classic representation of an American cowboy. Braxton soon learned, however, like his own, this cowboy's look was a facade.

Joe never mentioned he had a degree from Harvard, but when in conversation with Braxton he spoke to economics, politics and world history. Braxton soon came to learn he was also well-traveled.

Unbeknownst to Braxton, Joe had seen the prince from afar on several occasions while in Europe. He had also kept abreast of Braxton's travels via newspaper and magazine stories.

The prince, however, had yet to reveal his true identity to the rest of the mining party. As far as Braxton knew, they all, including Joe, thought him merely a wealthy English chap who wanted to invest in the mining industry and participate in the boom. Joe kept what he knew about the prince to himself and went along with his story.

Braxton could tell Joe had been raised in a learned environment.

Sometimes he let down his guard, betraying a classical education and alluding to great works of literature and some familiarity with the sciences. He invariably conjugated his verbs properly. Only rarely did he employ slang. When he and Joe were alone Braxton picked up on more inconsistencies in Joe's manner of speech. When with the other men, Joe was quite adept at expressing himself in their western patois.

The prince did not inquire into Joe's history. He watched as Joe made small talk and kept the conversations away from himself. In the company of others, they talked mining, cattle, and women. Braxton sensed Joe was not particularly interested in the latter.

———

Late one afternoon after a long day on the trail, Joe led the party off the path onto a level piece of ground. He told them to make camp for the night.

Braxton noticed two or three places where small rocks had been gathered in a circle, surely sites of previous campfires. Rusted tin cans littered the ground. Stubs of what had been scrub bushes dotted the area, along with grasses appearing less developed than those bordering the perimeter. Braxton observed, "Obviously, you or someone else has camped here before."

"Yes, once or twice prior to my purchasing an option on the mine.

There is a cave not far from here. That's where the mine is located.

It's a tricky trek. Shall we take a look before it gets

dark?" "Excellent, why not? I really did not want to have to wait until tomorrow to see the mine first-hand."

The pebble-mixed earth gave way to a rock surface as they rode their horses up a steep trail. Joe's horse's right rear hoof slipped, almost bringing it to the ground. Joe steadied the animal and then slid out of the saddle.

"It becomes increasingly difficult to remain on horseback the further we go. Loose rocks and sediment become treacherous. You can easily see why I didn't want to bring the wagons the rest of the way, since we were approaching nighfall. It is best to walk from here, my friend."

"Right oh," the prince said, and mimicked Joe's descent from his horse. Reins in hand, man and beast climbed the unstable wagon trail along the ridge of the steep ravine.

"Are there many avalanches here?" Braxton inquired.

"I have only experienced one or two. None right here. But look around, there is always the potential for a rock slide," Joe said, pointing to rocks and boulders that had been displaced from atop the hills and mountains surrounding them.

"The cave you spoke of. Is it truly a cave or a mine opening?" "Both, actually. The original stakeholder took refuge in it when a mass of falling rocks was determined to crush him. I understand the man ran toward the cave for protection. A lightning strike had initiated a rock fall forcing him to remain there for days. Unrelenting rains followed, flooding his egress. In the meantime, he kept himself busy looking around the cave. He chanced upon a silver vein; not very big, but large enough for him and a couple of drunk cohorts to work it for a while."

Braxton asked, "How on earth could that be? So many have searched for years for such a find, and he just chanced upon it?"

"Yep, that appears to be so. He eventually made a little

money but died leaving the stake to relatives back east. I bought the option after it had sat with no takers for three years. Sure hope there is something to it. Like I said back in Denver, I believe efficient mining techniques will make it worthwhile in the long run."

"Fascinating. Good fortune, that lightning strike!" Braxton marveled.

The crunch of rocks beneath the horse's hooves and the men's boots were interrupted by a distant rumbling.

"Thunder!" Joe declared.

"Coincidence? the prince asked. "We were just talking about that."

"Hopefully not, and hopefully further away than it sounds. With these high mountains surrounding us, it is hard to see where it is coming from. No way for sure to tell the wind's direction. We should consider returning to camp if thunder sounds again."

"Are we close to the mine opening, the cave?"

"Yes, just up a bit and it flattens out some in front of the entrance."

"Good."

They continued up the incline. Moments later the two men reached an area surrounded on three sides by millennia old sedimentary and metamorphic rock, common throughout the Rocky Mountains.

"This rock is not unlike some I have seen in Italy," Braxton observed. "Volcanic in origin."

Joe pointed to an opening in the side of the rock face.

"See that cave? That's the mine. I bet many a bear, maybe wolves, surely Indians have sought shelter there. Think of the tales that cave could recount."

"That is the mine?"

"Yes. We will return tomorrow and make camp here. At night, we'll bring the horses inside with us to bed down.

There is more than enough room. It's safer there. Damn falling rocks make for a poor night's rest. As you can see, we never would have been able to get the wagons up that rocky incline in time to make camp today."

"Can we spare a moment to take a quick look inside?" Braxton asked.

"Of course, why not. Just a quick look. We need to head back soon."

"You are correct. It looks large enough to get a full, horse-drawn wagon inside. Is it really that large inside?"

"Yes. Come, let's walk the horses. They need water and there is a small trickle running along one side of the cave. It's a bit salty. The horses love it. I am not too keen on it, but it is water nonetheless."

"They smell it, the water," the prince said, noticing the horses perking up, ears shifting forward, heads raising and their pace quickening.

Several small rocks bounced down the side of the mountain, catching Braxtons attention. A few larger rocks hit the ground nearby, causing Joe to whirl around and holler, "Braxton, start heading down!"

Suddenly the mountainside rumbled as boulders bounced and careened down the steep mountain's walls. The horses rose on their hind legs, protesting, their neighs sounding like screams. Dust filled the air.

Joe and Braxton grabbed their respective horse's bridles near the browbands and tugged the panicked horses toward the cave opening. They came to a stop ten yards from the darkened cave's mouth.

"Take your jacket off and cover your horse's eyes!" Joe was yelling but his voice was all but inaudible above the sound of falling stone.

Braxton and Joe fought to hold onto their horses, using one hand to cover the frantic animal's eyes as they tried to shake off their denim jackets. More than one attempt was needed to cover the horse's vision and jury-rigg the coats securely in place. The dust was so thick they could see nothing beyond three feet.

"Come on Braxton!"

Joe and the prince guided their confused horses and made their way to the cave entrance. Rocks the size of plums struck the animals; their saddles, blanket rolls, and saddle bags protecting them from injury.

An ear-splitting roar sent Braxton's horse toward the dark opening, an opening no animal or human being would venture into without checking to see if it was occupied; occupied by something ready to consume them - a bear, coyotes, or a mountain lion.

Just inside the cave entrance the horses planted their hooves, their eyes still covered. The opening they had passed through began to disappear as rocks and boulders piled higher. Stones, large and small, bounced several feet into the cave.

Joe shouted above the din, "Move back! We don't want any of those rocks to get lose and crush us."

The crashing sounds of smashing boulders and the peppering sounds of smaller rocks falling and dribbling down the mountainside gave way to silence. The thick dust settled. A small opening near the top of the cave mouth's apex allowed only a little light into the large cavern.

"What a fine mess we have here," Joe moaned, slapping the dust from his oil-skin leather coat.

"I agree. Should we remove the blindfolds from the horses?"

The horses moved their heads up and down, as if in agreement with what the English cowboy had asked.

A grating noise rippled from beneath the pile of rock covering the opening. Suddenly, several loose stones and large rocks shifted, releasing a huge boulder the size of a cow from halfway up. It ricocheted off the side of the pile and bounced, finally coming to rest on the rear haunches of Joe's horse, crushing its backside and pinning the screeching animal to the ground.

Braxton's horse shied away, breaking the prince's hold. Free but still blinded by the prince's jacket, the horse froze in place.

The injured animal clawed with both hooves, trying vainly to pull its pulverized backside out from under the massive boulder. The struggle lessened as the animal succumbed to shock, the jacket hanging around its neck. The animal's vein-popping eyes bulged wide. A dark liquid drained from its flaring nostrils. Air forced out of the horse's nostrils echoed off the cave's hard surfaces.

Joe looked down at the animal, drawing his Colt 45 from its holster.

"No! You cannot, you must not!" Braxton exclaimed.

"For God's sake, man! Consider the animal. It's dying, suffering." "That shot could set off another slide, an avalanche."

Joe responded, "Dammit! You're right."

Braxton withdrew a six-inch Bowie knife from the sheath at his waist. He walked over to the creature, strad-dled it, and placed both his knees on either side of its neck. He stroked the horse and spoke gently.

Braxton looked up at Joe. He grasped the knife with both hands and plunged it deep into the horse's neck. The animal's reflexive jerk was quick and strong, but not enough to unbalance Braxton. To ensure a quick and merciful bleed-out, he sawed at the neck, leaving a gaping wound, allowing the blood to gush forth and cover Brax-ton's hands and arms. The stench of death mixed with the dusty air, leaving a cloud of silence.

The prince wiped the blood off the blade on the horse's hide.

Joe stood with his fists clenched at his side, blankly staring at the dead horse. "Thank you, Braxton," a shaken Joe murmured. "My reflex was to put the horse out of its misery, but I'm glad you stopped me. I could have started another avalanche." He paused, swallowed, and drew one gloved hand across his eyes. "Genesis, that was his name. We had five great years together, first back East and then here."

Braxton stood, saying, "I understand. We will have to cover him with dirt to keep animals and bugs from feasting on the carcass." He returned the knife to its sheath. "Help me move him and I will do the rest."

Dark red blood had pooled beneath the horse's neck. Total silence permeated the dimly lit cave.

Joe murmured, "How did you think to stop me from shooting him? How did you know?"

"I knew, but I did not think. I reacted. I have experienced mining in a different part of the world. It is, for the most part, all the same."

Joe walked to the back of his horse and pushed on the boulder that pinned it in place. The boulder did not budge. "Help me. I need to get my gear before we cover him up with what dirt we can scrape up off the cave floor."

Fifteen minutes later, following a great deal of pushing and tugging, the two men had moved the rock off Joe's horse and had retrieved the saddle, tack, saddle bags, horse blanket and blanket roll.

Joe, still caught up in the loss of Genesis, hung his head and said quietly, "You'll find a couple of shovels in that wagon."

Braxton now saw a wagon on the back wall of the cave,

not 30 feet away. It appeared to be filled with supplies. "How did this get here? How did you know it was here?"

"My team and I left it the last time we were here in preparation for this trip."

"This just might be the ticket to keeping us alive, Joe."

"I am counting on it. We may be here for a while.'

Thirty minutes later a burial mound covered the stricken horse. The setting sun was taking with it their light source. Only shadows remained.

"There should be several lanterns in some of those crates. Some kerosene, magnesium strips, dried fruit and dried meat."

"And water?" Braxton queried.

"When we get some light, I will show you a spring. It is about forty yards back through the larger tunnel. We need to fill both our canteens. Let's break up one of those boxes and build a fire. We will need it to keep warm."

Shivering, Braxton said, "Yes, I was wondering about that draft. It is very cold. Where is it coming from?"

"I don't know. All I do know is that it may be the only chance we have to get out of here. No one is going to be able to move that pile of stone, even if they thought we were in here. I'll bet that entire area out in front of the cave is filled with rocks and boulders. They surely piled in, funneled by the surrounding mountains. No way the others will be able to get in here. There is no place to put the rocks when and if they can move them."

Joe located the lanterns while Braxton built a fire out of the wood from one of the boxes. Hoping to block the cold breeze whipping from deep within the cave, the prince commenced to position the boxes to build a break.

"As it's getting darker, the air is becoming colder and drier," Joe remarked. "That makes no sense, unless it is coming off the cooling night desert. It must be. Caves are not naturally this cold or arid. That hole at the top of those rocks must be serving as a flu, like a chimney. The tighter the hole the stronger the flow. It's stronger now that the sun has gone down. It seems to be pulling the cold air through at a faster pace. If I did not fear starting another slide, I would crawl up there and stuff that hole."

"Do not even think about it. Unless of course you want to join your horse under that pile of dirt."

"You needn't worry, Braxton."

Joe grabbed a lantern, two canteens and headed further back into the pitch-black cave. "I'll return in a minute."

Five minutes later, Joe was back carrying the canteens. He had obviously washed the dirt and rock dust off his face, as reflected in the lantern's light. He handed a canteen to Braxton.

"I was thinking, Joe said. "This cave has always been damp. The water that runs along the north side of the cavern is probably what formed the cavern and the tunnels leading into it."

Braxton had completed his make-shift wind barrier and now sat next to the fire. Joe soon joined him, both sitting, resting their backs against the crates.

"I could certainly use this air to cool some of my mining equipment and train engines," Braxton mused.

Joe smiled wryly. "So, you have an interest in trains as well as mines?"

The prince instantly regretted having thought out loud. "Some, yes." Clumsily changing the subject, he said, "I think we should consider going back into the caves to see where the air is coming from. I see no way for us to get out of here the way we came in. It is entirely too dangerous. If we were to get through this pile, what would we find? More mountains of rock?"

In reply, Joe removed a bottle of whiskey from the saddle bag lying next to him. "Well, we can't do anything more tonight." He cracked open the top of the whiskey and used a corkscrew to remove the cork from the bottle. "You know what they call this in the West?" Joe asked, pointing to the corkscrew."

Braxton chuckled, "I cannot say as I do." "The worm."

The men laughed. Joe took a swig and handed the bottle off to

Braxton. The two talked about everything but their predicatment of being trapped in a cave until they had finished off half the bottle. The cavern took on an eerie ambiance, with tall shadows, a chilling airflow, and a dwindling, flickering fire.

"Looks like we are getting into that bottle," Braxton slurred. "I haven't eaten since early this morning. That hit me hard."

"Yup, me too," Joe belched and laughed. Replacing the cork, he continued, "We are going to save the rest until the day we make it out of here. Or we call it quits."

"Suit yourself, Joe," Braxton sputtered, laying his head against the crates. "It is cold as the devil. There is not sufficient wood to get us warm." He rolled over on his side, reached inside one of his saddle bags and pulled out two bottles.

"I'll be god-damned!" Joe exclaimed.

"It appears we both are. Now give me that worm, cowboy!" "Naw, put those bottles back, we can work on this one some more."

"Yes sir! One arfarfan'arf to another" Braxton shouted playfully.

"What the hell is a arf barf narf?" Joe mumbled. "A drunkard," Braxton quipped mischievously.

Joe gave Braxton a friendly jab and said, "Drunkard is easier to say, what's with the fancy words, toff?"

Braxton thought to himself, he is a handsome man, intelligent, apparently well read, somewhat rough, but sophisticated. He felt a stirring in his loins, much like he had experienced with Aramis that night on the train between Berlin and Vienna.

Several swigs of whiskey later, Joe untied the leather straps holding his bedroll together. He spread his slicker out and laid his saddle blanket alongside Braxton. Joe then looked directly into Braxton's eyes.

Braxton did not look away. At that moment, Joe made a decision.

He positioned his bedroll and blanket against Braxton, then continuing to look Braxton in the eyes, he adjusted the blanket, running his hand down the prince's hip and leg. Braxton smiled.

Joe sat atop the bedroll, leaning against the boxes and covering himself with the blanket from the waist down. "I suggest you do the same as I and sit close to me. It's going to get a lot colder when we sober up, my friend."

Not wanting to risk standing and falling over, Braxton crawled the five feet needed to retrieve his bedroll and horse's blanket. He returned and placed them next to Joe.

"Good idea," he shivered and continued, "but I am still cold as balls."

"In America, it's called cold as a witch's tit. That's how cold I am. Sit closer."

The men moved closer, pulling the blankets up around themselves after placing their Stetsons atop their heads.

Joe leaned his head close to Braxton and slurred, "When were you planning on telling me who you are, Monsieur Prince?"

Braxton ignored the question, grunted, and reached

across Joe's body for the bottle lying on its side. Peering into the mouth of the bottle, he said sadly, "Empty."

The prince threw the bottle across the cave. It shattered on impact, startling the sleeping horse.

"You are in your cups," Joe slurred.

"Your question, me not telling you? Have not given it much thought."

"Horse shit, Highness."

Braxton snorted a laugh, "That was ripe! Horse-shit Highness!

Hope you do not mind my using that one on a few of my relatives." "Help yourself," Joe laughed back saying, "but only if you come clean and answer my question."

"Very well," Braxton said moving closer.

Joe said, "Hold still a moment." He took both of their blankets and spread them together across the length of their bodies.

"Lie down and put your head on this," Joe said, handing him a pair of rolled up jeans.

Braxton stretched out on the makeshift bed and placed his head on the pants pillow.

"Now turn on your side and face me, Braxton. Get as close as you can," Joe said softly. "We will need our body heat to make it through the night."

Moments later the men had arranged themselves, so they were pressed up against each other, Joe's arm wrapped around Braxton.

"You smell like a drunken whore," Braxton deadpanned.

"Look who is calling the kettle black. If your subjects could see you now!"

"I haven't any subjects, my father does, zounderkite. That means dunderhead."

"I know perfectly well what that means, your royal high

ass. Now answer my question. God I'm drunk," Joe belched in Braxton's face.

Braxton flinched. "Bugger off!"

Joe belched once more and asked again, "Why have you held your identity from me? I have known who you are since the day we met, yet you never confided in me. Why?"

Braxton stiffened, then relaxed. Joe's arms felt better around him when he was relaxed.

"Because I wanted to maintain an equal and level relationship with everyone. Never been able to do that."

Not certain it was the right time to surrender to his libido, Braxton, now aroused, reached down and adjusted himself. "Besides, I am hungry. I want to sleep now."

"We will eat in the morning. We will sleep after you fully answer my question."

The drunk prince sighed and said, "I wanted to avoid the anxiety and stress and just be whatever it is normal people are."

"Braxton, you are not normal. You are like me, and I am not normal."

"What do you mean, Joe?"

Joe ran his hand down Braxton's back and said, "I have been attracted to you for years."

Braxton shifted his weight, frowning slightly and in a confused voice asked, "Years?"

"Years," Joe confirmed. "At least five years ago. I was in Italy and finagled a way to crew on your uncle's yacht."

"My uncle? I have several. What madness is this?"

Joe slurred, "Your uncle, the Duke de Chiacontella, Cosimo." "Christ almighty," Braxton murmured.

"I was crewing on the yacht when he sailed to Capri. When you and Aramis were in Capri."

Braxton's head spun. He tried to push Joe away, but Joe latched on and pulled him closer, not letting go, forcing Braxton to grasp what he had said and feel Joe's arousal.

"A bit sobering, my knowing about Capri, isn't it?" Joe said softly, moving his lips inches from Braxton's, their steaming breaths mixing.

Pressed up against Joe's body, he allowed himself to absorb Joe's intimate revelation.

Joe continued, "I swam competitively at school and was able to follow your uncle at a distance when he swam from the yacht to the grotto. I remained in the grotto's shadows, but I was close enough to overhear your conversation."

Braxton wanted to hear everything Joe had to say, but now he also wanted to silence him with a kiss.

"Before then, I felt the fool following you about Europe. But that day on Capri, I fell in love with you." Still holding Braxton, he pulled the prince to him, touching his lips with his. The prince did not back away.

Slowly, their softly touching lips evolved into a deep kiss. A kiss that lasted longer than either of them could have anticipated.

"That was nice," Braxton said, giving the end of Joe's nose a kiss. "But you have me at an unfair advantage."

"How is that?" Joe asked, running his thumb along the side of his new-found lover's face.

"You know much about me. I know nothing of you but what you have shared these past few days."

"That, I cannot deny. How long I have yearned for this moment.

You now must know how much I love you."

Braxton sighed and cuddled closer. They soon kissed again, and then relaxed as the heat of their bodies pressed tight, warming them.

Unbidden, Valentina drifted into Braxton's mind. Oddly, he could not see her face as clearly as he thought he should. Indeed, her visage had clouded with each passing day over the year his letters had gone unanswered.

"Did you know I may still be engaged? The marriage is prearranged, but I love her nonetheless and will marry her if she will have me."

"I hope so," laughed Joe, "because if you did not, you would have to stay here with me! Besides," he said, kissing the prince softly, "who in their right mind wouldn't want you?"

Braxton smiled and thought to himself, that would be interesting. I once had the same wish to remain with Aramis.

Unknowingly, they each recalled Cosimo's last words in the grotto, warning of the consequences of forbidden love.

"You both have choices to make. Make them before they are made for you. You can choose to renounce your positions in the world. If you abandon your birthrights, you will, in fact, be forced to live a life much as you have these past three weeks, isolated from the rest of the world."

The thought of separation intensified their desire for one another.

They pulled each other impossibly close, their mouths passionately punishing one another. Hands grasping and exploring. Their bodies writhing, wishing they could rid themselves of their clothing. Their cocks yearning to burst through the clothes that bound them, each desiring to touch the other.

The heated, drunken lovemaking ended in release and gave way to inebriated slumber. Braxton and Joe lay together arms wrapped around one another, their unshaven faces resting together in sleep.

———

Braxton squatted next to an iron pot full of beans and set on top of the hot coals. He stirred the beans with a wooden spoon.

Joe raised himself up on his elbows and pressed a palm to his forehead. He groaned, "God my head is going to explode," then laid back, pulling the blankets up around his shoulders.

"I've cooked some beans and dried meat I found in one of those crates. I could not find the dried fruit and I was much too cold to keep looking." He kept stirring.

"I feel like crap, but I need to eat something to get over this hangover. Get my chow kit, yours too, we'll need 'em," Joe mumbled. "Balls it is cold."

I have already thought of that. I am warming up your plate now.

Rise and shine, it is time to eat."

Joe sat up and asked, "How long have you been up."

"I have no idea," Braxton said, handing Joe a tin plate covered with piping hot beans. Chunks of blood-darkened dried beef sat along one side of the plate. Joe took the plate and Braxton handed him a bent tin spoon.

"Not bad, English. Where'd you learn to cook?" "Siberia."

"Get off!"

"I found the beans in the crate, along with some seasonings. That was a bit of a surprise. There was dry mustard, salt, pepper, syrup and dried onion. I had to heat up the syrup, due to the fact it had become a bit hardened with age."

"How can you function? I can barely move," Joe asked, blowing on each spoon of beans. Don't royals get hangovers?"

Braxton chuckled, "Not this one." "You are damn lucky."

"So, I hear. You ready for more of this?" "Almost."

The prince took a few minutes to clean up around the fire, adding wood to the fire then refilling Joe's plate and preparing a plate for himself. He sat down close beside Joe and leaned against him.

Feeling Braxton's gaze, Joe looked over, catching Braxton watching him eat. They grinned. Braxton bent over and kissed Joe on his bean flavored lips.

"Not while I am chewing! I want to participate too, you know."

Braxton, popped a spoonful into his mouth, leaned back and said, chewing, "Sorry."

"When I finish, do you mind if I rest a bit longer?"

"I would like to join you in that rest," flirted Braxton.

"Ah, that would be nice. Then afterward I could actually get some rest."

"But I would like you to finish your story before our 'rest.'" "Capri?"

"Correct. And then what followed, if you don't mind."

Joe took his time eating. Braxton, finishing first, started cleaning up, busying himself while waiting for Joe to start talking.

Joe placed his empty plate down on the ground, took a couple of swigs from his canteen, groaned, and laid back. "So, where were we? Oh yes, the yacht, Capri. I did not want your uncle to see me swimming back toward the yacht, so I hid among some rocks and watched him make his way back to the boat. Then I followed him.

Thank God, I made it back before they weighed anchor." "Didn't the crew miss you while you were gone?"

Joe coughed a laugh, "Not that crew."

"Oh yes. Mediterranean crews can be a bit laissez-faire."

"We sailed back to Naples. I served them my notice, got

off the yacht and waited for the duke to disembark. I was surprised when he left unaccompanied."

Braxton interrupted, "So, all these years you have known the secret I share with my cousin?"

"Forgive me for being so forward, but after last evening's intimacy, I feel free to tell you I also know of your uncle's secret; that your father and he had an affair."

Braxton, astounded, did not know how to react. He stood with his eyes and mouth wide, staring openly at Joe. At last Braxton whispered, "I believed that might be the case. As I was growing up, my uncle and father would disappear for hours, sometimes longer when the families were on holiday. There are times when it is easier to push these thoughts aside; not to think about things one does not want to understand.

"Have you ever shared any of this with anyone?" "Yes, I have," Joe said, pausing.

The prince shook his head slowly side-to-side. "Dear God, who?"

"In Naples I registered under a fictitious name at the same hotel as your uncle. That evening at dinner I saw him sitting alone. I asked if I could join him. He did not recognize me as a crew member, of course. I'd visited a barber and presented myself dressed like any other gentleman."

"You sound dangerous."

Joe closed his eyes and continued with the story. "I did not hide my American accent. He must have been curious, so he welcomed me to his table. Our dinner was an unintended and surprisingly romantic encounter. We spent the next week together. Neither of us expected what happened to occur. Oddly, I liked the 'older man' relationship. At that time, and even to this day, he is quite handsome and easy company. I learned a lot about your family. It is amazing what older lovers will share with younger men."

Joe and Braxton sat silently for a while, Braxton thinking of what he had just learned about his Uncle Cosimo.

"You do have me and my family by the balls, do you not?"

Joe appeared not to have heard the remark. He had fallen back to sleep. Braxton went over and arranged the blankets around the sleeping cowboy, then pressed his lips on Joe's forehead.

"Maybe we can have that 'rest' when you awaken."

Joe, his eyes closed, whispered, "Yes, there will be more of that after I have rested a bit."

Braxton chuckled and said, "Indeed, there shall."

Braxton looked around the cave, Joe quietly snoring in the background. He headed over to the boxes and began opening them, absentmindedly removing items he thought useful for exploring caves.

———

Four hours later, Joe awoke. Alarmed by the silence, he sat up quickly and looked around for Braxton. Unable to see him, he shot upright.

My God! He has gone back into the caves. Without me!

Rubbing his eyes and attempting to get his bearings, Joe heard a scraping or dragging-like noise.

Braxton emerged from the cave's interior wearing a miner's cap and goggles, covered in dirt, his face an ashen white. In one gloved hand he carried coiled rope. In the other, a sputtering magnesium strip lantern. He pulled behind him a shallow, canoe-shaped canvas tarp strapped to his waist by a three-foot rope. It contained a short-handled shovel, a pick, two canteens, four spent magnesium lanterns and several rags. Three jagged pieces of rock the size of an apple nestled in a back corner of the canoe.

He spied Joe, rushing to put on his jacket. "What is the hurry, Joe?"

In a panicked voice Joe asked, "Where have you been? I was afraid you might have gotten lost in the cave and I was going to go look for you!"

Braxton grinned wide, his shining white teeth breaking through the gray mass that was his face. "Caving."

"I was worried sick. Why didn't you wake me? I would have gone along. You could have gotten lost or been killed! I was only sleeping a little while." Joe paused for a minute, then stuttered, saying, "You are not an experienced caver, right? You could not possibly know what you are doing?"

"I believe I do, and it has been hours."

Braxton removed his goggles, rings of relatively clean skin circling his eyes. He placed the lantern on the ground and removed the rope from around his waist. "I caved with Monsieur Martel, a French caver while in Northern Ireland on tour. It was fascinating."

"Okay, I guess you are somewhat knowledgeable," Joe admitted. He proceeded to organize himself, appearing to be deep in thought. "It must be getting warm in the desert; the temperature in here has become much more agreeable. Did you find anything? How far back did you go? I'm still surprised you didn't get disoriented or lost." He paused and cocked his head. "How did you find your way? You look like you've been to Hades and back."

Braxton leaned down and picked up a strand of colorful twine leading toward the back of the cave.

"Your version of bread crumbs," Joe said, a bit of levity finally showing in his tone. "Did you come across the witch and the gingerbread house?"

"Indeed, I did. Not the witch, nor her frozen tit. I did,

however, find the gingerbread house. And the treasure," Braxton said nonchalantly.

Raising his voice, flustered, Joe exclaimed, "Enough with the riddles! What did you find?"

Braxton ignored the questions.

"I need some water. Mine is gone. I finished off the canteens. What are we going to do about water? The mountain water is too salty. It shall surely be the end of the horse. Sad to say, I do not believe the animal will make it out of here alive."

Braxton slapped dust from his trousers and coat, then bent over stretching his thigh and calf muscles.

"I thought about that, Joe said. "It will be difficult for him and for us. As for water, we will distill it. I have a contraption for doing just that in one of the crates."

"Why did you not mention it earlier?"

"We were busy, don't you remember? I thought of it but was not interested in being distracted at the time." Joe smirked, "Do you blame me?"

The prince folded his dusty arms and gloves across his chest and replied in good humor, "Come to think of it, we were a bit preoccupied. Show me this machine. Does it distill whiskey as well? I will tell you my morning's adventure while you put the 'fresh-water well' to work."

Joe agreed and set about locating and unpacking the crates holding his mining equipment.

Braxton walked over to Joe and stood alongside him, watching Joe rummage around, observing his nervous energy and wondering when he would stop and pay attention to his adventure.

"Hello Joe. Are you listening?"

"Yes, I'm listening Brax. I can do two things at once. I am trying to get your water first." He continued combing through a crate.

"All right. Well, before I set about my journey, I fashioned the small canoe you saw out of canvas I found in the crates. It allowed me to drag my tools and supplies along with me as I explored. It had to be open and accessible so I could reach back when crawling and retrieve what I needed. It suited my purposes well."

Joe kept searching for the distilling machine. Braxton hoped he was still listening.

"Much of my journey was spent bent over at the waist; most of it was spent on my hands and knees. It was rather grueling."

Joe said, "Uh huh."

"Like I said, I was crawling, sometimes on my belly. I kept moving forward toward the breeze. When indecisive about which direction to take, I followed the wind pummeling my face. At times I felt blinded, as there was no light to be had. Then there was."

Braxton paused, waiting to see if Joe had heard.

Joe, his head down inside a crate, froze. He stood up, turned and took hold of Braxton's arm, giving it a shake, asking anxiously. "What?

"Did you dead-end? What was it?" "Light."

"Light? What light?" "Sunlight."

Joe dropped a piece of metal he was holding and wrapped his arms around Braxton. Dust flew about as he slapped Braxton's back. Holding the prince's upper arms, he stepped back, looking Braxton in the eyes, "I can't believe it!"

Braxton went on to describe having spent much of his time in darkness, conserving the lantern's light, not knowing how long they were good for and how long he would be exploring.

"It was the crawling on all fours and belly crawling that just about finished me off, but then, there it was, a distant bit of light. From there on I do not remember much, frantically making my way to the source. It was quite a crawl, but I made it."

Joe stood mesmerized, drinking in Braxton's account. "Oddly, I had not noticed the caves ceiling opening up, so transfixed was I on reaching the light. For most of the distance I could have gotten off my belly, stood up and walked straight for it!"

Joe offered, "Perhaps you were fatigued and couldn't think straight, in need of water, dehydrated as they say, and over wrought."

"No doubt. Realizing I could get up, I came to my feet and shuffled forward, weighed down by the canvas canoe in tow. I would have run if I could. It is my good fortune that I did not, for as I rounded a turn, an intense glow lit up the large cavern.

"Sunlight poured into the space igniting a shimmering web of silver veins lining the cavern's walls. The overwhelming iridescence nearly blinded me. Had I had taken another step I would have fallen to my death!"

"Explain man!" Joe barked excitedly, almost shouting.

"In the center of the cavern there is a very large hole, a vertical drop."

The opening spans at least twenty feet across. When I removed my goggles and peered down into it, I could not see beyond thirty feet. I took a melon-sized rock and let it drop. Perhaps eight seconds passed before I heard it hit what must have been the bottom.

"Soon my eyes adjusted, and all was revealed. The edge bordering the hole is wide enough to walk around to the other side, where an opening the size of a man admits the light. I spent time surveying the mountainside and the area below. From what I could ascertain, the opening is approximately a thousand feet above any walkable spot.

With ropes and pulleys, I am sure we can work our way down." Joe stared blankly at Braxton.

"The water, Joe, please. I am quite parched."

Joe returned to the crates, appearing to aimlessly fumble about.

The prince walked up alongside Joe and placed his arm around his shoulders. "Let me help you find it. This appears to be a daunting task. I certainly would not want you to be left to it with no assistance."

Joe turned and faced Braxton. In a slow steady tone, he said, "Thank you, Braxton. Without your exploration of the cave, looking for the source of the desert air, we would not have found our way out, nor would we have found the veins of silver."

The men then held each other, grateful there was hope they would find their way out of the cave.

———

Dearest Valentina,

Has it been almost two years since we have spoken? I have lost count of the letters I have written. And yet I write you again, not having heard from you since that fateful day prior to you detraining in Vienna. You must know I remain determined to recapture your love.

After two months in Canada, eight months in California, two months in the Rocky Mountains, and another nine or so along the way. I have had much time for reflection.

I am writing this letter in New York City. It is quite the metropolis. I do not believe there is anything like it in the world. If there is, I have yet to see it.

The last letter I wrote found me in Denver. Since then, I have survived a deadly rock slide in the Rocky Mountains, experienced the slaughter house capital of the world, Chicago, and am, as I mentioned, now navigating New York.

All this with no private train to call my own!

America is a paradise for conducting business. Opportunities abound. My efforts have centered around mining, cattle, and real estate. I would have loved to have been able to share this land with you. The vast plains, soaring mountains, thunderous falls, massive rivers, and its native inhabitants have become beloved to me. The American Indian has a fascinating culture I have never known before. They are introspective, spiritual, wise, and self-sufficient. I dare say, they appear to be getting the short end of the stick, much like the Irish have for centuries.

As you would have expected, I have purchased interest in lumber, oil drilling, and mining. The latter, mining, along with a friend.

Braxton paused his letter writing long enough to remove a gray crumpled envelope from his pocket. He withdrew a daguerreotype depicting him and Joe sitting atop a bar in some forgotten town, both hoisting beers, looking hard-ridden and put up wet, yet smiling broadly. He pondered it for a moment, kissed the likeness and returned it to his pocket.

This friend, one I hope to introduce to you, is a very special person, someone for whom I care deeply. His name is Joseph Richards, but I call him Joe. We experienced a most horrific accident. It is a miracle I am here today. We were imprisoned by an avalanche of rocks for several days. We managed to find our way out, the details I will share with you one day, and have since become business partners and the dearest of friends. I am currently staying with Joe and his family in a stylish home on Park Avenue in a part of the city called Manhattan.

It is somewhat interesting to learn the upper class is made up primarily of self-made businessmen, or at least their fathers or grand-fathers were. Many in the first generation are lacking in education and their manners are abhorrent, but their company, conversation and sports are stimulating. Some in the second and third generations have, unfortunately, assumed all the airs comprising Europe's most obnox-ious aristocrats.

Back to my friend, Joe. I thought him initially just a well-educated prospector. In truth, he comes from a generations old, prominent Boston family, educated at Harvard, and well-traveled. He has a charming and self-sufficient wife and seven children. I enjoy them immensely. I grow fonder of them by the day.

Since I arrived in the East, I have had to shrug off the freedom of the American West and assume my persona as royal envoy. My time in New York remains brief. Next week I depart with Joe for Washington D.C. My father's ambassador keeps me to task and has arranged for me to meet the president, senators, congressmen, and other Washington society while in the capital city. Joe will make introductions to business leaders, much as he has done in Denver, Chicago and New York.

In the meantime, I have purchased vast acreage in the state of Colorado and the Wyoming Territory, a territory soon to become a state. I have purchased farms in Illinois and large tracts of undeveloped land north of New York City. I hope to show these properties to you one day.

While writing the letter, Braxton felt compelled to share his life with Valentina. At the same time, he resented her continued silence; not writing and sharing her life with him. She could not ignore their relationship forever, whatever it may or may not be. Deep within his heart he felt wounded, even after having the affair with Joe. How were they to handle the matter of the marriage contract? Both of their fathers having signed the marriage agreement, Parliament's ratification of the legal and binding document had made their betrothal and marriage a matter of international law: a treaty.

I shall return to England toward the end of October. My feelings are mixed. Shall I be returning to a sticky situation concerning our marriage or shall you and I have decided to honor the contract? I know this sounds cold, but it is not without good reason, for I have spent the last two years writing and, in a sense, pleading for you to soften your heart toward me. As I have heard not the slightest sound from you, I harbor no expectations.

Know that I love you as I have always loved you. It is my deepest desire that we marry, have children, and spend the rest of our lives together.

He replaced his pen on the ink stand, rose from his chair and walked to the window. Looking out the window onto the expansive gardens behind the Richards' home, he saw Joe blindfolded, playing "Squeak Piggy Squeak" with several of his children. The object of the game was to make the one sitting on your lap accidently touch you, while you squealed as loud and often as possible, making the victim laugh hysterically, causing them to lose their balance and touch the squealing "pig." Braxton broke into a laugh watching Joe squealing loudly as his oldest child tried not to touch Joe while sitting on his lap and laughing uproariously.

In uplifted spirits, Braxton returned to his letter, but not before his heart twinged, thinking of Joe sitting on his children's laps, knowing he loves Joe and will miss him terribly.

Valentina, you must also know I would never take part in a marriage that you do not desire, regardless the consequences. I am prepared to accept those consequences, whatever they might be.

I will not hold you to the marriage contract. You are hereby released.

With all my love and best wishes for your happiness, Braxton

22

GOOD BYE AND HELLO

Braxton had not heard from anyone in his family during his last weeks in the United States. The few cables he had received dealt with diplomatic matters and his business affairs. Perhaps some personal correspondence had not found him, especially during the time he and Joe had broken away from their heavy schedules in Washington to ride horseback into the Blue Ridge Mountains.

For ten days they relived the time they had spent prospecting in the Rocky Mountains. They followed the C & O Canal's tow path from Georgetown to Cumberland, Maryland. Their mounts had been equipped much as they had been out West. Carrying a tent and camping para-phernalia, they vanished into the mountains. Armed with a map and compass, they chose to follow Indian trails winding through the rich, dry foliage bursting with autumn colors. The higher into the mountains they rode, the more brilliant the leaves and the more isolated from others they became.

A day into their journey, Joe turned in his saddle and

said, "That night, our first night in the cavern, I never finished my story. We became too busy trying to escape that cave. Would you like me to complete my tale?"

"Certainement! Tell on, ole' bard!"

"I will go back to the beginning, long before ogling you in the grotto,"

Joe said, smiling at his lover.

Braxton let loose a small laugh. They rode on for a few minutes before Joe continued with his story.

"My father was killed in a hunting accident just after I was born.

My mother had no real interest in raising me. She was more interested in New York society. My paternal grandfather offered to raise me and provide her an allowance if I could live with him. He was a kind old gentleman but was kept busy handling his vast business interests. I was essentially raised by servants. At age six, I was sent off to a boarding school.

"My family name and my mother's string of lovers provided access to the best families and business opportunities. My grandfather died three years after I graduated from Harvard. He left me his entire fortune."

Joe had first seen Braxton before his grandfather died, while on his Grande Tour during his college years. His trip happened to correspond with Braxton's Grande Tour. Fascinated by the stories of Braxton sweeping the Queen Anne Stakes as a young boy, Joe was determined to meet the handsome young prince. Their paths crossed briefly, but no matter how hard he tried, Joe was unable to garner an introduction.

"If I had had a bit more self-confidence, I would have found a way to introduce myself. At that time, royalty was mysterious and difficult for me to fathom. Not so much anymore." Joe grinned.

"My second trip to Europe was an experiment in living on the 'other side of the tracks,' seeing Europe from a different perspective. And thus, I arrived on Capri as a crew member on your Uncle Cosimo's yacht."

Braxton reined his horse to a halt and slid off. He looked up at Joe and said, "Shall we walk for a spell? I would like to hear more."

Joe joined him on the ground.

"Where did you go or what did you do following your assignation with my uncle?"

"When the papers reported you had headed off to St. Petersburg, I returned to New York and succumbed to societal influences. I married a woman I did not love but have grown to respect and care for. As you know we now have seven children.

"All the while, not a day passed without my thinking of you. It was difficult, but I buried myself in family, work, society, and an occasional assignation. I was not miserable, but I knew there was something missing in my life. I took a leap of faith, kissed my wife and children goodbye, and headed West, promising to return.

Perhaps I thought I would find what or who I was looking for there. I knew I liked men, real men, such as you," Joe said slapping Braxton on the shoulder.

Braxton, reins still in hand, clasped both sides of Joes unshaven face and kissed his lips. If the kiss had lasted much longer, they would have found themselves sans clothing. Braxton playfully pushed Joe away and said, "Continue with your story."

"I spent the next couple of years out West, returning home every six months to spend time with the family, but I always yearned to go back West. It was as if I had left something behind. Perhaps I was looking for you, or someone like you.

"I spent the years learning how to be a cowboy and, as luck would have it, investing in mining. By then I had pretty much forgotten about you. By that, I mean, not thinking of you daily. Upon learning you were in San Francisco, I set in motion a plan that might bring us together. My plan proved wildly successful. And here we are."

"And I am glad we are," Braxton said, taking Joe's leather-gloved hand in his. They continued their walk down the trail, hand in hand, canopied by the resplendent autumn trees.

When their passionate week came to a close, the men descended the mountain, walking again along an abandoned Indian trail. The crisp morning, caressed by a light breeze, ruffled the leaves, allowing dappled sunlight to intermittently envelope them and their mounts. A light rain the previous night had washed the sky, the trees and trails, the moisture muffling the sound of their boots and the horse's hooves.

In a quiet, uneasy voice, Joe said, "I imagine it will be a while before we see one another again."

"That is true, with an ocean between us." Braxton paused, and stared at the ground as they walked. "I could remain here in the states."

"No, you could not, and you know it. Your family, your country, and Parliament await you. Perhaps even the grand duchess." Braxton looked forward. Speaking in a stiff cadence he said, "This appears impossible. She has yet to reply to my letter releasing her. It is as it has always been since she left me in Vienna. I am not a part of her life. It is done. So be it."

In a pained tone, Joe asked, "What will you do? Find a different woman to be your wife?"

"I will run for Parliament. I shall most likely be

expected to marry someone of royal blood. I may be a bit too old for that. Everyone in my circle was married long ago."

"You are just breaking thirty."

"True." In an anxious pitch, stringing out his words, the prince offered, "Perhaps I will just wait for the times we can steal to be together."

"Oh Braxton, that we could find even a few hours, days, weeks or months to be together."

The lovers continued their journey down the mountain, having enjoyed all aspects of one another's company, their passion and desire well-suited to the wilderness.

When they returned to Washington, Joe boarded the train to return to New York. Braxton met the royal yacht in the Baltimore harbor.

———

Headlines trumpeted across England's newspapers:

PRINCE BRAXTON RETURNS FROM COLONIES TO LONDON ROYAL ENVOY PRINCE BRAXTON'S TOUR A SUCCESS!

AMERICAN WILD WEST CANNOT TAME ENGLAND'S PRINCE!

PEOPLE'S PRINCE RETURNS FROM THE AMERICAS TOUR OF CANADA AND U.S. WELL DONE!

PARLIAMENT? MARRIAGE? WHICH IS IT?

Braxton crossed the Atlantic aboard the recently commissioned Royal Yacht Mercedes. Accompanied only by his staff, the prince rarely left his cabin during the voyage.

The steam-powered sailing ship was 300 feet long and

50 feet abeam. It was 110 feet to the top of its mast. It drafted 14 feet and was powered by a 6,000 horse power, coal-fired steam engine. The efficiency of the ship's design complemented the sophisticated interiors.

Queen Mercedes had chosen to decorate the interior using a new, and as yet somewhat unknown, interior design style: Art Nouveau.

She encouraged the designers to add a Mediterranean flair, softening the hard-angled edges and sharp corners, giving the interior a more comfortable, relaxed and welcoming appeal.

The interior design's clean lines contrasted with the overdone palatial interiors Braxton had grown up with. He found the ship's essence in harmony with the workings of his mind; it was easier for him to think in less posh surroundings.

One evening, the prince sat at the large table in his parent's suite aboard the yacht, ignoring the week-old papers covering the polished ebony surface. What am I returning to? A future wife?

Politics? Why does that sound hollow without a wife and family? And Joe...have I made a mistake leaving him behind?

Braxton had anticipated he might struggle with the guilt of not being faithful to Valentina, unrequited as his love appeared to be. In fact, he did not feel guilty. He searched his mind as to why, postulating his exposure to so many different religions and cultures had played a part. Without question, the training with Master Seiko had unlocked his mind and soul, allowing them to be infused with ideas and concepts not heretofore extolled by western Europe.

Joe was married and accepted his family responsibilities. He also did not appear to have any guilt. They both embraced their duties and responsibilities. They both chose to fulfill them. It would be impossible to suppress their feelings for one another in the company of others. Their love had to remain separate and their secret.

Braxton realized another chapter had closed, as had been the case with Aramis. It had taken a long while, but he had learned to bury any thought of his first love. Now he was forced to do the same with Joe and with Valentina, though for altogether different reasons. Love is the devil's trick.

———

HRH Braxton, Prince Royal of Wales, dressed in honorary regimental commander's uniform could hear the canon's 18-gun salute pounding off in the distance. He gazed down the polished mahogany handrails lining the glistening metal stepped gangway.

On the London dock stood his parents, their majesties, the king emperor and queen empress, Richard and Mercedes. His brothers, Crown Prince Dominic, Prince John and John's wife, Frederika, had come to greet him.

Why were his sisters and their husbands, the Kaiser and Prince Maxim here, much less in England at all? They rarely left their own countries. They surely had not come simply to welcome him home.

Had someone died? I was in the mountains with dear Joe for weeks. Then aboard ship for a week. Anything could have transpired, though not a soul appears unhappy. So much for my arriving unannounced, slipping ashore and making straight for the Aurelio Palace.

Concealing the pain of having lost both Joe and

Valentina, he smiled, waved to his family and to the thousands of onlookers populating the docks. The Prince Royal faced the yacht's stern. He saluted the Union Jack, faced the ship's captain, saluted, then descended the gang plank to the cacophony of shouting and hurrahs emanating from onlookers crowding the dock and the smaller boats that had escorted the royal yacht into the harbor.

Descending the gangway, he noticed the king wearing the hat his father despised the most; the reviled white feather-plumed hat.

Braxton was not sure which order it represented. Mamma also wore a beastly chapeau, adorned with many feathers, ribbons and fruit.

She never wore festooned day hats, yet that is what she was wearing.

Were they holding hands in public? What on earth? They seem quite jubilant. I should return more often.

The prince stepped off the gangway onto the dock and saluted his father. The king returned the salute. The queen, her eyes sparkling and smiling broadly, extended her gloved hand. Braxton, leaning forward, tossed a discreet wink at his mother while performing the perfunctory kiss. She blushed as she often had when he had caught her unaware, her precocious son.

He remained facing his parents, both of them standing still and beaming.

Braxton wondered; this is most unusual. This is the time we make small talk, wave and depart. Why do we not get on with it?

Mercedes looked to her husband. He in turn offered her a slight nod.

Their majesties then turned to face one another and stepped back two steps.

Braxton's head spun, his chest tightened, he wavered.

There stood Her Imperial Highness, Grand Duchess Valentina, her lips curved into a smile.

Half in disbelief, Braxton returned her smile.

Is this my dream come true, or the mistake of a lifetime?

ACKNOWLEDGMENTS

This book, early on, took on a life of its own. How do you write the second book in a series and make it enjoyable for readers who have not read Braxton's Century volume one? Easy! Give them just enough of an overview to wrap their arms around as they jump in and throw them a life raft every now and then throughout the story to keep them afloat. I truly hope I have done this effectively. If not, please accept my apology and better yet, purchase volume 1!

Thank you so much to my team. Their professionalism, mentorship, expertise, and patience have once again been invaluable. Trisha Gooch Stein, content editor, Mary Criscenti, copy editor and Tamara Merrill: oracle, guiding light, and 'jack' of all trades.

As is my previous works, there are many people that have been there for me throughout the process of writing this novel: Mike Norton, Elena Bazhenova, Jae Barrick, Everett Hale, Larry Tritten, Josh Rutherford, Johnny and Jackie Lazootin, Craig and Alex Shaw, Dr. Virginia Foster,

Dr. Ann Gladys, Theresa Halvorsen, Sara Faxon, Valerie Alexander and the unnamed family and friends that are always there for me.

ABOUT THE AUTHOR

J.R. Strayve, Jr. was born to a nomadic military family, attending nine schools before entering college. Following service in the United States Marine Corps, he raised a family. It is here that he discovered his talent for "spinning tales," regaling his young children with spontaneous bedtime stories. Soon his passion for history spoke to him.

He spoke back and wrote the epic alternative historical series, Braxton's Century. Book 1 was published in January 2021.

He is currently co-authoring a sure-to-be best-seller blockbuster nonfiction detailing a Whistleblower's Veterans Administration exposé.

His first novel was and remains controversial: First Spouse of the United States, published in March 2019. A sequel is soon to follow. A short story, The Lieutenant & The Vintner and the novella, Vainglorious are available now.

Start your journey into history's most dynamic century through the eyes of an undaunted, rakish, youth today!

This first volume of four scorches a trail spanning from 1860 to 1880. The entire saga features a century of world wars and engineering marvels that one might recognize with requited and unrequited love, romances that defy social morays, death, revolutions, and espionage that casts this tale into one that could have been had Prince Braxton been real.

Braxton's Century Vol 2

When Prince Braxton departs Vienna, following a night of debauchery dressed in gold as the ancient God of War, Mars. He leaves behind a tangle of threats, promises, and compromised nobles, his trading empire intact. Or is it?

Braxton's larger-than-life wheelings and dealings take him from Russia to Japan, Hong Kong, and India. But it's sucking every ounce of Braxton's being from within.

Continue your journey of history's most dynamic century as Prince Braxton tears through life on his own terms. When life forces him to decide his path, what—and who—will he choose?

This second volume of four scorches a trail spanning from 1860 to 1884. The entire saga features a century of world wars and engineering marvels that one might recognize with requited and unrequited love, romances that defy social morays, death, revolutions, and espionage that casts this tale into one that could have been had Prince Braxton been real.

First Spouse Of The United States

They thought he had it all. But what he had was secrets in his closet.

Lt. Ricardo "Rocky" Chambers has always been the epitome of what women want and who men want to be. Handsome. Star athlete. Fighter pilot.

Heroism and prowess do not clear a path for happily-ever-after, as a dark secret could derail all this family man, captain of industry, and gay civil rights advocate has worked for.

And secrets aren't meant to stay hidden.

With adversaries lying in wait, the secret is exposed in the national media. Can Rocky and his husband overcome the fallout on the quest for the White House?

In a coming-of-age story that parallels today's political and social unrest, there are no taboo subjects.

———

The Lieutenant & The Vintner (A Short Story)

When SS Lt. Georg von Reichenau is assigned to the French Burgundy after recovering from his battle wounds, he laments not the loss of his fighting days but the loss of a trip to the Olympics and his future as a ski instructor.

Under German occupation in WWII, Andre Beaulieu, a gold-medal-winning Olympian downhill racer works to maintain his family's vineyard, unable to forget the woman he met at Olympic Village. He's been trying to find her for the last five years.

There's something familiar about the man who came to the vineyard after recognizing the name. But memory can be fickle. Can there be more to this recollection than either realize?